S0-AVS-665

THE GIFT SHOP

Charlotte Armstrong

THE GIFT SHOP

Coward-McCann, Inc.
New York

 Published on the same day in the Dominion of Canada by Longmans Canada Limited, Toronto.

Words to "Lullaby" by Charlotte Armstrong; music by Louise Matthews.

PRINTED IN THE UNITED STATES OF AMERICA

Chapter 1

THE first passenger off the jet came darting around the corner, well ahead of the pack, with his right arm folded to his breast like a broken wing. A pink lei was incongruous on his dark-suited shoulders and incompatible with his pinched and sallow face. He veered erratically between clumps of meeters and greeters; his eyes shifted as if he feared lest he be met, as if he were driven, and, although in a great hurry, not at all sure where he was going.

The waiting people had surged together behind him to absorb and impede the rest of the flower-decked travelers when, reaching the central space where the stairs march up and down, he took a sudden turn into the terminal's gift shop.

The fair-haired young woman who was realigning some costume jewelry on the counter did not look up as he entered like a blown thing, as if wherever a foot happened to come down there he must stagger. A low table of toys was placed against the high counter, near enough the entrance to lure children; he leaned over this to call to her.

When she did look up she knew at once that he was in trouble and pain. She saw his right arm slide downward from its crooked position, but she could not see how he began to walk his middle finger delicately over the top of a small ceramic piggy bank that stood on the toy table, and she did not see him very carefully, very precisely, with thumb and forefinger, guide a tiny, folded piece of paper into the slot on the pig's back and then, with his forefinger, gently push it through.

He had fixed her with his bright and feverish eyes that were burning with concentration upon this secret accomplishment, although he was carefully not watching his hand. The girl came closer. "Yes, sir?" All her attention was on his face, to help him tell her what (she supposed) he so desperately required of her.

But he said something quite foolish. "Where are the telephones?" And he stepped backward and gave her an owly look now, a momentary dimming and relaxing of his fierce gaze.

"Why, both ways. Just around there, sir." She pointed. "You must have passed them. Is something wrong?" He had turned his head to look behind him. "Hey, are you all right?" the girl said, stubbornly interested.

He didn't seem to hear. He turned his body and seemed to set his will for effort. By now a lean, middle-aged woman who had a child by the hand was standing in the wide entry. A purple lei and a white one framed her long plain face, which was composing to a simper, as if she intended to speak to the man.

But he put his right foot down far to his right, made a mighty lurch, and as he caught his balance he snarled at her in a voice that betrayed too much pain and no patience left, *"Get out of the way, sister, will you, please?"*

The tall woman bridled, blinked her pale lashes, and yanked at the child. The man went past them out the door, driving, with his head down, his right arm dangling, and now, from the ends of those fingers, there were falling slow drops of bright blood to make a trail along the floor.

The gift shop girl gasped. Her name was Jean Cunliffe. She had normal human feelings, and her first thought was that he ought not to be *allowed* to bleed like that. She said to the woman, "He's hurt!"

The woman's face had frozen. "Bobby, come see the pretty pictures," she said, and with a scooping motion of her arm she guided the sleepy child toward the magazine racks. To Jean she snapped, "Why don't you do something?"

Jean sidled along behind the counter in a hurry to the telephone. She certainly would do something. The little boy with the sleek flaxen head was being hustled away from blood and trouble. A worthy excuse, Jean supposed. But she, employed here, had the list of numbers to call in emergencies. So she called the Airport Medical Center. After all, after all, she was thinking, in a confusion of duty and dismay, this terminal can't have people bleeding all over its floor.

But she hung up with a feeling of having passed the buck. Where was he now? Surely she ought to go and see. Mrs. Mercer could mind the store. Jean simply went. Dodging for openings through the currents of people now flowing sluggishly around both sides of the moving stairs, she found herself entangled with a half dozen children who seemed to constitute a group, although they were of all complexions and racial origins: a little black boy, and one tawny, a freckle-faced redheaded lass, a small adorable Oriental female with a straight black bob. A blowsy white woman with a great knot of black hair sliding on her nape made admonitions and cheerful apologies as Jean threaded gently through.

Had she lost the poor man? No, no, there was his trail. Happy chatterers were not noticing; gay feet were scuffing and blurring it, but Jean tracked him to the left, along the row of phone booths. Was he in this one? No, it was a meek-and-mild felt hat. Then here? Yes. Light fell on the pain-ravaged face in which the lids were down. He was waiting for a connection—or else he had fainted—braced there in the corner. She thought of shouting, "Is there a doctor in the house?" But she did not. She hurried on, because she had spotted a Security man. She noticed in the next booth, as she passed, a big man with a bland and listening face, wedged in with cascading flowers.

Harry Fairchild was deep in a soft sofa that faced the glass wall of his high apartment below which the great carpet of the lights of the city of Los Angeles was beginning to set up its multicolored pattern. His well-shod feet were on the coffee table, his elegantly socked ankles were crossed. The girl's high-arched feet, in her pretty green slippers, imitated his position in a comradely fashion.

They had drinks in their hands, which they needed like a hole in the head, since she had (not very long ago) skillfully cut him out of the herd at the Winters' cocktail party and arranged, not against any serious opposition from Harry, to go on to dinner somewhere. Sometime, that is. Later.

Meanwhile Harry was worried about absolutely nothing. She was a very beautiful girl, about twenty-five years old (he presumed), with a natural self-confidence and even arrogance that he rather admired.

She had said the casual "Tell me what you do, Harry."

And he had answered . . . all this as soon as they had settled down . . . in his usual manner. "Well, my father is an ex-oil-tycoon. My oldest brother is the governor of one of these United States. My next brother is a very high-class surgeon. There's a whole lot of drive in the family, see, and I feel very strongly that this should be balanced off. So *I* don't do a damn thing."

"Do you know, I doubt that," Dorinda had said. Her smile was dainty. She gave him no wide view of too many teeth, too boldly white. On the whole, and so far, Harry was tending to approve of her.

But, with mischief, he had launched into one of his little testing devices. "As a matter of fact," he had told her, putting on his worried-cherub expression, doubly deceiving, "I more or less grub around in books, you know." And then he had gone into an account of the decipherment of Linear B, which he contrived to load with as many difficult details as he could remember, quoting lavishly from Ventris, and concealing almost all the true excitement.

It did amuse him to watch the dear creatures. They were so well-trained, so thoroughly indoctrinated. Eighty-five percent of the girls in the world, or so he had tentatively concluded from his private samplings, would hang upon a man's words, and no matter what words, with some semblance of fascinated attention, *if* the man happened to be a neat and clean fellow, only thirty-one years old, healthy, wealthy and unmarried.

True, about ten to eleven percent reversed violently and were rude, but he didn't doubt that this, too, came from the indoctrination. They were only being "different." He didn't know when he might come upon a truly different one, or what he would do, when he did.

He droned along now, watching this Dorinda Bowie, about whom he knew nothing, except that she had, at least, known someone who knew the Winters, that she was beautiful, elegantly groomed, and possibly intelligent.

She had a nice control, surely. She was hearing him out with serene and silent patience. Harry was beginning to think that if she were to allow one twinkling bit of humor, one clue that she was seeing through him, to cross her lovely face, why he might even take her to his other place, where he had no built-in chaperon and protector like Bonzer, his manservant, who was even now in the big room answering the telephone.

But she hadn't, up to the moment when Harry, with apologies, pulled his six feet from almost horizontal to moderately vertical and went to speak to whoever was calling.

"Harry? This is Bernie B."

"Bernie-baby, to what do I owe . . ."

"Shut up and listen."

"Is that any way to talk to an old school . . ."

"Shut up, for once in your life."

Harry shut up, for the moment.

"I've been after something for your daddy," Bernie said.

"Why sure, I recommended . . ."

"Ah, listen. Listen!" The voice was melodious with an important despair.

"Go ahead," said Harry crisply.

"I've got the dope your daddy wanted, but I can't deliver. They roughed me up pretty good in Honolulu."

"What? Who?"

"Some *swine*." Bernie's voice became explosive. "And one *swine* is right next door, listening *now*. So don't talk. Listen, will you please? Because I'm going to give you the word, brother, and you better catch on."

"What the . . ." Harry was feeling lost.

"Shut up. I'm at International. Pan-Am. And bleeding like a *stuck pig,* I am."

"You better get to a doc . . ." This was automatic.

"I sure wish I was at old Doc McGee's." The voice was beginning to wail drearily. But Harry bristled up, to listen hard. "You remember old Doc McGee? I wish I was making a phone call from old Doc's. Many is the phone call . . . You listening for the word?"

"That's all right, Bernie," said Harry. "So why don't you sit still, and I'll buzz right down?"

"Yah. Yah. Do that. But I'm not going to make it . . . all the way home." The voice was fading. "Harry?" It forced force. "You get the message to your daddy and nobody else—because there's got to be a rat in his house and I don't care so much about getting myself dead for nothing."

Harry, hanging onto the phone, heard something go away, some breath, some life, some sense of a tie, a communication.

In the airline terminal the man in the booth was collapsing, folding, sliding, falling.

In a moment Harry heard another voice, a man's voice, loud and urgent. "Hello? Hello, who is this?"

Harry kept shut up. Very gently he hung up the telephone.

"What's the matter?" said Dorinda.

"Damned if I know," said Harry, passing his palms over his thick dark hair. "Couldn't make a lot of sense out of it. But look, I . . . uh . . . guess I got to go somewhere. Raincheck, Dorinda?"

"Must you?" She stood up with easy grace.

"So let Bonzer put you in a cab. O.K.? And I'll call you."

Harry, who could move a good deal faster than most people suspected, was already at his door. And out of it.

He descended by elevator into the basement, winkled his car out of its slot, floated up the ramp. When he had to hesitate before entering traffic, the door on the right side opened and Dorinda got in beside him.

"I thought I might be helpful," she said gravely.

"You might?" said Harry. "That's possible. Also, we *might* just get that dinner date. Good deal, Dorinda. Me, I didn't want to presume on an old acquaintance."

He had never seen her in his life, before five o'clock that afternoon.

Now he was in the stream, driving shrewdly.

"Where are we going?" she said in a moment. "And why? Now, tell me." She was cozy.

"Going to International. And I wish I knew why, believe me." He was cordial. But he wasn't talking.

He had a word. He realized that he was the only member of his family to whom Bernie could have given *this* word, as he had done. Bernie Beckenhauer, the fraternity brother who had gone, quite freakishly, with dedicated drive, into the strange profession of private investigator.

Harry didn't know what he was going to do with the word. He'd have to see. Blood? Rats? What the devil was his daddy up to now? None of his seriously competitive, ambitious, driving, immediate relatives ever told *him* anything.

He said to Dorinda, "Just hold onto your hat, honey," and hit the freeway.

Chapter 2

IN the terminal most people had nervously retreated, leaving a clear space around the trouble, but some had been drawn to make tight arcs at either end of the passage behind the line of phone booths. They stood and stared. Jean Cunliffe halted at this line as the young Security Officer burst through to the core.

The door of the phone booth had been opened and the man's body had spilled out on the floor. All strain had been erased from his face. He was unconscious. The big chap from the adjoining booth, with white flowers still cascading around his neck, was in a half-kneel, half-crouch, and seemed to be fishing into the man's limp pockets.

"Excuse me," said the Security lad. "Look—uh—better not touch him, mister. Ambulance coming."

"Sorry," said the big man. "I figured we ought to get his identification. Poor guy." He rose.

"Yes, *sir,*" said the Security lad. "I'll take over. Please, folks. Please stand away now. Everybody." He was spreading official and guarding arms. The arcs of onlookers shuffled and retreated. Jean fell back with them. She had done all she could do. Better get back to her job.

But now a man in a gray suit, evidently a senior police officer, came bursting through. He exuded a dour patience, an air of weary experience. He knelt briefly. He conferred briefly with the Security lad. Then he said loudly, "Those of you who know anything about this man, I'll want to talk to you in a minute." His hard gaze told Jean that she was included.

So she drifted apart, to wait obediently, although surely Mrs. Mercer, her superior in the shop, would be having fits by now. Somebody behind her called, not loudly, "Oh, Miss? Oh, Miss—from the gift shop?"

So she turned and saw the angular, long-faced woman leaning through the glass doors to the waiting room proper and beckoning urgently. So Jean pushed through to her. Now the woman stood like a mountain peak among foothills of children. Why, there was that little Oriental, and the redheaded one! The children were tugging at garlands of flowers. The lean woman stood plain in her gray costume.

"How is the poor man?" she said to Jean with a greedy simper.

"I don't know, ma'am," said Jean honestly. "He's fainted or something. I don't think . . . I mean he isn't . . . hasn't died. And help is coming."

"You are a good girl."

Jean blinked at this. It surprised and offended her. She now saw that the white woman, with the falling-down mass of dark hair, was seated, holding on her lap the little blond boy whose gray eyes were watching everything drowsily.

Jean was about to excuse herself when the big chap with the white lei was suddenly before her. "Excuse me, Miss." He seemed to surround her. His little eyes licked at her from his heavy flesh. "I wonder if *you* have any idea what could have happened to my poor friend from the plane. He spoke to you in the gift shop, didn't he?"

"Why, yes, he did," said Jean. "But he just asked me where the phones were. I guessed he must have been a little bit blind, you know? Of course, then I saw that he was hurt so I . . ." She felt herself embarrassed.

"I see," said the big chap. He seemed to assess and dismiss

Jean's soap-and-water-fresh young face. "You were in the shop," he said, turning so abruptly as to seem to accuse. "Did he speak to you, ma'am?"

The lean woman's face was bleak and hostile. "He did not," she snapped.

Now the police officer in the gray suit was coming toward them. "Word with you?" he said to the big chap. Then to Jean, "And you, in a minute."

"Sir, could I go back on my job. I work in the gift shop."

He nodded permission; the two men stepped back into a clear space near the phones.

But the lean woman said fiercely in Jean's ear, "That man's a liar! *He's* no friend. He's a liar!"

Jean looked up at her grim face. "Some people are," she said softly, and set off.

Now the children surged suddenly in a mass and went scampering past her. The pack of them began to froth around a newcomer, rather a startling figure. This was a man, a burly fellow with a perfectly bald head and a whiskered chin, dressed in a tight-fitting knitted orange sport shirt and a pair of tight black trousers that did not quite contain his paunch, which hung over at the beltline. He had a guitar case slung around his neck. His expression was either sleepy or "way out."

The children—he seemed to have two on each hand and one around each knee—were bubbling. (*All* of them, black, brown, pink and tawny!) "Papa, here we are." "Here we are, Papa." "Aunt Emaline is here," they said. "Mama's got Bobby." "In here, Papa."

Jean, changing course to get around them, found herself slipping under the noses of the conferring men and she distinctly heard the big one say to the policeman, ". . . stranger to me. Didn't even notice him on the plane. I'm very sorry."

Well! Jean Cunliffe was just a poor girl trying to get along; she had a summer job she had better keep; she hurried back to it. If she didn't understand what was going on here she probably never would—and such was life. But people—although it was none of her business—people lied like breathing! Darned if they didn't!

Harry Fairchild pulled up right behind the waiting ambulance at the entrance to the International Carriers building and said to Dorinda, "So be helpful! Park the car?" He thought she looked a little stunned, or a little miffed, as he nipped out of the driver's seat and raced around the hood. He went sailing down the long tiled passage and up the moving stairs faster than they were moving, and straight to the trouble.

Harry said to the white-coated backs bending over poor old Bernie, "His name is Beckenhauer. What's wrong with him?"

"Knife wound," said one of the men, glancing upward. "Not new, either."

A man in a gray suit beamed his attention on Harry. "Who are you, sir, if you don't mind? I'm police."

"Fairchild. Friend of his."

"You supposed to meet him?"

"He phoned me."

"He tell you what happened?"

"No. Fact is, he didn't make a lot of sense." Harry wasn't going to talk, but he had to say something. He didn't want to make himself sound too mysterious. There were bystanders, for instance. Big chap, wearing sad white flowers. A fat lady. A little man. "He mumbled something about being roughed up in Honolulu," said Harry, owing this much to the authorities. "I just got the idea that he was hurt and where he was. So I said I'd come. How is he doing?"

"They'd better take him."

"Right," said Harry. "Hey, can they take him to St. Bart's?" He touched one of the white shoulders. "Can you do that? I'll call my brother, the doctor. He'll be taking care of him. How about me setting it up? You tell St. Bart's, Dr. Richard Fairchild." There was doubt. There was discussion. There was compromise.

The policeman said, "Pardon me, but are you *Harry* Fairchild?"

"That's right."

The magic of that moneyed name received a brief ceremonial silence, during which Harry got down on one knee and looked intently at poor old Bernie, at his gaunt face and the faint stubble on it, at his frightening and uncharacteristic helplessness, and the flowers around his neck. His jacket had been pulled open. An envelope was coming out of his inside pocket. Harry's hand went out, but the policeman, breathing on the back of his neck, said, "Don't touch."

Harry rose and said somberly, "What do you call this?"

"Foul play," said the policeman. "I'll want a few more answers, in a minute."

"If I have any more," Harry said morosely.

He stepped out of the way as the white-coated ones prepared to shift the unconscious man to a stretcher. The policeman snatched at the envelope and kept it in his hand. Harry, feeling very uncomfortable about poor old Bernie, shifted farther out of the way and began to stand as tall as he could and look carefully around.

He had a word and he was supposed to use it to find some kind of message and take that to his father. Cautiously. So much was clear. But how was *that* word going to lead him to a message, here in these marble halls? And where was the one "swine"—which plural Bernie had significantly used as if it were singular—where was the "swine" who had been eavesdropping?

People were moving, but leaving one wide way. Harry turned to watch the stretcher-bearers. Wait. Had they understood? He took a few quick paces; he seemed to be wading through children. "Hey!" he called, loudly enough for those men to hear him. "Dr. Fairchild is going to want him in St. Bart's. So bear that in mind, right?"

"Yes, sir, Mr. Fairchild," said one of the men.

Then Harry saw the policeman cutting across over there, going to the bar, or the coffee shop, or . . . ah, the gift shop!

Then Harry caught, through its glass walls, a promise in the bright clutter of its wares.

The gift shop was unusually crowded, especially by children. More than one set of parents had shepherded the young into this shelter while the wounded man, the stretcher—those distressing tip-offs to the existence of pain and trouble—were going by.

Jean Cunliffe, who was talking to the man in the gray suit, saw this tall young man come in. He pushed through the milling people and established himself as if to stand in line and be next. This brought him close enough to overhear, and she hesitated. But the man in the gray suit gave the newcomer a permissive nod and said to Jean, "Go on, Miss."

"Well, I knew right away that there was *something* the matter with him," she continued. "I couldn't tell what. All he said, all he *did,* was to ask me where the phones were. So of course I told him. But I thought it was funny because he'd just walked by the phones."

"How do you know he had just walked by the phones, Miss?"

"Oh. Well, I didn't *know* it. I guessed it, because he must have just come off the plane from Hawaii. Because he was wearing flowers."

"I see."

"Of course, maybe he came up the stairs. I don't *know.*" Jean strained to be perfectly honest. The policeman almost smiled at her.

"And then, Miss?" he said, almost gently.

"Well then, he just turned around and went away, and I saw that he was—you know . . . It's still on the f-floor. I called. But then I thought I'd better find him. And the Security man came."

"I see. Thank you very much, Miss."

"What did happen to him?" she burst out.

"We don't know. But we will." The policeman turned to Harry. "We're not going to get much here. It didn't happen here. Looks like Honolulu, all right."

"I'd like to have your name," said Harry genially, "and give you my number."

Jean watched the exchange of cards and couldn't help thinking that this was odd. Shouldn't the encounter have gone the other way? Why wasn't the policeman demanding information?

The policeman said, "We'll be in touch, Mr. Fairchild. Soon as we have a little news from the Islands. Couple of wheels I better get turning. Excuse me?"

He left the shop. But the other one stood where he was, staring at the floor. Jean gave him a curious look; then she hurried behind the counter. She was about to wait on somebody, but he was quicker. There he was, standing over the toy table, exactly where the poor man had stood, and he was calling to her. "Miss?"

"Yes, sir," she said in her salesgirl voice. He was very nice-looking, very well-dressed; he had a nice smile. He had something—some kind of presence.

He said to her benignly, "You were a good girl to take that trouble for my friend, and I appreciate it."

Jean felt herself turning a hideous red. She had put up with being called a good girl by that antique female, but to be so called by this character was simply humiliating. "Think nothing of it," she said fliply, and thought hostilely, probably *he* isn't a friend, either. How do I know?

"Hey, don't be so mad at *me,*" said Harry. "I can't help it if you did a good deed. Listen, right now I want to buy something. How about everything on this table?"

"What?"

"This table," he insisted. But he didn't make a gesture, he didn't sweep with his hand to indicate his meaning. "The one I'm leaning on," he said. "Everything that's here."

Mrs. Mercer had approached.

The man said, "Here's my card, and here's—what's this?—forty dollars on account. Now, I want the whole works packed up and sent to me, collect for the balance. Will you do that, please?"

"Why, I—don't know," gasped Jean, who had never heard

of such a deal and had no precedent. But Mrs. Mercer was peering at the card and the two twenty-dollar bills in Jean's astonished hand.

"Why, certainly, Mr. Fairchild," she purred. "Just do what he says, Jean."

"Right away, Jean?" He had a flying eyebrow.

"You mean *tonight!*"

"Well, why not?" said Harry, with an air of sweet reason. "Send it by messenger, collect. That's easy, isn't it? There'll be somebody there to take it in," he soothed. "I feel, you know, that good deeds should be rewarded."

Then he nodded, gave Mrs. Mercer a nod and a smile for her very own, and strode away.

"Is he crazy?" said Jean.

"He's Harry Fairchild," said Mrs. Mercer with a gleam in her eye. "He can afford it. Meantime, these people need a little service. Do you mind?"

Jean turned to obey. She was thinking. Somebody there to take it in? That will be his wife, of course.

Out in the concourse Harry stopped in his tracks. Dorinda, graceful and elegant in her green brocade cocktail suit, was stepping off the moving stairs. He waved and she saw him. Her pretty slippers were so quick to change course toward him that she walked right into a little boy in a cowboy outfit who had judged it possible to scoot across her former path. He was a sturdy little fellow, but she almost bowled him over, and he clutched at her skirt. Dorinda looked down and said something with a twist to her mouth that was not pretty at all. The child got his balance and Dorinda brushed by with an effect of having got rid of some annoying piece of dust. Harry Fairchild, who was not in the habit of making sentimental judgments, smiled at her.

She came smiling. He held out his palm and she dropped his car keys into it. "What's it all about?" she asked.

"Fellow who phoned me passed out," said Harry with a small shrug. "So I dunno. They carted him off in the ambulance."

"Yes, I passed them," she said a bit breathlessly. "Who is he? What happened?"

"Nobody knows what happened. Excuse me, Dorinda? I said I'd phone my brother, the doctor."

"Well, surely," she said, with a puzzled frown.

So Harry tore off to the phone booths. He felt he had the situation well in hand, insofar as he understood it. He'd done all right, so far. But he had better get his wits together. He still mustn't talk, and he still had to say something.

Dorinda waited. The crowd was thinning. There was a little man, a nondescript little man, wearing a felt hat that was somehow more like every other felt hat in the world than felt hats are like each other. He was reading a newspaper, a nondescript newspaper somehow grayer than most, and he was ambling along, unregarded by anybody. He drifted. He halted. He continued to read.

Dorinda spoke to him softly. "Excuse me. Do you know what happened to the man on the stretcher?"

"No, ma'am, I don't," he said mildly. "I know he was making a phone call, right in the booth next to me."

"Well, *yes.* He made a phone call," she murmured, shifting restlessly, "but what . . ."

"Just gibberish, really," said the little man comfortingly. "They took him to the hospital." He nodded pleasantly and began to drift away. "To St. Bart's," he added, with a certain brightness.

The man with the white flowers went by, mopping his face with a white handkerchief. He stepped upon the moving stairs and was borne downward.

Then Harry was bearing down upon Dorinda and the policeman in the gray suit was bearing down upon Harry. They converged.

"Just one more thing, Mr. Fairchild," said the policeman. "Excuse me. This Beckenhauer was a private investigator. I guess you'd know that. On some job for *you,* was he?"

"Hey, not me," said Harry recoiling. "I never did have occasion to hire one of those. But I'll tell you this. Bernie is a good man, I've heard."

"Well thought of," said the policeman gloomily. "Something a little bit peculiar." He turned his back on Dorinda, and Harry turned with him. "Just spoke to his partner," said the policeman in a low voice. "Five days ago they had vandalism in the offices. Files torn apart. Records burned. Partner says Beckenhauer's secretary can talk to us in the morning. But he thinks the case he was on was 'Fairchild.' "

"Is that so?" said Harry. "Is that so?" He sucked a tooth. It gave him a thoughtful air.

"You see my point? So why did he call *you?*"

"I thought I had that figured out," said Harry pleasantly. He turned, as if out of politeness, and included Dorinda within the group. "See, Bernie and I went to school together, same fraternity and all that. I'm figuring that he knew he needed some kind of help, in his condition, and . . . Well . . . there was my phone number, handy in his head."

"That could be," said the policeman grudgingly. His eyes were steady.

"I guess Bernie will tell us, soon enough, when they pull him out of it. Like tomorrow?" Harry sounded on the hopeful side, but his eyes kept a serious and steady communication going.

"Could be," said the policeman with a bleak smile. But his eyes said, don't hope too much.

"I wish I knew," said Harry, in all truth. "I wish I knew what's going on here."

"If you find out, let me know," said the policeman with a glum sarcasm which was, nevertheless, an indication of his willingness to wait, if Mr. Fairchild said so.

"And vice versa," said Harry. (Then he had a flash.) "Oh, say, your people will notify . . . uh . . . Bernie's people?"

"Right."

"Then I guess this is where I came in," Harry sighed.

He knew he had the man's permission to go. He took Dorinda's arm and turned her toward the stairs.

Jean, in the gift shop, was staring over the heads of some small customers. Who *was* he? And if he had a wife at home, then who was *she?* Jean certainly wished she knew what was going on here.

Dorinda said, as they set off in the car, "I certainly wish I knew what was going on here. What in the world did the poor man expect you to do?"

"I wonder," said Harry, whipping into traffic.

"He'll be all right, won't he?"

"You know, I don't think they're so sure."

"Oh. I'm sorry. Then are we going to the hospital now?"

"No, no. Look, Bernie's got a . . . Well . . . uh . . . There's this girl . . ."

"Oh?"

"Doesn't seem *she's* going to get officially notified. If you . . . uh . . . take my meaning." He was making things up as he went along.

"I see," she said thoughtfully. "But you know about her? You think that's why he called you?"

"I wouldn't be surprised," said Harry. "She's carrying a bit of a torch, too, poor kid."

"And has," said Dorinda dryly, "no telephone of her own."

Harry said quickly, "How did you know that?" and rushed right on. "Looks like Bernie's been took bad, so maybe it's not much of a mood for dining and dancing. Besides—I better go see this chick, don't you think, Dorinda?"

"Of course," she said agreeably. "Raincheck?"

"Good girl."

"Good guy?" she teased him.

"Just a little old friend to all the world, that's me," said Harry, a touch bitterly, as he patted her knee.

When he let her off at the bright entrance to the Beverly Hills Hotel he watched her turn her elegant back before he whisked away. It struck him as a little bit odd that a girl as smart as Dorinda hadn't wanted to discuss a P. I. engaged in a case that bore the name of Fairchild. Surely she had heard what the policeman had said. Oh, well . . . Put it down to tact or something. He drove fast. Of course, he wouldn't be *surprised* if poor old Bernie did have some girl, someplace, but not having the faintest idea who or where, Harry was off to see his daddy and find out what was going on here.

Dorinda Bowie walked about fifteen feet. Then she turned all the way around, and walked back to the attendant. "Do you think you could find me a cab?" she asked sweetly.

"Yes, ma'am."

A cab came and discharged passengers. Dorinda got into it in her graceful fashion. "St. Bart's Hospital?" she let her voice question. "Do you know where that is?"

"St. Bartholomew's? Yes, ma'am."

She smiled at the driver and settled back.

Chapter 3

EVERY time he put his foot into the downstairs of his father's fine Georgian house Harry was forced to remember the day of his mother's funeral. It had been an experience he didn't wish to relive, if he could help it. He had fallen out of the habit of coming here very often.

Cousin Elaine opened the door for him tonight. She was fortyish, a spinster related on the Fairchild side, and the very way she wore her hair clued Harry, the connoisseur, to the fact that this poor female had never had a clue. She had come blowing along from someplace—to attend the funeral possibly—a long twelve years ago, and she had ever since run this house, bossed the staff, and "taken care of the old man," an arrangement pleasing enough to all, since servants come and servants go, but blood is thicker than wages.

Now Elaine peered at him in her nearsighted way and exclaimed, "Oh, it's you! Oh, I'm so glad. Your brother is here. Your brother Dick phoned. You were at the airport, weren't you?"

Elaine always called his brother the governor, "your brother," and his brother Dr. Richard Fairchild, "your brother Dick."

"We are all just as anxious as we can be," she went on. "Your brother Dick is operating. I'm so glad you've come, George."

She called him "George" because this happened to be Harry's right name, but with the brothers *he* had, there was no fighting the inevitable. In fact, even his family called him "Harry," and only Elaine seemed to remember an ancient truth.

"Take me to your leader," said Harry blithely, perhaps because poor Cousin Elaine was about as unblithe a character as ever breathed, full of duty and ancient rigidities. He followed her gladly up the sweep of the staircase. Harry didn't mind upstairs so much, where the old man lived these days.

But he was thinking about a rat in this house. Now who would that be? The servants were not visible at the moment. There was a couple, there was an in-and-out cleaning person. There was the chauffeur-gardener, who didn't live in the house. Anybody else?

In the wide upper hall there was a woman. She was an Oriental of some sort, perhaps partly Polynesian. She was not young. She was slim and dressed in a fashion that suggested the Chinese. Her manner was gracious and deferential. Harry had never seen her before.

"Oh, Mei," said Elaine, "here's Mr. George. This is Mei Fong. Now come, George."

Harry could only grimace at the stranger; he went after Elaine into his father's enormous bedroom.

Paul Fairchild was sixty-six years old and in the process of skillfully, with expensive advice, surviving a distress of his heart that had given him warning some months ago. He was sitting up in his thronelike bed, an antique piece of furniture with a towering headboard of carved dark wood. His face was pink and his flesh was firm; his white hair was up like a crest. "Harry," he barked, "what's been going on? What happened to your friend Beckenhauer? Dick says he's been knifed."

"Dick should know," said Harry amiably. "Hi, Tom."

His brother, the governor, was sitting in a big soft chair beside the fireplace, where lamplight was doing no damage to his handsome face. He was the very image of the noble young statesman. Clean-cut about the nose and mouth, glinting gray at the temples, compassionate and humble about the eyes. "Harry." He smiled his famous smile. "It seems you know something."

"How come Beckenhauer phoned *you?*" their father cut in. "Why didn't he phone *me? I* hired him."

"Ah," said Harry. "You did, did you, Daddy?" He sat down in the chair that was a twin to his brother's chair. "Tell me about it."

Tom said, "Let's not be coy. We'd better be sure that this man's injuries are not in any way related to the job—"

"What's the job?"

Paul Fairchild said crossly, "All right, Harry. Come in, Mei. Come in. Now . . ." He fidgeted. He seemed to pout. He cast a baleful look at his youngest son and said, "I don't know how you got in on this. I didn't even tell Tom, until he came by yesterday. Or Dick, until last evening. It's my business. I don't know why there should be any of this damn trouble. I don't want the whole thing spread around either—particularly." The old man was frowning fiercely.

Harry thought fondly, the old man's made a fool of himself, somehow.

His father said, "You boys! You three big louts! That's all very well, and I don't complain. But I always did want a little girl. And I want her now. All I want is my daughter."

Harry felt the shock all the way to the soles of his feet.

His brother Tom said, "We are rumored to have a little sister, you see?" The governor's head was trembling in a slight negative.

"A half sister, you see?" said Elaine, as if to enlighten Harry to the fact that his mother was long dead.

Harry fought away his shock by pretending not to have felt it. "How did we come by this sister?" he drawled. "The usual method, I presume."

His father said, "Do you want to hear about it?"

Harry slouched a little lower in the chair. Elaine had perched near his father. The woman, Mei, had seated herself apart, near the door. All of them, even the stranger, seemed to resign themselves to hearing what they already knew told over again.

His father began, staccato. "Eight years ago. Still had the yacht. Went around the world. Put into a place called Dolabela. Oh, it's off the tail end of the Philippines, somewhere. Very nice little place, very pleasant. There was a young woman. Well, the upshot of that was—I married her."

"According to some local rites," said Tom, "the legality of which I haven't yet been able to determine."

"If *I* took them as valid, then they *are* valid," snapped the old man.

"Certainly," said Harry encouragingly.

"I rented a house ashore. She . . . uh . . . wasn't so sure she'd like it here. Anyhow, honeymoon." He glared and Harry took care to move no eyelash. His father looked away, down at his own hands where they trembled slightly upon the bedclothes.

The woman called Mei spoke softly. "One day soon Miss Marybelle is gone."

"Yes, yes," said the old man. "Mei, here, she . . . uh . . . took care of us during that time. But I don't want to get ahead. All right. One day Marybelle was gone. Didn't know where she went or how. Did my damndest to find her—until at last, well, finally, I got the message. Marybelle was just plain disappointed in her bargain and that's the size of it."

It was costing him something to tell this story.

"So I wrote the whole thing off and sailed for home," Paul Fairchild said, "and when I got back I didn't think it was necessary to yak about it."

"Why should it have been?" said Harry easily.

"Now *you* . . ." said his father in exasperation, as if he had begun to say, "That's enough sympathetic understanding from you, little boy." But he caught himself and said, instead, "Well, it was about three weeks ago that Mei showed up. She came to the U.S.A.—looking for the usual milk and honey—and had got herself into a bit of a financial bind. Naturally she thought of me. Looked me up. That's when Mei tells me that there was a child. A little girl."

Harry was forced to blink, whether he wanted to or not, as his father's face softened to a foolish shy delight.

"Even if there was a child," said Tom with an air of quiet wisdom, "you must see that there can be no proof."

"Where is she now?" said Harry. "The little girl?" And then he added, partly to tease his brother Tom, "Our little sister?"

"That's it," said his father gruffly. "That's the problem. Mei says that Marybelle . . ." He swallowed and then he said it bluntly, "went into hiding to get away from me. She was pretty upset to find out she was pregnant. She didn't want the child. But she bore it and gave it away. Now Mei got all this from some kind of grapevine, but the tale was that the child was given to a bunch of American missionaries."

Harry suppressed a groan. He stopped believing a word of it.

"Some kind of more or less broken-down group," said his father, "who were scraping along without money or support, and who finally had to give up. Broke up. Last year. Dispersed. Vanished. And my daughter with them."

The old man looked very grim.

"And it was three weeks ago," said Harry, "that you asked me if I knew of a good private investigator."

"That's right."

"Asked *him?*" said Tom, with faint surprise.

"And Bernie went after the child," said Harry, ignoring this. "Did he find her?"

"That's what I want to know. I think he might have."

"What makes you think that, Daddy?"

"You don't think so?" The old man looked bleak. "He didn't tell you?"

"Just go on," said Harry.

His father beetled his white brows, glared awhile, and then went on. "Well, he found Marybelle all right. I had his report. It seems . . ." This was something else hard to swallow, but the old man swallowed it and continued. "Later on, she—uh—married another fellow, who wasn't exactly starving in this world, and off she went with him to New Zealand. And never had told him a word—either about *me or* the baby. Fact, she won't admit it now."

"Bernie found her? Bernie talked to her?"

"Right. And she went into hysterics and this so-called husband put Bernie out of the house. But Bernie thought that Marybelle was scared about the legality of her—uh—present marriage. So she . . ."

". . . went into hysterics," said Harry. "Naturally. A pretty woman, Daddy?"

His father glared at him.

"What color, by the way?"

"Damn it," said his father, and then he howled, "I want my little girl. If I've got a little girl in this world and her mother doesn't want her, then *I* want her. What's wrong with that?"

"Not a thing," said Harry.

"If," said Tom with a sigh. "I'm glad to hear that 'if,' Daddy. Even you, Harry, ought to be able to see that someone may have heard about this—uh—marriage of Daddy's and is trying on a little flimflam of some kind." The governor flashed his smile. "Of course, Mei is only repeating what she has heard."

"Flimflam?" said Harry thoughtfully. "With what object? Money?"

"What else?" His brother sighed for the sordid souls of men.

All the Fairchild boys had always had plenty of money, so that when Tom devoted himself to the service of mankind, via his political career, and Dick devoted himself to service in the field of medicine, they could afford the luxury, just as Harry could afford to do what he called "not a damn thing."

Their father said grumpily, "You don't know beans about money, any of you."

"Just a minute," said Harry. "I may be confused. But how is somebody going to get money out of knifing poor old Bernie?" He was having quite a few second thoughts. Bernie was not an idiot, after all.

"No way," said Tom, with his hard head showing. "That's why I'm inclined to think the knifing is not related."

"Of course not," said Elaine. "It can't be. This Beckenhauer had an enemy." She nodded sharply, as if this settled matters.

Mei said, "But it makes me fear . . . It makes me fear very much . . ."

Harry discovered that he didn't know what to think about this woman. It occurred to him that she (a former servant) had certainly known all about his father's wealth because the old man didn't mind throwing it around when he happened to feel like it. And she was in a position to tell a tale of far away and long ago, with nobody to contradict her. Evidently she had landed herself in this house, well surrounded by milk and honey. Maybe that was all there was to it. Or what about this Marybelle's new husband? He might have been enraged to the point where some henchman of his had set upon Bernie for having accused and insulted a cherished wife. Was this an operating human motive anymore? Anywhere?

The old man in the bed said, "Be quiet. Done is done. Harry, I've told you, and now you had better tell me. Why did Bernie call you and exactly what did he say?"

"He was in bad shape, Daddy," said Harry gently.

"Then why didn't you call the police? Get some real help?"

Harry rode over the implication of incompetence. "Why don't I call the hospital?" he said and rose.

"Damn it," roared his father.

But Harry went to the phone that was on the table at his father's bedside. "What's the use of guessing," he said soothingly, "when Dick may know all about it?"

But Harry was more or less stalling, in order to pull his wits together. He didn't know all about it, but he knew something. He knew that Bernie must have believed in a connection between the attack on him and this quest. Bernie had been roughed up by some "swine," and "one swine" had been eavesdropping on the phone call. Bernie had used cryptic means to tell Harry how to get the message. If the message had something to do with the dope for Harry's daddy, then Bernie hadn't wanted some "swine" to find *that* message.

It was not for Harry to undo all Bernie's pains unless and until he found out for sure that Bernie had been in some way deluded. And if he took Bernie seriously at all, then he took him seriously all the way.

So there was a rat in this house, and for all Harry could tell the rat might be in this very room. Therefore he could not speak up and say that he, and he alone, had been given a word and would soon have in his hands whatever message Bernie had so desperately wanted delivered.

"Dick?" he said when he had his brother's ear. "Harry here. Daddy wants to know . . ."

"He didn't make it," said his brother, the doctor. "Died on the table. Sorry. Tell Daddy I'll be right over."

"Did he talk?" said Harry with some difficulty.

"Never came out of it," Dick said. "Not a word."

Harry hung up. He was tingling. He was hearing that fainting voice on the telephone. "I don't care so much about getting myself dead for nothing."

The lobby of St. Bart's was very quiet and deserted except for the pretty creature in the green brocade and the woman in white who was saying, "They did all they possibly could. It was just too late. I'm very sorry."

The girl's head had bent with the blow. Her dark hair was perfumed. The woman could smell it and it smelled good. "I was at a party," Dorinda murmured. "I . . . we kept expecting him. Could I have . . . do you think . . . if I had got here sooner?"

"Oh no, no, no," said the woman, happy to nip guilt in the bud. "He never did recover consciousness. Nothing you could have done, dear. These things happen."

"I wonder . . . Could I see . . ." Dorinda looked up as the woman began to shrink away from what was morbid. ". . . his things?" breathed Dorinda. "Something to keep. Because we . . ." She put her hands over her mouth.

"Well, I'm afraid—" said the woman, who hadn't been young for a long time but who could dimly remember that the young suffered very much. "Of course, later. But right now the police are going to be in charge of everything, you see. So I couldn't really. But would you like to talk to Dr. Fairchild? I may be able to catch him."

"I don't think . . ." said Dorinda in a moment, turning away. "No. You are very kind."

"Have you a way to get home, dear?"

"That's . . . all right," said Dorinda wanly. She walked away and the woman in white felt as sorry as (within her professional obligation to detach) she dared to feel for the poor pretty thing, so young and too shocked and upset to have given her name, even.

Chapter 4

DR. Richard Fairchild, lean and fair, his skin tight to the bone, came in a hurry and fell upon the sandwiches and coffee that Elaine had summoned up. Between sip and bite he regaled the assemblage with some gruesome details, mercifully obscured by the jargon of his trade.

"Oh, he got it in a struggle," Dick announced finally, "or so I opined to the cops. He must have busted somebody a good one with that left hand."

"Could he have been saved had he gone to a doctor at once?" the governor wanted to know.

"Doubt it," said Dick. "In my opinion, no. Little surprising that he lasted out the flight. Of course he was immobilized. He loosened trouble when he began to move again." Dick's good teeth embraced the bread and chicken. "He was a mess," the doctor said. "And now what?"

"I'm sorry the man is dead," the old man said dully. "I want my daughter."

"Hey, Daddy," Dick said alertly, "You've about had it, for one day. Pack it up. Beddy-bye. The cops will find out who done it. How about letting the cops find the kiddie? If that's what you want."

"It may be news to you, Dick," said Tom, "but the legally constituted law-enforcement bodies are there to deal with law breakers, not to go hunting the world for . . ."

"Some old man's fancy, eh?" Dick said. His jaunty bluntness was not malicious. It never was. "Besides," he added, "the cops would be sure to leak the whole affair to the papers. I forgot that. Send another private eye, then. Somebody a little brighter, maybe?"

Harry said, "Yup. Bernie was dumb enough to get on that plane without the benefit of your opinion."

Dick stared at him. "Do I follow?" he said, in a minute. "So he was hero? Oh, come on, Harry. He was jumped by some hoodlums and put in such a state as not to be able to think at all. Sure, that passes for heroism, on occasion."

"If you want my opinion," said Tom earnestly, "I say wait. I can't understand why there should be any connection between this crime and our business. The police will investigate the crime. Since we don't want . . . uh . . . our business kicked around in public . . . wait awhile."

"Sure. Play it cool," said Dick. "That's the way. Go to sleep, Daddy. What's dead is dead."

Harry discovered that he had been good and mad for quite a few minutes already. He put on his worried-cherub look and said, "But Daddy only wants his daughter. Why shouldn't he keep on looking for his daughter? A man is dead. What of it? Or don't I follow?"

"Well," said Dick, "gossip being what it is (and no offense to Mei), I'm not so sure that Daddy's *got* a daughter."

"In your opinion, Doctor?" said Harry. "Really? He was only fifty-eight."

"Boys," said their father.

"How did *you* get into this, Harry?" said Dick. "And what are *you* so excited about? What did this fellow tell you on the phone, by the way?"

"Not much," said Harry, seething.

His brother, the governor, said severely, "Do you mind, Harry? If you know something, say so. And if you don't, then have the grace to admit it. This is no time to play on-again-off-again, now-you-do and now-you-don't."

"I have an opinion," said Harry slowly. "Bernie knows . . . that is . . . he knew where to find the little girl."

"Do *you* know?" cried his father.

"No, sir," said Harry. "However, I'll see what I can do."

"What is this?" said Dick in a moment. "A caper? Come *on,* Harry."

"I talked to his partner," said Paul Fairchild with new energy. "Did I tell you? No reports came in from Bernie within the last three days. They knew he was in the Islands, but not where. Or even why. You're thinking there'll be some clue in his office?"

Harry said nothing. He let his father see that this was not what he had in mind. His clever brothers didn't miss what he was doing.

Tom said, "Harry, if you take it into your head to bumble around in this affair, you're going to make an open exhibition . . . This isn't a game."

"Oh, I'll play it cool," said Harry. "Believe me, I'll remember that somebody on the other side knifed Bernie and got him dead."

"You're saying it is connected," burst Dick.

"Oh, yes."

"How do you know that?"

"He told me."

"What else did he tell you?"

"Not much," said Harry. He had talked. Well, that came of letting himself get angry when he shouldn't have. They didn't know Bernie as he did. He was on his feet. He had better go.

The woman named Mei said to him, with signs of anger, "You are being very cruel."

"Me? I only said I'd see." He edged to the door. "There may be nothing in it."

"In what?" snapped Dick.

"I'd rather not say."

"George!" roared his father, in ultimate severity.

"Until tomorrow, Daddy," said Harry. "I've got my reasons." As long as he was making a jackass of himself, he might as well do a thorough job of it, so he hammed it up and slunk dramatically out of the bedroom door.

He ran downstairs, out the door, leaped into his car and roared off toward his apartment where by now, or surely very soon, he would find all the piggy banks from the gift shop. *Pig!* "Pig" had been the word. One of the pigs, then. There had better be something in it.

The other Fairchild sons took a hasty leave. Dick didn't like his father's look. He said he hoped his daddy wasn't taking the man's death too hard. Crime was crime. In a violent age people took their chances. Tom, who was catching an early flight in the morning back to his own capitol, enjoined his father not to take Harry too seriously. He must realize that Harry might sometimes need the spotlight, under an emotional pressure, sibling rivalry, probably unconscious.

Elaine accompanied them down to the door with cries of reassurance. Harry couldn't possibly be sure that the poor man's death had any connection. Why, it couldn't have! There *must* be another explanation. They needn't worry about Uncle Paul. She would attend to the old man's bedding-down at once. At once.

But when they had gone Elaine slipped along the dark and somehow tomblike lower rooms to a telephone. She dialed by the light of the moon through a window.

"Yes?" said the voice.

"The man . . . the agent they sent is dead."

"We know." The voice was calm.

"I didn't expect . . . I don't like . . . It makes me very . . ."

"Nothing to do with *us,*" said the voice, becoming hearty. "Very unfortunate. We are quite upset. After all, how can he tell us, now, what he did with her? We still need to know. Have you picked up anything helpful?"

"Well, George . . . I mean *Harry* Fairchild, the youngest one . . ."

"Yes?"

"*He* knows something."

"I see."

"He wouldn't say what. Of course, he may have been just clowning."

"We'll keep an eye on him," said the voice in a businesslike manner.

"Don't—"

"Don't worry."

The line clicked dead.

Elaine retraced her steps and went upstairs to the old man. He was very, very tired.

"You mustn't worry about a thing," she said to him. "Please, Uncle Paul. Haven't I been the same as a daughter to you all these years? Haven't I?" She thumped his pillows.

"You're a good girl, Elaine," the old man said wearily, "and I'm grateful. But you know, she'd be . . ."

Elaine began to tidy the big room now, making it dark for the night.

"Her mother was a pretty woman," the old man said. "Her hair . . . the palest . . . flaxen, they call it. Silk, I'd sooner say. She'd be . . . My little girl would be seven years of age. With flaxen hair, do you suppose?"

There was an old frame house, tucked away at the bottom of what Southern Californians call a canyon, that had to be sturdier than it looked from the outside, since it had not, obviously, yet fallen down. Inside, it was very spacious. The room where Miss Emaline Hanks was reclining wearily on a dilapidated couch was so large that she could not even see all the way into its poorly lit corners. It was night, of course, but she wasn't sure how far into the night. Her time sense was all askew. She had been so tumbled, and batted about in such turmoil, that she had to make an effort to realize *where* she was.

She was in her sister's house. And there was her sister, Callie, plunking herself into a canvas chair, tugging at the tab on the top of a can of beer. What could be seen of the room was insanely cluttered. But Callie was making no effort to tidy up, now that the children must be in bed at last. Now that the buzz and movements of so many children had been subtracted, Miss Emaline was even more painfully aware of the anxieties and indecisions that were batting at her from within.

"You look awful beat, Em," said Callie. "Relax. Relax. Maybe you aren't used to the noise, eh? I'll try and get them to be a little quieter tomorrow. Of course they'll make a lot of noise shushing each other." Callie grinned and stretched out her legs in their laddered stockings. "Quite a group, aren't they?"

"Where did you get all these children?" Miss Emaline said feebly.

"Oh—here and there," her sister said. "We can't have any. We should know. We sure tried. But we can raise them."

"I know." Miss Emaline tried not to wince at Callie's vulgarity. "I know they are adopted. But so near of an age. And so *different*."

"Oh, well, I kinda got to wanting the ones that were too mixed-up to be wanted," said Callie, "and the wrong age, and all. Rex, of course, *he* doesn't care."

"But so many," murmured Miss Emaline.

"I'd just as leave have six more. There's plenty of room."

"What are you *ever* . . . ?" Miss Emaline's imagination boggled at the thought of all these children growing up and having to be schooled at about the same time. Her anxiety veered to her own problems. "Is Bobby all right? Can she possibly go to sleep?"

"Why sure she can," said Callie. "The whole mob is going to get sung to sleep in a minute. Rex will do it. You'll hear." Callie sipped. Then her wide mouth widened. "How come her hair is cut like a boy's, Em? Fooling somebody?"

"I can't tell you about her, Callie," said Emaline with agitation. "I've promised. I dare not. There are wicked people. I even know exactly what I *ought* to do. There was a man, a good man . . . but he can't help right now, and I'm afraid . . . I hope . . . Nobody knows we are here?"

"Who's to know?" said Callie.

"Oh, Callie, I didn't mean to dump us on you like this, for a night. I only wrote because I thought you and I could visit a little while at the airport. I hadn't seen you . . ."

"Been fifteen years, or something like that," Callie said. "So this is a whole lot better, I'd say. Don't worry so much, Em. Everybody's gone but the two of us, from the olden days. So tell me how you've been. You never did get married or anything?"

Miss Emaline said, in a whimper, "No, I never did. Or anything. All we tried . . . It was wasted. We only wanted them to live as the Lord would have them live. But they didn't . . . they wouldn't . . I came because I am hoping . . ."

"You're all wore out, Em," Callie said kindly. "And I think I'm going to bring you a little glass of wine now."

"No, no." But Miss Emaline's protest fell feebly from her lips. How could she tell Callie that a good woman didn't drink alchoholic beverages? Emaline, confused and exhausted, had been taken in here. Very kindly, although it did seem effortlessly. Callie, who had just fed seven children and three adults and then merrily trooped the children to seven baths and seven beds, did not seem in the least fatigued. While Emaline felt ready to turn her face to the wall and give up the ghost. Did Callie, then, flourish like the green bay tree? Of course she's ten years younger, thought Miss Emaline, and bashed the ugly head where it was rising.

"I will not judge," she said to herself.

Callie came with the wine and put it on a table. Miss Emaline did not touch it. Callie did not urge her to touch it.

There was a continuing sense of voices, exchanges, laughter, hanging above this room. Now Miss Emaline heard a chord of music from up there.

"Hah!" said Callie. "Now you got to listen. I guess you wouldn't know about the entertainment world. Rex is kinda great, Em." Her plain face was radiant with pride.

"I don't know *what* to do," burst Miss Emaline, who wasn't in the world to be entertained.

Her sister tilted the beer can and looked at her calmly. "Why don't you just goof off for a couple of days. You'll probably figure out what to do when you're feeling better."

"Will I?" said Miss Emaline pathetically. "But you have such a houseful—"

"Oh, well," said Callie. "I'm not the greatest *house*keeper in the world, I'll clue you. But there's room—So why not?"

Miss Emaline thought, if I stay, maybe I can help her. I can be *useful*. The big house was not dirty, she had noticed that. But it had no order. "You may be right, Callie," she said, sinking back. "Maybe a few days. I don't feel awfully well."

But Callie had tilted her head. Upstairs, the guitar was stringing chords into a sequence.

Miss Emaline had barely spoken to Callie's husband. Nor he to her. A strange man. A man who didn't seem to be quite on this earth. Miss Emaline had noticed how the children seemed concerned to guide him, to shepherd him into the everyday small routines, as if he could not be expected to remember all these *little* things. "Papa, can we close the car windows? Or do you want to put it in the shed?" "Papa, if you'd just pull the end of the table, we can put the leaf in." And even, "Papa, did you wash your hands?"

He wasn't slow-witted. Emaline knew that. On the contrary, he was very quick to understand, but he understood on another level. It was obvious that the children both respected and adored him. As for Callie, Callie was . . . content.

Miss Emaline said, in decision, "Then we'll stay, just for a while, if you'll have us, and if he doesn't mind. I don't know where else to go, Callie. I must not make a mistake."

"Stay forever," said Callie carelessly. "But listen. Listen!"

The man had begun to sing. He was far away. He was up there, where the children were lying in seven beds. But all of the big old house fell into a hush, in which the singing voice was not loud, yet every note fell like a separate drop of gentle rain and every syllable was clear.

A feeling of softening came upon Miss Emaline. It was like fainting. Her arm and hand went reaching, to be taut, to resist. She picked up the wineglass in tight fingers.

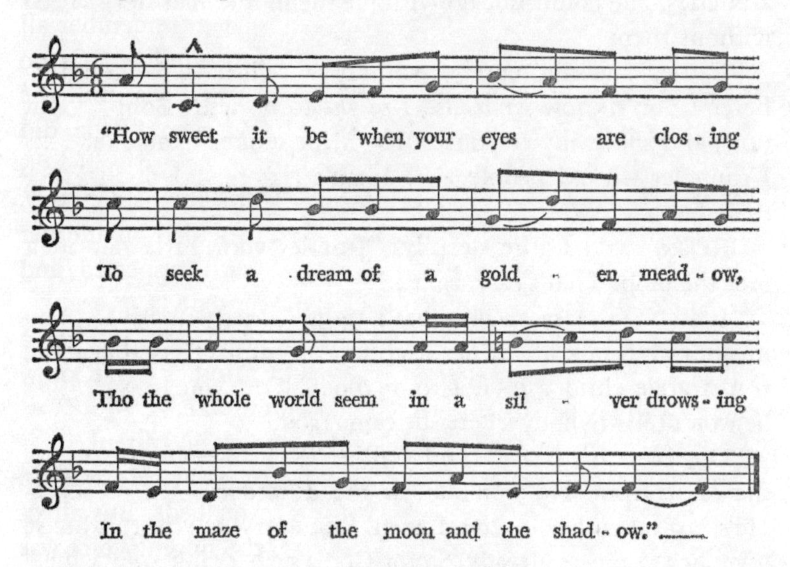

Miss Emaline felt her eyes swell, tears start. But this was childish! She wished he would stop.

The music had fallen as the rain falls, and now, as it ceased, a silent peace flooded the house. Miss Emaline was adrift in the quality of this silence. She was lost. She clutched for her anxieties. She could not do without them. She had never been without them.

"Callie," she said tensely, "you know we'll have to be hiding here? I don't know what else I *ought* to do with Bobby, right now, and she is my responsibility. Mine alone. I can't let . . . I can't let wicked people . . . I can't risk . . . I don't know their faces—"

"Relax," said Callie sleepily. "Just let your little one melt into the mob. That's easy, isn't it?"

"It is NOT easy to do what's right," cried Emaline. "You mustn't even talk about her, Callie. You mustn't say that there is a strange child . . . not to anybody! Can you be sure that he won't tell anybody where she came from?"

"Oh, bless *his* heart," said Callie. "Rex doesn't care where she came from. He won't know the difference—six or seven. He's just taken her in, *too*. Listen, Em, everybody in this house loves her to pieces already. So for God's sake, drink your wine."

Chapter 5

JEAN Cunliffe worked the late shift all weekdays but Friday. She came on early then, and afterward had the long weekend off. She had already been on duty since 6 A.M. when, at about a quarter to eight, Harry Fairchild came swinging in, directly to her. He did not smile. "I have to talk to you. Can you take a break?" He read her doubt before she could voice it. "What is the other lady's name?"

She told him and he swung away. It took him only a few seconds to achieve a signaling, although martyred, nod of Mrs. Mercer's head. So Jean found herself, in some bewilderment, hurrying around the corner and into the coffee shop.

"How did you work *that?*" she gasped.

"It doesn't matter." He took a table apart from any other customers. He ordered coffee for them both, and then he said to her, severely, "You did not do what I asked you to do."

"Why, yes, I did, Mr. Fairchild," said Jean earnestly. "The box should have been delivered. I gave it to the messenger myself."

"Oh, the box came. But you didn't send me everything that was on that table."

"Well, I sure did," said Jean, bristling up. "I sent exactly . . ."

"Oh, no, you didn't. Not exactly." There was a lot of green in his grayish eyes. He wasn't being particularly charming.

"Well, I'm very sorry," said Jean, thinking seriously of getting up and walking out of here. "But to the best of my knowledge . . ."

"I suppose it isn't altogether your fault," he said with a pained smile that was only the token of an effort to be fair. "What about those pigs, for instance?"

"Pigs? You mean the piggy banks? All right. I remember that there were exactly four pigs on that table. Pink, green, yellow and ivory. And that is precisely what I sent you. Did you ask your wife if she counted them?" Jean was becoming a little annoyed herself.

The coffee came. He seasoned his, in silence. Then he said, "What did you do? Sell one?"

"Sell one what?"

"Piggy bank? From that table."

"Since they are there for the purpose of being sold . . ." she began stiffly.

"That's what *I* thought, when I bought them," he snapped. "And I've got no wife. I unpacked the box myself."

"All right. Then you know you got four of them. I took the same colors, even, out of stock."

But he was shaking his head with a look of I-thought-as-much-you-poor-benighted-soul. "How many did you sell and to whom? You won't know, naturally. So you've messed things up, but good. You managed *not* to send me the only thing I really wanted."

"What only thing?"

"One of those pigs."

"If you wanted one pig, why didn't you buy one pig? Why did you say you wanted the whole tableful? I think you can kindly stop bawling me out, and many thanks for a delicious cup of coffee."

Jean Cunliffe wasn't taking on any blame she didn't deserve, and the hell with him and his big fat, wealthy, unmarried charm.

He didn't speak for a moment. Then he let one eyebrow fly. "What kind of girl are you anyway?" he said. "Do you suppose you can resist blabbing to The Group? Or, in the vernacular, can you keep quiet?"

Jean glared at him, keeping quiet in eighteen languages.

"The trouble is," he said ruefully, "you don't know me and I don't know you—but I don't see how I'm going to get any help from you, at all, if I don't tell you a little bit."

"I don't see how, either," said Jean promptly.

"All right," he said. "Here's the point. And keep quiet about it, will you? I have reason to believe that there is an important message for me in one of those pigs. I wanted it, and I still want it."

Jean's face changed. Her thoughts were racing. She knew immediately who was supposed to have put a message there. Or so this Harry Fairchild thought.

She said, with no huffiness, "You should have told me that last night."

"But I didn't think I'd better," said Harry. "I didn't know who might be watching and listening. Not a living soul knows about that pig but me—and now you—and let me say that you'd do well to keep things that way."

Jean's mouth fell open. She didn't laugh aloud, but she wanted to.

"He's dead, you know," said Harry somberly. "Bernie. The man in the phone booth. 'Foul play,' the cops call it. In other words, 'murder.' "

She picked up her coffee with a steady hand and drank some of it. "I had no idea," she said, in a moment, "and you admit you didn't give me any indication." His face kept that somber reproach. "But I can try to remember," Jean said. "That is absolutely *all* I can do *now,* isn't it?"

She gave him a sharp, challenging look and then squeezed her eyes shut.

Harry Fairchild watched her. This was a nice girl, perfectly ordinary common-or-garden-variety of nice girl. Young and breezy. Healthy. Pretty. Probably what is known as "wholesome" (within reason, of course). She had meant no harm in the world. Oh, he knew that. But when he had hopefully smashed four piggy banks to bits and found absolutely nothing in any of them, he had been a pretty frustrated fellow. Then he had figured out what might have happened. Called to find out her hours. And here he was—and he had been right, all right—but what did that matter? The whole thing was fairly hopeless.

He had spent an early morning hour with the cops. He had admitted to them what they already knew. Yes, Bernie had been on a job for his daddy. But the cops must query his daddy about that. It had been personal, Harry told them, and threw no light, as far as he could tell.

But now, from what *they* had told *him,* he knew that somebody was up to something, all right. Murder, plus. The word was that Honolulu police had found indications of a struggle in the parking lot at the airport there. In Bernie's pocket there had been some hotel bills, marked paid, and the Honolulu police, having been informed of them, were going back on Bernie's tracks. The police here had done about all that they could do. A stewardess, for instance, had testified that she had thought Bernie hadn't looked well, she had queried him, and been sent about her other business. Bernie had not spoken to another soul on the plane, in her recollection.

But the upsetting "plus" was that, in the airline ticket envelope from Bernie's pocket, there had been no baggage ticket. And Bernie's baggage had been claimed by persons unknown in Los Angeles. When Harry had pointed out that one scarcely needed a ticket, the whole business of claiming being run on as jolly and informal a basis as it was, the policeman had said that one might need a ticket if one had *no other way of knowing which bag* belonged to Bernie. So something was up. Somebody had acted and was still acting. But Harry didn't think there had been any "dope" in Bernie's baggage.

Among Bernie's other effects, there was a small notebook which he had kept in some strange cryptograph of his own. His secretary couldn't read it. The police had tried her on it. So it began to look as if there existed no formal or even informal record of the "dope" that Bernie had been trying to deliver.

Unless it was in a pig. In a pig, that had been sold in an airport.

Persons unknown, for what reason Harry couldn't imagine, were after that "dope" with violence, theft, or anything else that might serve.

But it was in a pig! And who could say where the pig was?

Then Jean Cunliffe opened her blue eyes and said, "The place was full of kids last night, and you see," she explained, "*children* want the one in hand. *Children* don't always believe in the fact that the one from stock is going to be just the same." She bit her lip in the middle and her smile flew up on both sides.

"You didn't suspect me of being a child, naturally," said Harry bitterly. "I understand that. Go on."

"Oh, I like children, on the whole," said Jean condescendingly. "Now please don't interrupt me. I am remembering that I sold three of those pigs. Because I remember remembering the colors so that I could *conscientiously* substitute the same colors in *your* order."

He took no umbrage. His eyelids may have flattened a little.

"All right," said Jean. "There was a pink pig, and there was a little girl who screamed and howled and stamped her feet and had to have that pink pig, even though her parents were knocking themselves out to convince her that a breakable ceramic piggy bank was not an ideal toy to take on a European tour," she wound up, out of breath.

Harry had a pencil in his hand, and he wrote on the paper napkin, "Pink. Girl. Europe." He met Jean's eyes. She was defying him to speak, but he did not.

"Of course, I don't know the name," she said, "but they wanted me to hurry. They told me not to bother to wrap. Their plane was boarding. Their tour was leaving. One of those guided, scheduled, packaged tours, you know. Does that help any?"

"Could be I can find that one," he said. "Go on." Now his smile was real, and a very warming smile it was.

"I also remember," said Jean, "*because* this little pink-pig-purchaser was so mean and ornery, that there was another little girl who had wanted the pink pig in the first place. But she had to make do with green. See, I had to save our one remaining pink for you."

Harry scribbled on the napkin. "Girl. Green."

"Green was appropriate," said Jean. "Her name was Deirdre. She was from Ireland."

He looked up quickly.

"I thought it was so pretty. I was listening to her mother's accent. I knew they were Celts. I had got as far as deciding they weren't Scots."

Harry blinked. She hadn't said Scotch.

"Then the other mother asked," said Jean with a grin. "That's how. Oh! Oh, wait! Now it comes back. The Irish mother said something else. Ballycoo. Bally-coo. A place name?"

Harry grinned this time. "Good going. Now, that's possible too, isn't it?"

"Is it?" said Jean doubtfully. "Let me see. I'm afraid I'm hazy about the third one. There was a yellow and an ivory, and I sold the yellow. I know that."

"Two out of three is fair enough." He shrugged.

"No, no. I remember a little bit," she said. "I thought it was sissy. I mean, I remember thinking that at the time, but I can't 'see' that little boy. But one thing. I do know that his father, or whoever the man was, paid for the yellow pig out of a ten-dollar traveler's check."

She looked sideways at him. And I'm not as dumb as you thought I was, am I, Buster? she was thinking.

"Where is that traveler's check now?" he snapped.

"At the bank, I suppose."

"Which bank? Never mind. I'll find out." He studied the marks on the paper napkin.

"Pink. Girl. Europe. Tour."

"Girl. Green. Deirdre. Irish. Ballycoo."

"Yellow. Boy. Check."

"Why in the world did your friend ever put a message in a pig?" she asked softly.

"You didn't see him do it?" he countered quickly.

"No. I guess he could have done it. I can say that much."

"That's what he did, all right." Harry moved restlessly. "Drink your coffee, Miss . . . Jean?"

"Jean Cunliffe."

"Miss Cunliffe. And thanks very much. All that you could do turned out to be quite a lot." Well, he *could* be charming.

Jean lifted her cup. She couldn't help preening herself. She had remembered a lot more than she could have been expected to remember. This affair was really very strange and interesting. She wasn't at all anxious to finish her coffee and go back to work and hear no more about it. She was reflecting that Harry Fairchild would be called a good-looking man, yet, if you analyzed, there was, in his amiable assortment of features, not one of any classical beauty. His nose, for instance, was too short. He glanced up impatiently. Not to be caught studying him, Jean gazed afar.

"That's funny." She put her cup down carefully. She'd caught a glimpse of something, out in the concourse. "There's one of the passengers from the same plane last night. What's he doing here, I wonder."

Harry's neck seemed to stiffen and resist the impulse to turn and look. "Perfect recall, eh?" he said skeptically.

Jean gave him a look meant to wither. "Since *this* man pretty much got in on the act and was the first one to kneel down over your friend, I tend to remember him."

"Describe him. Where is he?"

"He is wearing a brown suit," she said, shortly, "and he is standing right smack outside, looking at the back of your neck."

"*That's* what he's doing here?" said Harry softly. A very odd look came over his face, but he still did not turn around. He began to shred the paper napkin in his fingers. "Can you, with a happy, happy smile, tell me all about this man and exactly how he got in on the act last night?"

Jean beamed upon him. "Why sure," she said. "He was just trying to be a Samaritan, I guess. Said he was looking for identification. Afterward, he came over and asked me what his poor friend had said to me. There was this old bid . . . I should say this lady, from the plane, who took it upon herself to tell me he was a liar, but . . ."

"A liar?" Harry was taking the paper napkin down to confetti.

"Oh, I suppose she thought he meant it literally. See, he called your friend his 'poor friend' and she said that *he* was no friend, if," she continued, "you can disentangle my quotes and my pronouns, Mr. Fairchild, which I will admit is not going to be easy, off paper."

"If I follow you," said Harry, meeting her eyes with a curious sense of companionship, "this chap was just too, too terribly interested? Where was he looking for identification? In Bernie's pocket?"

"Where else?" said Jean. "Of course, *I* heard him tell the policeman he didn't know your Bernie. He just happened to be there, is what I think."

"Be where?"

"In the next phone booth," Jean said.

Harry leaned back and blew breath out. He said, "Where do you live?"

"In an apartment," she answered, with cheerful evasion.

"Do you live with a man? I mean, are you married? Or do you live with your father? Or a couple of large brothers, or *somebody?*"

"I live alone," she said coldly.

Harry was worrying the confetti to powder. "I should have my head examined," he said gloomily. "What the dickens am I going to do with you now? Is he still out there?"

"He is," she said. "Why should you do anything . . . ?"

"All right," he cut in. "We're going back to the gift shop and you're going to resign and then . . ."

"Hey! Not so fast. I happen to have to work, to pay the rent. You may not—"

"Ah, but you've got a new and better job." He got up. "You are now first assistant to an idiot. So come along."

"What are you talking about?" she said indignantly.

"You're working for me. The pay's not too bad. Say a thousand a week? Is that okay?"

"Just what," she said icily, "am I supposed to be doing for you, at those prices?"

He sat down again. "I don't suppose you have a passport," he said moodily.

"Oh, you don't?" said Jean.

"You do?"

"I do." He gave her a look that made her think he didn't believe this. "Even poor folks, these days, often take the three-week high-spot-hitting European jaunt," she said. "You'd be surprised. I did it last summer. In the winters, see, I go to college."

He looked at her gravely. "It might save time. You might be useful. You could recognize those kids?"

"What kids?"

"The ones who bought pigs."

"Well, the little girls, maybe. I don't guarantee . . . Now *what* . . ." She pushed her chair back, both hands on the table edge, feeling alarmed. "What do you mean, passport?"

"O.K. You can choose one," he said. "You can let me take you to my daddy's house, and you can stay there, where there are servants all over the place and no danger of white slavery, by the way." His look withered her. "Or else you can go along and help me spot the right kids."

"Go *where?*"

"Wherever we have to go. I can find out what tour flew out of here last night at . . . whatever hour it was. Sevenish? Right? And where the tour is now and where it can be caught up with." He was standing and pulling at the back of her chair. "Your first duty, Miss Cunliffe, is to find out which bank has that traveler's check, so that we can locate Pig Number Three. You are vice president in charge of pigs, so come on."

Jean got up on shaky legs. "I think you're crazy."

"Just stupid," he said glumly. "But not quite stupid enough to leave you around to get beaten up, the way Bernie was."

"Oh, for heaven's sakes!"

"What do you suppose," he said crossly, "that some spy thinks you and I have been talking about all this time? And me taking notes, idiot that I am." There was no longer anything legible on that paper napkin. Or any napkin, either.

"*What* spy? Spying for *whom? Why?*"

"Never mind. I'm not going to . . ."

"You're darned right you're not going to . . ."

"Come on," he cut her off. "Let's go tell your boss you quit."

"Why bother?" she said sarcastically. "Why don't you just drag me off by the hair of my chinny-chin-chin?"

"Because it's not courteous," said Harry, "and you are sure proving to me that you *can't* keep quiet about you-know-whats, can you? Anyway, I've got to find out about the check."

Jean weathered his reproach and went beside him to the cashier. She had to get out of here anyhow. While he paid, she looked out into the concourse. The man in brown, the big one who had worn the white flowers last night, had bent his head and was pretending (Now why was she even toying with the notion that he was *pretending?*) to study a timetable.

When Harry turned she said cordially, "Protect me back to work. Then I'll be glad to ask about the traveler's check. I'll do it for free. How's that?"

"Dandy," said Harry. "And the villain asking, right behind you. Deviosity. That's what we've got to learn *and* practice."

The shop was almost under their noses. They had a walk of about ten feet. The man in the brown suit was watching them idly.

"Very devious type spy," Jean said softly. "He's standing there *spying*. A double bluff, don't you think?"

Harry cast her a look. "Just a clown, eh? All right for you."

Chapter 6

AS soon as they were within, he put her aside and went sailing over to where Mrs. Mercer was waiting on a woman. He said, loud and clear, "I guess you'll be able to get along without Miss Cunliffe, won't you? She and I have made a little arrangement. I'm sure you'll explain to the powers that be. Please, Mrs. Mercer? I'm setting her up in a bit of a love nest, you see, and naturally we'd like to get on with it."

Mrs. Mercer turned a rich purple. Jean herself was seeing several other colors, including red. The woman customer tittered nervously.

But Harry Fairchild spun the book of sales slips around and read off the name of the shop's owners, and the business telephone. "On second thought," he said kindly, "I'll phone your boss and do it myself. So please, take no trouble at all. Come along, sugarplum."

Jean came closer. She was *trying* to form a sentence that would say, he's joking. It isn't true. But there was Mrs. Mercer, hissing at her like a snake. The look on her face was as mad a look as Jean had ever seen in her life. It had in it all the envious loathing of lusty youth (and somebody else's sex) that Jean had ever heard rumored. Jean felt herself turning cold. The fact was, she suddenly didn't want to work here anymore.

Harry was turning her rather gently. "Just a minute, precious," said Jean coolly. She went for her purse and then—in the sulphurous evil of the smoldering atmosphere—she let him whisk her out of there.

"Okay," said Harry briskly, pretending not to notice that she was absolutely numb. "Now let's see if we can get rid of *him*."

He hustled her directly over to the man in brown. "You are just the fellow I want to see," said Harry sternly.

"Pardon?" The man blinked.

"This girl tells me," said Harry, "that you were first on the scene last night, when Bernie Beckenhauer went down. So, if you don't mind, will you tell me why you stole his baggage check? And just exactly what you did with his baggage?"

"You must be making some kind of mistake," said the man dourly. His little eyes flickered between the two of them. Jean's face wasn't telling him a thing. She was more bewildered than he was.

"What's your name?" said Harry imperiously, stepping forward.

"Who's asking?" The man stepped backward.

"Fairchild. Harry Fairchild."

"My name is Varney. Victor Varney. I don't know what you are talking about."

"On that plane, were you? From Hawaii? Last night? *She* says you were."

"So? What's the matter with you?"

"So? What are you doing here now?" Harry was pressing him, moving in on him.

The man said in disgust, "I think you're nuts. Excuse me. I got no time whatsoever for nuts." He turned away. Harry let him go. The man stepped onto the moving stairs. He was wafted down, his stare thoughtfully upon them, until he disappeared.

Harry said, "I don't know. I don't know." He looked down at Jean, who was trying to get the breath to speak at all. "Deviosity," he explained. "He may think that, now, he knows everything you told me."

"Then he won't . . . uh . . . bother to beat me up?" she gasped.

"Atta girl," said Harry admiringly. "Of course, as I say, I don't know."

She let him lead her around to a phone booth. He put her into it and sat her down. So there she was, stuffed in, and barricaded by his body, half-listening to his further antics on the phone.

She was thinking, well, he is a fun-type madman, anyhow. But that Mercer! What a creep! She shivered a little.

Harry called the number from the gift shop. He got the name of a bank. The bank was not open yet. By another phone call he got the president's name. He called the bank's president at home. Told him a pack of lies. He then hung up and asked her solicitously if she was still breathing.

She said she hadn't given it a thought, but she would and let him know.

Harry opened the door and wagged it like a fan. Then he shut them up again and called the terminal's authorities for last night's schedule. He got it. He called a travel bureau for a tour that fit the schedule. He called another. He found one that knew. He asked for the tour's itinerary. He discussed it.

Jean was thinking that she'd have to hunt another job. She'd find one, of course. And she'd have to get away from Harry Fairchild in a minute. She'd watch it, and not get into a car with him. She had better not even leave the building. She knew the rules for nice girls, more was the pity.

But when Harry finally finished his telephone marathon and took her arm and walked her away, she was in no fit state to notice the felt hat in the next booth over. Or under it, the inconspicuous little man, as quiet as a mouse in a mousehole.

She had begun to think that Harry Fairchild *couldn't* be crazy. He was probably just rich. There was no other explanation.

He encouraged this idea by whirling her downstairs, through the tunnel, and then along the row of counters, shopping among the international carriers for seats to Europe as soon as possible. At last he found a seller and negotiated for two . . . not one, but two . . . to Copenhagen and he inquired about connections on to Amsterdam. Jean made no protests. He could afford his fun. She wasn't going, of course. She found herself watching for the man in brown. But the long building was sparsely populated. He was nowhere to be seen.

Harry said, "Well, that gives us four hours to get back here. Can you make it?"

"No," she said stonily.

He began to walk her to an exit. "Don't be mad. Sure, that was a dirty trick I pulled upstairs. But you're on salary. Let me get you away from here safely, and then we can discuss . . ."

She stopped walking and dragged him to a stop, too. "You won't take me anywhere at all," she said sadly.

"You don't want to fly off into the wild blue, eh?" he said, riding swiftly over the total negative. "That was for you to say. He travels fastest, and so on, anyhow. Okay. What I've decided to do, then, is hide you somewhere, with a trustworthy bodyguard. But not in my daddy's house."

"No?" she said thinly. "Well! Why ever not?"

"Because there's a rat in that house." They were standing in the middle of the space. He wasn't touching her. He went on chattily. "I'll admit that our so-called villain in the brown suit may be only an innocent businessman—if such there be. I'll admit further that you might be entitled to take your own chances, villains included. But, if I put you in my daddy's house, where I'm *sure* there's a rat, then you'll *surely* be set upon and made to spill what you know. I can't have that. Sorry."

"What makes you think . . . ?" She began to sputter.

"Oh, come on," he said pityingly, "you'd spill. No offense. So would I. Didn't I explain that 'they' are ruthless?"

"Whee!" said Jean. "Less ruth than you, even?"

"Oh, shut up," he said. "I hate this kind of nonsense, believe me. At my age it's bad enough that I have to go tooting around the world after a piggy bank. I purely resent having to be the misunderstood hero, on the top of it." Then he was impelling her out of the building and, suddenly tickled and ready to whoop with laughter, she went.

At the ticket counter the little man who had stood inconspicuously behind them sidled up to make a purchase.

When they came out into the non-air-conditioned air, Jean flared into speech. "You mean to say you are really going to Am . . . ?"

"Shush!"

There were people disembarking from an airport limousine. Jean lowered her voice. "How can you be sure he ever did put . . . ?"

"Shush!"

"I told you," she stormed, "I did *not* see him do it."

"Oh, he wouldn't have let you see," said Harry, who was scanning the sidewalks and the pavements. He looked across to the peaceful parking lot, where the docile machines stood in their ranks. It was a bright day. He tugged at the girl gently. She wouldn't move. He looked down and said impatiently, "He told me he did, on the phone."

"Now *that,*" said Jean immediately, "is ridiculous!"

She had her heels dug in. He was looking down at her. His eyes were greener than ever. The weather was bright. There was a breeze. His dark hair was stirring. Jean put up her hands to hold her blonde tresses. A jet screamed off into the sky.

As the noise died, Harry bent and said close to her startled ear, "They got Bernie in a parking lot. Did you know that? Better wait for me here." Then he was gone, across the pavement. Then she could see him running down an aisle between the automobiles.

When he pulled up and leaned to open the door, beaming at her cheerfully, Jean got in. She really didn't know what she was getting into. (It was Harry's Mercedes-Benz 300 S E convertible roadster, off-white with black leather inside.) But Jean was furious. She could have nipped off and hidden from him in half a dozen ways. And hadn't. She said, as this astonishing car whipped away, "Hah! Hah! Tell me this. If your Bernie took the trouble to call you up on the telephone and tell you that he had put a message in a pig . . ."

Harry was slipping from lane to lane, watching behind.

". . . then," cried Jean, "*why* didn't he *tell* you, right there on the telephone, what the message was?" She thought she would have died if she hadn't got to say this.

"Oh," said Harry. "I see what's bothering you." But he went right on. "Now, if you don't want to fly off, that's perfectly understandable. I'm thinking the best idea is for me to give you some hiding money and let you hide yourself. That way," he glanced at her, "*I* wouldn't even know where you were. Okay?"

Jean said, "I don't want money. I want the answer to my question."

"Yes, but where shall I . . . Look, if you have a car I would suggest that you leave it . . ."

"I came in a car pool," she said. "Would you mind driving me home? I live at 28479 Painter."

Harry said nothing.

"As you could find out, in five seconds on the telephone, the way *you* operate," she sputtered.

He said, "How do I go, please?"

So she told him. This surprising automobile—surprising because it was not long-snouted, rip-snorting, or bright red, either—began to follow her instructions. Jean Cunliffe happened to hold the theory that drivers reveal their inner selves. She had plenty of time to observe that Harry Fairchild was a fast, a safe, and a very shrewd driver, because he didn't say another word and, stubbornly, neither did she.

He pulled up in front of her modest apartment house, handed her out of the car, and went with her into the lobby in what seemed to be automatic courtesy. But when she had used her key on her first-floor private door, he stepped into her one-room-kitchen-bath, right behind her.

"I won't ask you to come in," she said sweetly. "You must

have so much to do. Please, try not to worry about me, Mr. Fairchild." She pitied him, kindly.

Harry sat down in her one upholstered chair. "To answer your question . . ."

Jean sat down on the edge of her daybed. She was dying to hear this.

"I went to school with Bernie," he began. "We had a fraternity brother and patron. We called him old Doc McGee. Fellow had a house that was our hangout. So old Doc got sick and tired of paying the phone bills all us undergraduates kept running up on him. So he put a big piggy bank next to his phone and nobody got to make a call until he'd put his contribution in the pig. That's background. Now. Bernie said to me on the phone last night that 'one swine' was right there, eavesdropping. The point being"—Harry was being very patient and *too slow,* thought Jean, trying not to fidget—"that Bernie thought he had to be cryptic. That's why he didn't tell me what the message *was.* He told me he was giving me a word that was going to clue me. Let's see if you can guess. He said '*some swine*' had roughed him up. '*One swine*' was listening. (Maybe in the next booth, hm?) Bernie said he was '*bleeding like a stuck pig.*' " Jean shivered. "Then he talked about old Doc McGee and phone calls, which brought into my mind what he knew it would bring into *my* mind. After that, he even said he wasn't going to make it '*all the way home?*' Can you tell me what the word was?"

"All right," she said meekly.

But Harry was suddenly dumb—just sitting there with his dark head tipped a little, his hands together. It had occurred to him that he had been talking again. And why should he have been?

"I'm sorry I goofed," she said, in a moment.

"Oh, that's all right." He was pressing his ten fingertips, the left against the right.

"I hope you'll be able to find the one pig you wanted, Mr. Fairchild."

"I'll move fast," he said listlessly. Now she believed that there was something in a pig, and why the devil had he gone to work and convinced her? He didn't know what he was going to do about her. Nothing, probably.

"What's *in* that pig?" she wanted to know now.

He groaned within. The trouble with talking was that one thing led to another. "Oh, I'm only guessing," he shrugged.

"Why do *they* want whatever it is?"

"That I can't even guess," he said bluntly.

"But who *are* they?"

"*I* don't know."

Jean had begun to bristle. He could almost see her brain going around. "Did you make that up about the baggage check and the missing baggage? *Did* you?" She was pouncing on the point of suspicion.

Harry saw no point in lying. "No, I didn't make that up," he said monotonously. "The police told me."

Jean rose and went to look out of her window. "Then why didn't the man in the brown suit follow us here?" she demanded.

"Maybe he did."

"Oh, he did not."

"Then *I* don't know why not," said Harry. "Listen, I am a quiet fella. This isn't my forte. I don't know that I've got a forte, when you come right down . . ."

"Now see here," Jean blazed at him. "You lost me a job and threatened me with villains and I don't know what-all, and you're *not* chickening out now—or are you? Do you intend to take that plane?"

"Well, Bernie gave *me* the word," Harry said helplessly.

"All right. And *I* sold the pig." Jean hauled her suitcase out of the closet and put it on her bed.

She wasn't going to kid herself any longer. She could not sit this one out. She'd never forgive herself. She saw herself a grandmother, mourning, in her shawl, the missed merriments of her youth. The fact was—supposing the worst came to the so-called worst? Some people might still think that there was a fate worse than death. But there wasn't. And she wasn't afraid that she was going to die.

She was a brilliant packer, swift and decisive. Fast, eh? she was thinking. She knew how to pack for travel. Very little.

With increasing uneasiness Harry watched the performance, as graceful as a dance, not one wasted motion. She didn't change her dark blue linen working costume. She didn't even primp. At last, she whipped her suitcase shut, dumped away the milk and cream from her small refrigerator, yanked on a travel-wise knitted hat, tweaked it to a becoming shape, opened her top dresser drawer, took out a clump of beads and baubles in one hand and her passport in the other—all this in one fast sweep around—and then she bowed to her audience.

Harry rose and said, "I appreciate this, Miss Cunliffe, very much. I am trying to think where you'll be perfectly safe and comfortable."

She bounced her passport on her palm. "You'd better not risk it, had you?"

So Harry put on a look that was a combination of innocent wonder and deep trouble. "But listen to this. Now, please be serious. I think I've had an idea. Supposing they do get after you, to tell them all you know. Okay, I'll be on my way. So what you do is, *you tell them!* Hah! Instant safety! So simple, it's hard to see, isn't it?" He was beaming on her and also drifting backward toward the door. "Please don't worry about me, Miss Cunliffe."

"It's not done," she said severely.

"What?"

"That sort of thing. Not by the good guys."

Harry winced.

"Of course, I'm only guessing that *we* are the good guys." She dumped the beads and the passport into her handbag and took up her coat. " 'But you need me,' she said simply," said Jean. "So we'll both guess. And there is absolutely no need for *me* to know what *you* guess *might* be in the pig. Is there?"

He rolled his eyes to heaven, signifying defeat, and then he sat down and told her.

Chapter 7

THE sun was lowering; its slanting rays were trapped now against the hill that bounded the raggedy back yard, and the children were scampering in a golden light, making ghostly rainbows with the garden hose.

Miss Emaline, limp in a garden chair near the house wall, was running a fever; she knew that. She was coming down with something. She hadn't been able to help Callie all day. She had tried not to complain. She felt guilty and miserable now as her body alternately shivered and burned; her mind was not even as clear as it ought to be. It ran in circles.

Sometimes she tried to attach their names to the children. The little black boy was Carl. The red-headed lass with the skinny legs, she was Alice. The boy who might be an Indian, wasn't he Lenny? No, he was Joe. No, Joe must be the boy with the very *white* skin and the huge black eyes. There was a Rebecca. The little Korean? And a Nancy. Nancy must be the one who seemed to be honey-colored—skin, hair, and eyes, too. There was Bobby, of course, screaming and giggling and scampering as fast or faster than the others—the boys or the girls.

They were having a water battle and Rex, the grown man, bald head, beard and all, was in the midst of it about as wet as they all were, ducking and dodging over the rough turf, and the noise was making Miss Emaline's nerve ends wince, and wince again, with that sick feverish running shudder.

But there sat Callie, rocking and watching, not seeming to care how noisy they were. Or how soaked, either. "It waters the plants," she had told her sister complacently. "They sure do need it."

Miss Emaline had done the best she could . . . the best she could . . . all this day. She had had a talk with Bobby this morning. Bobby was an intelligent child, respectful, well-behaved. She had taken everything so well, so quietly. Just as she had taken the death of Mrs. Webb, the Reverend's wife, who had been the one to raise her. Poor Mrs. Webb, worked herself to death, she had. Well, that was what raising a child could do to you. The Reverend was so lonely and defeated now. Helpless-seeming. Miss Emaline had had such hopes of helping.

When Mr. Beckenhauer had come to them and said that Bobby was really the child of a very, very rich man, they had all agreed that they had no right to keep the child from her natural opportunities. Mr. Beckenhauer had thought it proper for the little girl to travel with a woman and he had said that the father would be, without a doubt, most grateful to such a woman. They had all agreed that Miss Emaline should be the one to go. She was the most hopeful, the most aggressive, or perhaps the most anxious. She wanted to make her way to the former mother-churches and try what she could do. Miss Emaline had dreamed of saving their mission. Even now, she might make it possible for them to re-form and continue the holy work. Somewhere. Somehow. They were all praying for her.

When Mr. Beckenhauer had asked Miss Emaline privately, that night, to cut Bobby's hair and dress her in shorts and shirt and use the male pronoun during the journey because, he said, some things had happened that were making him rather nervous about the child's safety, Miss Emaline had not permitted herself to be daunted. He had given her money for their fares, and a good deal over. The seats had been taken in the name of Mrs. Webb. He had told Miss Emaline not to appear to be acquainted with him on the plane. He had promised to be on the plane and that he would contact her soon after they arrived in Los Angeles. And he had said that it would be all right for her to write her sister. A good idea, actually, he had said. A good man.

Oh, she had trusted him, and taken the money, and allowed him to convince her of the need for all such secrecy, for the child's sake. Because of certain wicked people. So Miss Emaline had not told the others very much at all. Just that she was taking the child where the child belonged and she would, once magically transported to the Mainland, do all she could to plead, to raise funds, to save the holy work. She would be back as soon as possible. She would never desert them.

But now . . . Oh, that bright blood dropping! The evil that must be in this terrible world! But Mr. Beckenhauer had told her what to do, just the same, and she had done it. She knew that, now. He knew where she was. He would contact her as soon as he was better, and instruct her. She knew where he was. At St. Bart's, of course. She'd heard that. She'd taken pains to listen. But Callie had no phone. Miss Emaline hadn't been able to call. When she felt better . . .

At least for now, Bobby was safe. Such an untroublesome child, as children went, taking everything in stride. Miss Emaline had told her, this morning, that she might just begin to call Callie "Mama" as the others did. If Bobby didn't mind? Bobby had asked if she could call Papa "Papa." And had promised, with a lighting up of her small face, that she *would* do so, and had skipped off to join what Callie called the mob. She hadn't had much chance to play in her little life so far. She was playing now, with great gusto.

It was Bobby who was guiding the hose at the moment. She was in the fore and sending the stream of water after the big man who was jumping it as if it were a rope. But Bobby was going to "get" him. Her little face was glowing with determination. When the man went looping off in a trot to the side of the house Bobby tugged on the hose and the children, accepting her leadership, all helped her, and they staggered like a many-legged dragon in pursuit. They'd get him—this large child who played as hard as they. They'd drench him. Miss

Emaline shuddered at the chilly thought. Her head ached. Her eyes ached. Her chest ached. Then Rex turned on an outdoor faucet, there at the house wall, and he put his big thumb over it and made a great fan of water catch the children in their laughing faces and they ducked and tumbled, shrieking with delight.

"Hey, that didn't get *you,* did it, Em?" said Callie, beside her.

"No, no." Miss Emaline's very voice ached in her throat. "But Callie, I'm afraid . . . I'm feeling quite ill." Miss Emaline's head rolled. "And how can I ask you to nurse me? I can't do that."

Callie didn't speak. She rose and put her hand on her sister's forehead. She looked smilingly into Emaline's tired, aching eyes.

"Callie, what if I'm contagious? You *have* to think of the children."

"Don't worry. I will."

"Do you think . . . a hospital?" Miss Emaline's heart fluttered.

"We'll ask the doctor."

"The Mission did have insurance," Emaline rambled on, "long ago. It wasn't kept up. How could we? I have *some* money. Would there be a charity ward? At St. Bart's, Callie? Do you think so?"

Callie had her fingers on Emaline's wrist and was frowning a little.

"Because I've heard of St. Bart's. It's a good hospital? If I could only . . . I can't impose. I can't impose."

"I wish you'd told me you felt so bad," said Callie. "You're sizzling."

But Emaline was trying to think of a name, Bobby's name. She ought to tell Callie in case she, Emaline, was dying. Mr. Beckenhauer had asked her not to tell anyone either the name or where the wearer of the name was to be found. Not even to write the name down anywhere. So she had not. But she knew it. She'd have it in a minute. "Was it 'Just?' " she murmured.

"Justice? No, no, it was Fair. Fairchild," she said to Callie, "That's to remember for Bobby . . ."

"Bobby's okay," said Callie. "They are all fair children."

Miss Emaline burst into weak sobbing.

"Don't cry, Em. I'll nip down the block and call the doctor."

"You are a good woman," wept Miss Emaline. (Oh, she ought not to have risked this dangerous business for the child. Oh, she ought to have been daunted. But now—now!—she must protect the child with her life, if necessary. It was the only way to redeem herself.)

"Let me get you inside, where it's higher and dryer than it is out here," said Callie. The back yard was a tumble of sun and water and children. You couldn't tell one from another.

Miss Emaline said craftily, "Callie, could you drive me to St. Bart's? Couldn't I just go there? Wouldn't they take me in? I don't want . . . *your* doctor. I don't want . . . anybody to know where she is. I know it's an imposition."

"Sure, I can drive you, if you want," said Callie.

Miss Emaline leaned dizzily on her sister. She tried to take her own weight.

"Impose. Impose," said Callie gently.

Chapter 8

THEY traveled first-class, Harry on the aisle, Jean at the window. As the big plane slipped along toward the top of the globe he couldn't be rid of the sense that she was bouncing. She didn't, of course, literally bounce but she was so . . . *thrilled* was the word, he supposed grimly.

He had told her to go to sleep. She'd said she couldn't. It was too early. He'd said she'd be sorry if she didn't. Then he had taken out the paperbacks that he had selected haphazardly. John Donne? Okay, he'd refresh his soul in decent silence, whether she bounced or no.

He conceded that Jean had not, obviously, done much traveling. He knew now that she was an orphan, on her own, with limited resources, and, he presumed, narrow horizons. It wasn't that Harry minded traveling, but he'd had it. He, for instance, felt that he could take the North Pole or leave it alone. Even if the romantic idea, that the polar route went over the Pole, had been true, the North Pole, he reasoned, was not perceptible to the unaided human senses. Even if you were standing on the thing, you would have to imagine it. Harry felt that he could imagine the North Pole as well, or better, in his chair at home. But there she was, hanging out the window as if she were going to see something.

Oh well, here they were. Harry had very little doubt that he was making a monumental fool of himself. Chasing a pig! But one could make a fool of oneself with a certain amount of dignity and aplomb, by not compounding folly with a wiggly enthusiasm. So he read, with stern diligence, trying his best to ignore his companion.

Now she was definitely wiggling. "Oh," she said, "Donne? Oh, the line I love above all lines . . ."

He cocked an eyebrow. Now what?

"Bracelet of bright hair about the bone," she quoted.

He gave her a look of terrified disdain and she subsided.

Jean snuggled down into her seat and told herself she had better stop acting like a puppy dog. All right, she couldn't help being excited, but she had better simmer down. The trouble was she'd had so much fun. Quite a day, this had been. She smiled to herself over the story of the old man and his unexpected little daughter. She thought it was touching. She wished she could have met Harry's daddy. But Harry wouldn't have that.

He hadn't even gone to see his daddy, himself. He'd spoken on the telephone, said he'd be away a couple of days, might have something to report, didn't know, wasn't sure. Harry really believed there was a spy in that house, close to his father; he wouldn't say a word that might be revealing.

The Gospel According to St. Bernie, thought Jean. But she had to agree that, if you believed any of it, you had better believe it all. She did believe firmly that there was something in a pig.

There were three of them now who knew about pigs. There was Bonzer. Harry had told him all, and nothing in Bonzer's mien betrayed whether or not he had already suspected that pigs mattered. Jean liked Bonzer; she thought his manners were elegant. He looked like the White Knight, but with a higher I.Q. He had a calming effect, as if absolutely nothing would ever surprise him. He *sat* on improbabilities and kept them in their places as perfectly reasonable possibilities, at least. He made everything respectable, somehow.

So she had sat happily on the big couch in Harry's apartment, looking over the city, listening to Harry explain what Bonzer was going to do about the traveler's check. Bonzer was to go to the bank where the president, having been told a tale, would have culled out the check in question. Harry had put up a yarn that there was a young lady in whom Harry took some discreet interest, who was very much concerned lest she had been conned into taking a spurious check, a forgery. She did not wish to be in trouble about it, on her job, and Harry did not wish her to be in trouble, either. So Harry, although feeling it his civic duty to give warning, nevertheless proposed that he, personally, would supply the ten dollars, so that the accounts of the shop would not be short and the girl home free.

Bonzer, therefore, was to appear in his employer's behalf, and insist upon handing over ten dollars in cash, which the banker would not take, of course. Harry said that this was *not done*. Bankers were very suspicious, especially about *given* money. But the device, although very silly, would serve to get Bonzer a good look at the check. He was to make a note of the name and also whatever identifying numbers there might be on it. If there were two or more such checks submitted by the gift shop, then Bonzer was to take notes on all of them. He could choose any one upon which to fasten the banker's suspicions. Harry had no qualms. The false accusation would prove false, of course, he said airily.

Having secured this information, Bonzer was to go to Bernie's office and consult with Bernie's colleagues in the matter of locating the man who had signed the check. But Bonzer was not to tell even them why he wanted to know this.

And the word "pig" was not even to be breathed.

Harry thought they had covered the pig's tracks. Bonzer had already divided the box of toys into two sections and sent one to each of two children's hospitals. Even if the toy transaction were to become known and arouse the villains' curiosity, they could not discover which of the toys Harry had really wanted. The pigs would have vanished, fallen into a crevice between hospitals, as it were. Harry himself had already cleaned away the crumbs and pieces in this apartment. (Bonzer accepted this statement impassively.)

Furthermore, Harry had explained with satisfaction, Mrs. Mercer would no doubt understand that toy-buying spree to be Harry's reaction to a sudden overwhelming yen for a pretty girl named Jean Cunliffe.

Also (Aha!) if anybody inquired of Mrs. Mercer how come Harry Fairchild and Jean Cunliffe seemed to have vanished, Mrs. Mercer had a full-blown explanation ready and willing to explode from her lips.

"Deviosity," he had beamed.

Jean couldn't help smiling, remembering the argument that had ensued. Bonzer had rustled up a delicious meal and she had enjoyed it very much, meanwhile telling Harry that there was no such word as "deviosity." What he meant was "misdirection," a technique used by magicians. Harry had said he liked his own word better. Had there ever been, at any time, any question in her mind about what he *meant* by "deviosity"? Well, no. All right, then. It was not progressive—in fact it was pretty stuffy—to discourage a man who could coin a word with an immediately obvious, perfectly clear meaning. There ought to be more such words, Harry said, and he would have to see what he could do.

They had then discussed a code word for "pig" that might be useful on occasion. They could not, Harry declared, discuss the matter in any even partially public place. But some emergency might arise. So they made hilarious suggestions to each other, but settled on none.

Armed with passports and documents, they had taken a cab at the last minute. Jean had tumbled lightheartedly into the beginning of this journey, as frisky and friendly as a puppy dog. They'd boarded swiftly and been more or less shooed into their places just before takeoff. Harry had shaken his head at her to indicate that he had seen no villains on their heels, but they both knew that this didn't mean a thing, since they had no idea who the villains were. Or, for that matter, how many.

The mystery of why there should be *any* villains was unsolved. It could be, of course, that Bernie had other information to interest villains, about some entirely different matter, even though he had said in his famous phone call that Harry was to take the message to his daddy. Still, Jean was thinking, wasn't it at least possible that the message would explain itself as having nothing to do with the Fairchilds? Bernie had seen those pigs in the gift shop. The syndrome, pigs-Harry, Harry-pig, had leaped into his mind. Bernie may have pressed his old friend Harry into service just *because* of a coincidence.

"Is this a coincidence, Harry, darling?" a voice was saying. There was a female standing in the aisle. She was wearing a soft gold-colored wool dress, cut in such a way as to set another female's teeth on edge with sheer despair.

Harry, struggling, with a threshing of limbs, out of his seat, was bleating, "Well! Dorinda, darling!"

Who is *she?* Jean wondered with ferocity.

Harry floundered around making introductions. Jean smiled. Dorinda smiled. Then Jean lay very low, listening, naturally, as hard as she possibly could.

Harry said, "I will admit I am a charming fella, but isn't this going a little far, Dorinda, darling?"

"Something came up. I tried to phone." The lovely face was smiling daintily.

"That was awfully nice of you."

"How far are you going, Harry?"

"Just as far as the plane goes. You too, eh?"

Well, either they weren't going to tell each other a thing, or else they understood each other very, very well, indeed.

"How sad," Dorinda was saying, "that we didn't know. But, of course, you already have someone to talk to."

"Oh, yes. Oh, yes. Jean's my best girl Friday. And this, of course, *is* still Friday."

Harry could be such a silly ass. Jean said aloud, without having known she was going to say it, "Would you like to take my seat for a while?"

"That's very, very sweet of you," Dorinda said to her. "And you must take my perfectly good seat, back there. Oh, thank you."

So Jean found herself inserted into another window seat, beside a little man who was reading a nondescript grayish magazine. He had let her past him without any fuss. His no-colored hair was thin on the top of his hatless head, combed in the usual parallel strands to cover the usual bald spot. Jean paid no attention to him.

She was thoughtful. She'd had a moment of truth, a kind of sinking down. She was here by a regrettable necessity. Harry Fairchild hadn't known what else to do with her. That was the truth of the matter. She would not, she felt sure, act like a happy puppy dog anymore.

She sighed and thought of the map she had in her handbag. It was a large-scale map of the British Isles. Jean wasn't going to sleep, that was for sure. She was feeling too upset, or to use a better word, downcast. She might as well see whether she could be useful. It would serve him right if she earned her salary. So she unfolded the huge thing and, struggling, finally managed to fold it so as to reveal Ireland as conveniently as could be, and she settled down and began to run her eyes very carefully over all the place-names, beginning at the top, or north, and going on down. There were hundreds of places beginning with Bally. Maybe thousands. She studied diligently. She felt it had been very thoughtless of her to have enjoyed herself so much.

Dorinda said, "How nice for me to have somebody to talk to! I didn't mean to put her out."

"She doesn't mind," said Harry carelessly. "You know, it comes over me, Dorinda, that I was rudely interrupted the other evening. I never did finish telling you—"

"Oh, yes, what was that all about?" she said lazily.

"You don't remember? And here I thought you were fascinated. All right. Never mind." Harry prepared to rise above hurt feelings.

"But I remember every word you said, darling. I meant the interruption. Your friend—wasn't he?—at the airport?"

"Oh, that. We'll never know. Poor chap passed away." "Gone and forgotten" his tone implied. (He hoped.) He was not going to let any more young women in on the act. He had enough trouble.

"And how is your daddy?" said Dorinda softly.

"Fine." Harry blinked.

"And your brother, the doctor? And your brother, the—oh, yes—the governor?"

"Fine. Fine."

"And the little girl?"

"Fine," he said automatically, and then he said, "Uh—what little girl is this, in particular, Dorinda?"

"Why, Bernie's girl."

"Oh. *OH!*" said Harry. "Oh, *she's* fine. Heartbroken, naturally. What—uh—threw me off—Bernie's girl happens to stand five-nine in her socks." Harry checked himself. Better not toss these inventions around so carelessly. The day came when you had to remember what lies you had told to whom. And he had enough troubles already. Hah! He'd fix Dorinda. He'd talk about *her*.

He leaned back and said, "Dorinda Bowie. Any relation to the knife of the same name?"

A funny thing happened to her face. It was gone in an instant. "What was that?" he said. "Was there a flash of light, or something?"

Dorinda was smiling in her dainty way. "I don't think so." She snuggled down. "Now, you must tell me more."

Harry, snuggling down, said, "Why sure enough. Where was I? Now Linear B, you see, turned out to be syllabic."

Jean finished the map of Ireland, having found no such place-name as Ballycoo. So she sighed and refolded the map in its original creases. The man in the next seat stirred slightly and she thought *he* sighed.

She looked up and realized that the whole planeload seemed to have gone, in some sophistication, very early to sleep—except for herself and her seatmate. She gave him an exasperated glance, got up, and wormed out into the aisle. It had suddenly annoyed her to imagine that, while she had conscientiously *not* gone to sleep in somebody else's chair, that Dorinda whatever-her-name-was *had.*

But when she came to where Harry was still talking, this annoyed her very much, too. "It's getting late," Jean said. "May I have my own seat, please?"

"Why, of course." Dorinda agreed at once. Harry rose to let her out and, standing there in the aisle, he kissed her a gentle goodnight.

Jean crawled into her own seat, which was disgustingly warm. Harry sat down and said with gusty relish, "Well, that was nice and rude!"

"Would you mind very much not talking, Mr. Fairchild?"

"Delighted," said Harry, with heartfelt sincerity.

Chapter 9

"IF," said Jean between tearing yawns, "you care to remark that you . . . oh—ah . . . told me so, pray do."

"Brace up," said Harry. "It is your duty to pick up firsthand impressions, and write a book."

"Um." She couldn't prop her eyelids up. "But a hotel is a hotel is a hotel . . ."

"I'd better get you a room with a bed in it," said Harry crossly.

"No, don' . . . They mi' . . ."

"A fat lot of good you'll be."

"Just pinch me," she said, "when ti' . . . come . . ." and off she went to sleep, where she sat.

He *had* told her so, damn it! Here it was almost 1 P.M. in Amsterdam, but Jean, at 5 A.M. Los Angeles time, was conking out. He'd pinch her, all right, when the time came. And violently. They were both going to have to look sharp. Harry was foreseeing problems.

Once on the plane from Copenhagen, Harry had cast the past aside and contemplated the future. Dorinda had bade him a gay *hasta la vista* in Copenhagen and gone off to parts unknown. She'd be back in Southern California before him, she had threatened. And there went the last link. Now they were just travelers, strange among strangers. And now what?

They were in the right hotel, but the American tour had gone off to "take in" the diamond cutters. It was scheduled to return briefly for "freshening up" and then in the afternoon it would "take in" Volendam. American tourists don't kid around. The only thing to do was catch them during this brief but scheduled recess. So here they sat, where Harry (provided that he could keep awake) could watch the entrance.

But he was brooding. Having caught the tour, having recognized the pink-pig little girl, then what? He had called a discreet and low-voiced conference on the second plane, when the future had begun to puzzle him. Jean was all for a direct approach. Deviosity was not called for. Surely he wasn't planning to steal the hippopotamus? He was rich. So *buy* the mountain lion. *She* wasn't worrying. They needn't tell the whole truth, she'd said.

He wasn't worrying about telling the whole truth—which was impossible, since they didn't know it. But Harry was wondering what part of any truth would serve. Oh, definitely, this sort of thing was not his forte. He had not done what he ought to have done, and so on. He fidgeted.

And she didn't have the decency to stay awake and worry with him. She was real gone. Well, poor kid. Harry felt a not unpleasant, almost fatherly, pluming up of a protective instinct. In fact, he had been a little troubled when she had stopped bouncing. She had been almost merely patient in Copenhagen. Of course, an airport was an airport was an airport. Yet, flying into Amsterdam, Harry had even tried to poke up her enthusiasm, pointing out the waterways, the half-a-spider-web the city made. She had been very polite. He'd felt a bit of a sense of loss.

He had been touched, too, by her report of her faithful and minute study of the map of Ireland. But, in view of the results, he wondered what the devil they were going to do if they did get their clutches on the pink pig and it turned out not to be the right pig. He would then phone home, he decided. Bernie's partner had gone—no doubt fuming—off on Bernie's tracks. Perhaps he had found them. Perhaps the message in the pig was no longer of any importance. If it ever had been.

When a little man in a felt hat came into the hotel, looked vaguely around, and settled down unobtrusively to wait, Harry paid no attention.

At the next arrival, however, Harry Fairchild sat up with a violent shock.

She came in, attended only by the porter with her bag, yet also by an invisible retinue, as she walked, in the arrogance of her beauty, her taste, and the money on her back. Dorinda Bowie!

Here! Of all—! *Here?*

Harry took the flesh of Jean Cunliffe's upper arm between his thumb and finger, held his breath while Dorinda walked, placing her pretty feet just so, calmly across his cone of vision and disappeared, having not so much as turned her elegant head.

Harry pinched.

"Ow! Hey! What?"

"Dorinda. Just came in."

"Huh?"

"And-that-is-too-much," said Harry heavily. "By gosh, I can believe the traditional six before breakfast. But not this." He was looking wild.

Jean rubbed her arm and squeezed her eyes open and shut, and wide open. "Did you say *Dorinda?* But she's in Copenhagen."

"The heck she is. She's around that corner."

"Who *is* she?" said Jean at last—as fiercely as she had long wanted to say it.

"You know something," said Harry. "I haven't the faintest idea who she is."

They both sat very still for a moment.

Then Jean said, "Hey, I'm a little bit scared."

"I know," he said. "I know."

"Somebody *told* her which flight, in the first place."

"I know."

"Because she *wasn't* there. But then, there she *was*."

Harry followed perfectly. He remembered how they had

been the last to board in Los Angeles, how he had scanned the faces, how he had not seen Dorinda's face, although it must have been there.

"Watching us now?" said Jean. "Do you think? Somebody?"

"Could be. Could be."

Jean closed her eyes and let her head droop. She swayed toward him. "I won't go up to them, if somebody's watching. I won't even point. I just won't do it."

Harry bent over her. "I'll get us some rooms. We'll have to kick this around a little bit."

"Um, hum," she murmured and swooned as if to sleep again.

"Oh-oh," said Harry.

The American tour was arriving. The hotel braced itself but, nevertheless, it reeled with the impact. Camera-slung, they entered with hoot and halloo. They milled. They were about thirty strong, predominantly female. The tide of sound tended to be soprano, with islands of baritone. A few dragged-looking children, too bored to be shrill, were appended to them, here and there.

Jean Cunliffe blinked and roused as if the racket had disturbed her. She gazed upon the scene with heavy-lidded eyes. "I see her," she murmured. "The one in the red coat."

"Don't look."

"I'm *not* looking."

Harry patted her knee and rose. "Follow me," he said. He took up their bags and set off through the crowd to the registration desk.

But Jean lingered. She poked at her hair, settled her handbag on her arm, got up uncertainly, blinked and craned her neck as if to get the kinks out of it. She soon saw, motionless in the midst of all the motion, the little man in the felt hat.

Oh ho! she said to herself. His faded eyes were on her casually. He wasn't the type one would notice noticing, ordinarily. But Jean noticed. In fact, she smiled at him and ducked her head in a bow of recognition. He looked blank. Then, very grudgingly, he nodded and his gaze scurried away.

Oh, she'd spotted him. Her seatmate! *Dorinda's* seatmate!

Oh ho! But her heart sank a little. Well, deviosity, she thought.

Jean started to wend her way through the turbulence toward the tour leader. He was easy to spot, wearing the correct harassed look, besieged by questioners. Jean pushed up to him. "Excuse me," she said, as rudely as anybody else. She began to make up questions. Had this tour been taken at the same time last year? Had it made the same stops, seen the same sights? The poor man was not sure. She insisted that he ought to be sure. He was sorry.

Out of the corner of her eye Jean was watching the little man sidle and drift until his ear was in a position to hear everything that she was saying.

Well, she *might* be misdirecting him with this nonsense. But she was scared. It was one thing to play hide-and-seek with hypothetical villains, quite another to know that you were being followed, watched, and listened to besides.

Harry, arranging for rooms, was glad that Dorinda had already disappeared. He asked for Miss Bowie's room number and got it. He realized that no one was standing within ten feet at the moment, so he said, "I wonder if you could tell me the name . . . The little girl in the red coat? I know the family. I know their faces, that is, but I'm—uh—kinda embarrassed not to remember the name."

"Edwards, sir," the man said, smiling understanding.

"That's it. Thanks a million." Harry was the very image of the jolly American extrovert. "Certainly want to say hello. Oh, by the way, which room have they?"

He got the number. It could not be far from Dorinda's. Well . . . He looked for Jean, and threaded to her.

"Now, we'll get you to bed," he said in a masterly manner.

Chapter 10

THERE was a bed in Jean's room; it might as well have been a stone.

It seemed to them, and no use wondering why or even how, that they had been followed here. The man in the felt hat had followed them, Jean was sure. Why, she'd seen him before, *too*. Somewhere else. She'd think where, in a minute.

Harry began to amplify his suspicion that Dorinda Bowie had followed them. He could think of a lot of funny little things about Dorinda, come to think of them. Dorinda—insisting upon going to the airport that night that Bernie had phoned. Dorinda, annoyed at having to park the car. Why? Because she might miss something? By golly, she had missed the toy-buying incident. That's what she had missed. Then, of course, Dorinda's picking Harry up, that very day, with such single-minded determination. Harry cursed himself for an innocent lamb. An unsuspecting fool.

"Who's Dorinda? What is she?" He paced. "She's damned good-looking. That's all I know."

But there was no use wondering. What, then, to do?

They had about thirty minutes before the tourists were scheduled to take off again. Might it not be best to wait and simply get into the Edwardses' empty room and steal the pig? There was no use wondering whether three dollars and ninety-eight cents would imperil their immortal souls. The question arose, how does one steal a pig? Harry was frank to declare that he was *not* going to climb, by ledge and balcony, across the façade of *any* building if he could avoid it. He'd sooner pick a lock, or seduce a chambermaid. Of course, he didn't know how to pick a lock. And furthermore, even if they succeeded in such thievery, they'd risk a hue and cry which would give away the importance of pigs. Harry cursed himself for not having brought along some substitute pigs. Why the devil hadn't he thought of that?

Jean, who had given him the floor for some minutes now, said sadly that she hadn't thought of it, either. She hadn't *been* thinking. She had just been enjoying herself, and she was very sorry. She would try to use her head, which was on the whole pretty clear—or so she had been told in her day.

Harry stared, winced, sat down, and held *his* head.

"Here's one idea," she said. "We could give up."

Harry straightened and gave her a keen glance. "Is that . . . uh . . . done?"

"If we give up, then *they'll* never find out what we were after."

"True. And we won't find it either." Harry found this idea very unsatisfying. "What if they already know what we're after?"

"Then they've probably got it, while we've been up here moaning and groaning and carrying on. *They'd* steal, in a minute."

"Is it necessary to be all that clearheaded?" groaned Harry. "You're right. You're right. That's the trouble."

"No, I'm not, and that's not what troubles me," cried Jean. "Harry, supposing they are after the little girl . . . your little sister. What will they do with her?"

"I don't know."

"You do believe that they killed Bernie. *Killed* him?"

"He was killed. I believe that. And they . . . *they* stands for whoever did it."

"Then . . . Oh, listen, they can't know what we are after. There is just no way they could know about pigs. They followed us. And here we are, where there is a little girl. And just about the right age, too. Didn't you say seven?"

"*You* think *they* think we're after the *child* . . ." Harry was agog. *"Here?"*

"Why wouldn't they think so?"

He couldn't answer that. In a moment Harry said, "All right. We have to get to the Edwardses, get the damn pig, and get out of here, without anybody ever knowing we went anywhere near the Edwardses."

"Right," Jean said.

"Let's just go where the Edwardses are, then," he said recklessly.

"Dorinda's room is on their floor, you said?"

"She's probably not going to be hanging out her door."

"But she could open it, at any moment," Jean said, "unless we penciled her in."

"Unless we what?"

"It's a trick. The kids do it in the dorms. Let me see if these are the right kind of doors." Jean went to look. "We could. It takes a plain wooden pencil. Then she *can't* open the door."

"Maybe Dorinda has nothing to do with it."

"It won't hurt her," Jean said patiently. "And here's a thing. The Edwardses should recognize me. After all, I waited on them. That might make it easier. I mean, if it looks as if we ought, probably we could warn them."

"If you think we ought—" Harry watched her young face.

"I certainly don't think it's fair to put their child in a possible danger, and not even let them know it."

"What about old felt-hat?" said Harry tensely.

"We can't worry about *him*," said Jean. "We don't know where he is."

"What's all this about penciling Dorinda in?" Harry's heart was lifting. "Sounds like a nice dirty trick," he said cheerfully, "and a nice high-principled reason to use it."

Jean gave him a glance of sudden mischief. "That's what comes of being clearheaded," she said, and took the yellow wooden lead pencil from his fingers.

They were two floors too high. They found stairs. Dorinda's room was only four doors away, and across, from the room they hoped to enter. All was still in this corridor except for the sense of the buzz of life behind walls. Nobody was lurking. So Jean rammed the pencil, full length, on its side, into the crack, the leeway that existed between the edge and the jamb of Dorinda's door. This wasn't done noiselessly, and a voice within called sharply, "What's that?" They didn't answer.

"It works. Don't worry," Jean whispered as they crept away. "She can't turn the knob. Somebody has to practically kick it out." Somebody would, of course. Dorinda would be on the phone for help. They had only a few minutes.

Mr. Edwards opened his door willingly to the voice of an American female and reacted at once. "Say, don't I know you from someplace?"

"Of course you do," gushed Jean. "May we please come in? May we please close the door?"

"Who is it?" said Mrs. Edwards brightly. She had been lying down with her shoes off and she was readjusting her girdle as best she could in the very act of sitting up.

"Oh, Mrs. Edwards," Jean turned with a sure instinct. "I'm the one who sold your little girl a toy, in the gift shop in Los Angeles."

"Well, for pity's sakes. Sally Jo?" said the mother, nervously continuing her struggle.

"Hi, Sally Jo," said Jean. The child was sitting cross-legged on the third bed in the room. She was a lanky child with limp brown hair and a pouting lip, and she was bored stiff.

"Who—uh—is this?" Mr. Edwards had an eye on Harry's size.

"My name is Fairchild," said Harry quietly, keeping himself background.

Jean said, "We'd like to buy the little toy back from you. It's very important to us and it's a long story. We haven't much time. We'd like to pay anything you think is fair. So would you? Please?"

"You mean the piggy bank?" said Mrs. Edwards in astonishment. "Well, for pity's *sakes.*" Her plump legs were now dangling off the edge of the bed; her plump feet were stockinged lumps.

Jean rushed on. "I sold it to you by mistake. I'm so sorry. I'll see that you get another one, exactly like it. I promise. I'll mail it wherever you say. And we'll pay you whatever you think . . . It's just that we haven't time. You don't mind . . . too much . . . do you?"

The whole Edwards family stared at her. Mrs. Edwards reached for one of her shoes.

Harry, who stood close to the inside of the door, with his ears tuned for any unusual sounds in the corridor, said, "Do you still have it, by the way?"

"Well, Sally Jo has it packed someplace. I never heard of such a thing in my life. I haven't had any sleep." Mrs. Edwards passed the buck. "Daddy?"

Mr. Edwards swelled and took over. "You're talking about a piggy bank? A mistake, you say?"

So Jean kept on talking, saying the same things over again, while the child did a kind of rolling flip off the bed and began to delve into a suitcase.

Harry sensed that these were amiable people. They had the impulse to be obliging. They didn't need the pig; it would be no hardship for them to surrender it. But they had a natural curiosity and they had, alas, the obligation to take time and be "wise." So they would go around and around and, in the end, act on pure impulse, just the same.

It was going to take too much time.

"How could you—uh—make a mistake?" the man was saying, still friendly.

"Well, you see, it belonged to Mr. Fairchild," said Jean, giving a little more, "so I shouldn't have sold it to you at all."

"There must be something in it," said Mrs. Edwards flatly.

And Jean said quickly, "Oh, we'd return everything the little girl put in it. She won't lose . . ."

"You're not going to get anything out of that thing without breaking it, are you?" said Mr. Edwards.

This chatter was suddenly getting nowhere very fast.

Harry fancied he could hear some banging afar. He took out his wallet and extracted an American one-hundred-dollar bill. "There's not much time, really," he said. "Will this be okay?"

ERROR. It was too much.

"Say," burst the man, "what's in that pig anyhow? Diamonds?"

The woman licked her lips and said, "Daddy, do you think we ought . . . ?" (She meant she didn't.)

"No, no," cried Jean. "It's only because we haven't time to explain." And there was some generous quality of understanding, some recognition of the pain of unsatisfied curiosity (for which they offered recompense) that caused a moment's trembling balance.

Then Sally Jo took the reins of power into accustomed hands. She turned around and stood with the small saucily painted pink pig cradled in her arms. "They can't have my pig and break it. I don't want my pig broken. It's mine."

"Ah, I know," said Jean warmly. "But listen, you'll have another one . . ."

"I don't want another one. I want my own pig." She stared at them with hostile smolder. Sally Jo was nobody to miss a chance to dominate. It was her forte. She was going to make trouble if she could. And she could. "You're going to make me give them my pig," she whined to her parents, "and you said it was mine. You *promised*."

This tore it.

"Now, sweetheart," said her mother, "Mommy and Daddy are not going to *make* you do anything. We wouldn't do that."

Jean said to the child directly, "Won't *you* please sell us the pig? And have a newer one for yourself?"

"No. You can't have my pig. I don't have to sell it to any old dumb . . ."

"Sal," said her father, "now just a minute. Just don't worry. Let Daddy talk. Look . . . uh . . ." He turned to Harry. "I'd sure like to know a little more about this." His eye was on the money.

"May I see the pig?" said Harry, severely. He aimed to raise doubt, to hint at one hundred dollars withdrawn. He pinned his hopes on the man.

"Let me have that a minute, Sal?"

"No." The child hugged her property even tighter and turned a defensive hunching shoulder. "No. You can't have it."

"Listen, Daddy's not going to . . ."

"No."

"Now, Daddy," said Mommy. Sally Jo teetered on the brink of tantrum and the threat was paralyzing.

Oooh, that little pig! thought Jean. Then the mother met her eye and betrayed her child with a grimace. Can't do anything with *her,* the glance said.

"I'll tell you," said Sally Jo's father with a hint of apology, "Why don't you folks get in touch a little later on? And we can talk this over a little bit more, okay? Fact, we're due on some trip. There's no use, right now." His brows, his glance, his voice, betrayed his child. "She gets set . . ."

"Don't *open*!" Jean cried. Too late.

Mr. Edwards was opening the door to show them out.

"Hey, what's up, out there?" said Mr. Edwards at once. There were people out there. There was some unnatural commotion. An incident was happening. It was the breaking open of Dorinda's door.

Harry, who was standing a few feet within the room, looked behind him. He met the mild eye of a little man who, holding his felt hat to his breast as if the flag were going by, was standing across the corridor, looking in.

Harry suddenly took control of the door and closed it.

"Hey, now, just a darned . . ." Mr. Edwards flared.

Jean said, "Oh, now . . . Now there may be *trouble,* and we didn't want . . ." ERROR.

Mrs. Edwards reacted instantaneously. "I'm very sorry, but *I* am calling downstairs." Her tongue licked at her lips. She reached for the instrument. Oh no, no trouble. Nothing like that. Mrs. Edwards washed her hands of trouble. Mrs. Edwards was upright and law-abiding, and authority was on *her* side.

You may or may not be desperadoes, her eyes said, but I want no truck with trouble.

Jean didn't know what to do. Harry, tempted to have the game as well as the name, regarded the child and the pig with violent impulses. And the child, either reading him loud and clear, or possessed of her own devil screamed, "He's a bad man. He's *bad*. Mommy! Mommy!"

And the mother, reacting like a tigress, with one shoe off and one shoe on, came lurching out from between two beds to protect her young. She was off-balance. She fell upon the child. The child's sturdy young legs held them both up, but the little pig, as if it had been greased for rustic sport, rose out of the child's grasp, described an arc, and fell to the floor, where it separated rather demurely into two large pieces. The hindquarters rocked reproachfully.

The child took air and bawled, "See what you did!" The mother, clinging to her instinctive purpose, staggered backward and the two of them fell in a heap on the bed.

The father took protective strides and thrust Harry aside. "Okay, what's in it?" he barked, and crouched to see.

Jean, who was looking down at the eight American pennies, the two American dimes, and the one American twenty-five-cent piece that lay at her feet, said over Mr. Edwards' bald spot to Harry Fairchild, sadly, "Nothing."

All this, then, for nothing?

The mother was writhing on the bed, trying to hang on to the child and also reach the telephone. The child was squirming and threshing, feeling, quite intelligently, that there was no particular safety in this heap of limbs. The father rose, red-faced and furious. "Now that's about enough. Now what is this? Some gag? Now, you two better get out of here."

He went defiantly past Harry. Harry was younger. Harry was bigger. But Harry was not a desperado.

Harry was rich. He let the hundred-dollar bill flutter from his fingers and said, "That's for the damages. Thanks very much. Come on, Jean."

"You keep your—" Mr. Edwards, to prove his manhood,

called the money a dirtier name than he ought in the presence of his family.

Harry got the doorknob first.

And just there, right in position to be framed by the doorway, stood Dorinda, with not a hair of her head ruffled. "Why, Harry Fairchild!"

"Oh, hi, Dorinda," said Harry wearily, not bothering to pretend a happy surprise.

"Oh, so *you* know this bird?" fumed Mr. Edwards. "Well!"

"But what is the matter?" Dorinda was inspecting the inside of the room with bright interest. Mrs. Edwards babbling into the phone; Sally Jo only half-disentangled from her mother, snuffling and whimpering. "Is something wrong with the little girl?" said Dorinda brightly. "Can I help, at all?"

Okay, thought Harry, there it goes. Whole thing blows up in our faces. Of all the inept, the stupid, the feeble, the worse-than-futile performances. He cursed the day he was born.

But Jean, still standing in the middle of the room, drew in her breath and cried, "But you just have to realize—why, the poor little thing. She's on an awful spot."

To Harry it was a miracle that in her voice there was no note of sarcasm. "Poor Sally Jo," cried Jean. "Oh, I tell you, *it's rough.*" She seemed to mean it. The child hushed to listen to this. "It's just *awfully* hard on her," cried Jean, "don't you see? To have to run the whole world? When she isn't even seven years old?"

The parents were completely bewildered. Dorinda frowned slightly. Harry didn't get it either; then he got it.

Because Sally Jo turned bright pink and shouted, "I am, too. I'm eight and a half, you dumb nut! I don't *like* you. I am so eight and a half. Mommy! Mommy!"

"Of course you are," said Mrs. Edwards in the voice of one too exhausted to be alarmed much longer. "Will you please hand me my other shoe? The man *is* coming. What her age has to do . . . I don't know. I think you people . . . Daddy?"

"*I said* you people better get out of here," Mr. Edwards sputtered, but the edge was off his righteous indignation somehow.

"Very sorry for the misunderstanding," said Harry pompously. "Come on, Jean."

It was Dorinda who stirred, as if from a spell. She turned as if to take Harry's arm, as if she expected to be escorted. Jean was moving toward the door and not looking forward to the immediate future or any other, when Sally Jo shouted behind her in tones of utter condemnation:

"Yeah! She doesn't even have our address. And she *promised!* She said she'd mail me a new pig. She *promised*." Sally Jo had a feud on.

Jean turned quickly. "Oh, yes, I'm sorry." But it was too late.

Dorinda said, "Pig?" and turned, too, all bright and interested.

Behind her Harry caught Jean's eye. He moved both arms in a curious way. "See you in church, Jean," he called out loudly, and then he vanished.

Chapter 11

JEAN stood, drooping, just within the room. Maybe this child was no longer suspected of being *the* child, but Dorinda was on to pigs, all right. That is, if Dorinda had followed them and had wanted to know what they were after.

Sally Jo was watching Jean, like a wrestler hunting advantage. Jean winked at her. She didn't know why. Neither did Sally Jo, and it shut her up.

Dorinda was busy being charming to Mr. Edwards. "My name is Dorinda Bowie. I'm from Chicago."

"Is that so?" said Mr. Edwards reverently. "I'm Ken Edwards."

"Daddy," said his wife, a trifle brittlely.

"Now you say you know that crazy character? That what's-his-name?" Mr. Edwards became more or less businesslike. He leaned out the door to peer this way and that after Harry—which brought him very close to Dorinda. "Where'd he go?"

"I do know him—casually," Dorinda said, "but whatever was he up to, Mr. Edwards?"

"Wanted to buy a *pig*."

"Really?" said Dorinda. "Oh . . ." She had managed to step gracefully out of Mr. Edwards' way and therefore a half-step into the room, and now she spotted the remains. "Was that a pig? But how very, very strange."

"I figured he must have thought there was something

valuable inside the thing." Mr. Edwards had himself an anecdote, at least.

"And was there?" Dorinda was absolutely fascinated.

"There was *what? Look?* Twenty-eight—twenty-five—fifty-three cents! Now you tell me . . ."

"But why in the world? Where did the pig come from?"

"We bought it in a gift shop in Los Angeles," said Mr. Edwards chummily. "Now, if this isn't the darndest . . ."

"Daddy," his wife said, with ominous patience.

"Now, Miss," said Mr. Edwards, speaking to Jean, "if that man is crazy you better say so."

"He's harmless," Jean said.

"Oh well, now," said Dorinda, allying herself with Jean, in a way, "he is a very rich young man. Possibly a bit eccentric. Wouldn't you say, Jean?"

"Possibly, Dorinda," said Jean stoically.

"Spoiled. Right?" said Mr. Edwards, viewing with alarm. "Probably always got given whatever he took it into his head to want. Well, if you ask me, he ought to have his head examined."

"Ken . . ." His wife spoke with deadlier sweetness than before.

"How come you were going along with the gag?" said Mr. Edwards, turning on Jean again. He seemed to think that it took the lightning off, if he included her.

"I have been employed," said Jean stiffly.

"Well, you better watch it, young lady. That's all I say. Don't you agree, Miss . . . uh . . . Bowie?"

"Oh, I think he is probably harmless enough," said Dorinda with her dainty smile. "But whatever do you suppose he imagined could be in a pig?"

"He didn't say. What about that, Miss?"

And Jean smiled upon him. "You were awfully smart, Mr. Edwards." She could purr, too, if she liked. "You guessed it."

"I did?"

"Well, there were no diamonds, were there?" said Mrs. Edwards with a curling lip. "That hotel man should be here. Now we'll miss the tour, I suppose. Such a fuss! Would you *mind* closing the door, Ken?"

"Surely. Surely."

"I *would* like some privacy," said his wife. ERROR.

"Say, let me ask the guide if he can hold up the tour a couple of minutes, Mother. Shame to miss it. I mean, the fellow is gone. Maybe I can head off the hotel man. No use of a fuss." Beaming with kindness, Mr. Edwards closed the door, leaving Jean on the inside, and himself on the outside with Dorinda.

"I never," fumed Mrs. Edwards, "heard of such a thing in my life!"

Stoically Jean took a small pad of paper and a pencil out of her handbag and wrote down what Mrs. Edwards dictated spasmodically while she bustled. "All this way and to miss Volendam. We live at 1541 . . . Now Sally Jo, stand still, dear. You want to see the people in their wooden shoes, don't you? Park Way, that's two words."

"*I want* some wooden shoes," said Sally Jo, whom her mother had by hair and hairbrush. "*I want* wooden shoes."

"Now, dear, we'll see. Park Way, Petaluma, California. Now you will mail it to Mrs. Kenneth Edwards. I think that's fair. It was your fault that the pig broke."

"Of course," said Jean. "Thank you. I'll mail it to Sally Jo." She bent to pick up the hundred-dollar bill and she put it on the dresser.

"Oh no, really," said Mrs. Edwards after a startled glance. "You take that."

"It's not mine," said Jean. "It's Sally Jo's. Why, she can buy enough wooden shoes for all her little friends, can't she?" Revenge, however small, was sweet.

Mrs. Edwards' eyes glazed. The phone rang. The poor woman sighed, harassed on all sides, and went to answer. The child was eyeing Jean thoughtfully. Then, holding her half-braided top hair in one hand, Sally Jo began to kick a piece of the pig around on the carpet.

Jean didn't want to go out into the corridor and encounter

Dorinda or the little man or anybody. Harry was off, doing something about flying away. She knew that because he had flapped his wings. She didn't particularly want to encounter him, either, until she felt more . . . Well, she wasn't ready.

She said, "Shall I pick up the pieces? Or may I finish doing her hair?"

Mrs. Edwards was saying, "Yes, Ken. Yes, I suppose . . ." She was nodding.

Jean took this for permission, and put her hands on the child's hair.

"Don't pull," said Sally Jo.

"Well, I *won't*," said Jean, sorting the strands in competent fingers, "but I'd sure *like* to," she added honestly.

The child's eyes met hers in the mirror. (Oh, you little pig, thought Jean. What you're in for, someday! You poor little pink pig.)

Mrs. Edwards, on the phone, was promising to try. She hadn't had a bit of rest, but she would try. She would, in fact, be right down and Ken had better be ready to go.

Dorinda must be somewhere in the picture still, Jean guessed.

The mother hung up and, seeing her daughter placid and Jean skillfully arranging the hair, she sighed. "They do say to change your shoes." The harassed woman rummaged. "They do say it is wise."

The child said, "How come you'd like to pull my hair?" This child could read emotional states? Had read Jean's pity?

"Because you didn't care about the pig. You never did. You only wanted somebody else *not* to have it." (So preach, thought Jean. That'll help, that will.)

"Well, but she was so dumb," said Sally Jo. "Her and her old caw-sill."

"I'm such a mess," cried Mrs. Edwards, hands to her head, "but there's no time." She put hairpins into her mouth.

"What," said Jean softly, "is a caw-sill?"

"A castle, silly! Castle," Sally Jo translated by using the American flat *a*. "She talked dumb, like that, all the time. She didn't fool me. Nobody lives in any old caw-sill anymore, do they?"

Jean couldn't speak.

"Boppy-goo. Bobby-goo. *That's* the silliest name I ever heard in my life.

"Petaluma," murmured Jean. "Now, there's a sensible name for a place to live."

"Of course, stupid."

"And Sally Jo. There's a sensible name for a girl," said Jean, concealing hope, fear and astonishment as she struggled with a hair clasp. "Not like Deirdre."

"*That's* the silliest name I *ever* heard in my *life!*" cackled Sally Jo. "She didn't fool me."

Jean sighed. "No, I guess not. I guess nobody can fool you, now that you are—*thank God*—eight and a half years old." She took her hands away. "Okay?"

But the child had been startled by her vehemence. Mrs. Edwards said, "Oh, thanks very much. That looks very nice. Sorry we are so rushed, but they'll only wait ten minutes. Oh—" She caught herself being automatically social. "My dear," Mrs. Edwards *had* to be wise, "ought you to be traveling with that . . . that person?"

"He isn't interested in me," said Jean.

Mrs. Edwards' eyes rolled, contemplating horrors of abnormality. "But how could you have taken on . . . ? You are so young. Did you say employment?"

"The salary," Jean said, "is a thousand dollars a week."

"Ah, but you must remember," said Mrs. Edwards, when she had come out of shock, "that money is not everything. But I thought . . ." This woman was about to remember that Jean had been working in a gift shop.

Jean said vaguely, "I'm sure you are right." And started for the door.

Sally Jo said, "Hey, aren't you going to Volendam?"

Jean shook her head.

"*I want* you to go, too. *I want*—"

"But I," said Jean gently, "*don't* want. Goodbye. Good luck, little pig."

Mrs. Edwards was mumbling around her lipstick, but Jean let herself quietly out of the room.

There was no one lurking. She found the stairs again and toiled up to her room. Her coat and her bag were gone, as she had more than half expected them to be. Jean turned away and decided against the elevator. She went slowly down all the stairs and there she found a door to a narrow hall and, at the end of the hall, the light of day. So Jean crept out of the hotel. Here she was, all alone by herself, on the streets of Amsterdam.

She knew she ought to ask, but not in the hotel where the watchers and the listeners were. She came around the corner and saw the Americans milling around their bus. No use asking them, they wouldn't know. It would be the nearest one, naturally. She'd find it by herself. Or else she'd never find it.

She walked on. It occurred to her that she had not seen this lovely old city; she had heard hardly a word in the language of its people. Maybe she would. Maybe she was stranded here and she would simply stay. She might get a job. Who was to say that she might not try? She was all alone in the world. She had her Aunt Jessie in Denver, Colorado, who didn't really care very much.

Then she saw the steeple. So Jean walked slowly over the bridge. She saw a boat below, in the canal. She saw the row of tiny cars along the embankment. She saw the tall and mellow old façades. Then she saw Harry Fairchild.

She ran and he grabbed her. "About to come after you. Cab's waiting. We're on a flight to Dublin. Barely going to make it."

They tumbled in and the driver took off.

Harry was busy looking behind. "Anybody follow you?"

"It doesn't matter much." Jean was quivering like a rabbit in its burrow. Safe, at last? Oh, nonsense!

"I'm calling home as soon as I can do it with any peace and quiet," he went on. "Meantime, we're off. May as well be. And no hot pursuit, that I can see."

"It doesn't matter," she said. "They know where we're going next."

"Huh?"

"They'll *guess,*" she said turning on him fiercely. "Do you think that little man missed me poring over the map of Ireland for hours and hours? Stupid that I am!"

Harry put his hand around her wrist. She was throbbing.

"Hey, soldier," he said.

"It makes me nervous. Excuse, please, but this isn't my métier. I don't think I'm devious enough, for one thing." Jean was afraid she might start to cry, and this made her sound very cross.

"Oh, I don't know," he drawled. "Duck to water, I'd have said. You sure got that miserable brat off the hook. How did *you* know she was eight and a half?"

"Because she might not have been seven."

"Again, please?"

"There was a chance, wasn't there?" She bit his head off, figuratively speaking.

"Good thinking."

"Oh, stop trying to cheer me up. Please. We blew it and you know it." She looked at, but couldn't see, the city of Amsterdam and environs.

Harry leaned back. "Always look on the dark side. Okay. So Dorinda now knows it's . . . alligators. That is, if she cares."

"She seemed to know that somebody *ought* to be seven years old," said Jean grimly.

"She did, at that. She did, at that. Well. Well. We'll just have to look out for Dorinda-baby, and the man in the hat, and whatever other assorted parties there may be. Still—why should we worry too much, when we don't even know ourselves, once we hit the ould sod, where to begin to fight? Answer me that."

"I *will,*" said Jean, "but not now."

"Huh?"

"Not in a cab. Not here. I don't trust anybody." She fought tears.

"All right," said Harry gently.

"I do know where to begin," Jean said in a low voice. "I got . . . a word."

"The green—"

"Shush!"

He said in a moment, "Honey, did you think I'd run out on you? If you had a bad minute there . . ."

"You *were* waiting at the church, weren't you? Oh, be quiet." By a tremendous effort she did not cry.

"Oh, I don't know," said Harry. "No use moaning and groaning and carrying-on, that's true. Still, to while away the journey why don't I change the subject? Did I ever tell you about the decipherment of Linear B? It's one of the most fascinating—"

Jean said coolly, "I've read the book. If you think it's so darned fascinating, why don't you go to work and decipher Linear A?"

Harry was stunned where he sat.

"Well?" She turned her head and smiled. (She was okay now.) "You're rich," she argued. "You're not *too* stupid. Maybe you need a hobby."

Harry sat very still. Chow-ee! This one was different.

At that moment, in the city, Dorinda was on the telephone to London.

"Pig," she said. "Can you hear me? P for Polly, I for Irving, G for George."

"Oh, *pig!*" said the man's voice.

"Don't come here. There's nothing here. Any news?"

"Not by me."

"I'll phone. Now, how fast can you get over to Dublin? Can you hear me?"

"Dublin, Ireland? Can't say . . ."

"They'll be in the air within the hour. Vance made a good guess. Got their flight number. Can you get there first?"

"It'll be close. No, I guess—"

"Don't guess. Get there. Pick up their tracks. Leave a message for me at the first hotel in the book that begins with A. I'll be there in the morning."

"Shall I meet you?"

"No, no, no."

"Tail them? Right?"

"Save time, if you can," said Dorinda. "Get hold of the girl-guide he's got along, that baby-faced blondy. *She* knows where the pig is."

"Pig?" said the voice, cautiously, still incredulous. "P for Paris?"

"I for idiot. G for get going."

Dorinda hung up. Her beautiful face was smooth and cold. But her very fingertips seemed to drip her overflowing will to power. She placed a telephone call to New Zealand.

Chapter 12

THAT night, in Dublin, Harry was on the phone to Los Angeles, where it was midday. "Not a lot of luck," he told his daddy, "but some. What's the news there?"

"We know more than we did, and it's not good," his father said. "Wait a minute and I'll read you a letter. Came from Beckenhauer, written in the Islands. I'm glad you called, because you'd better know what we're up against. Listen to this."

Harry seemed to hear the rattle of paper, then his father's steady voice became Bernie, speaking from his grave.

"Dear Mr. Fairchild:

"I have good hope that if all goes well and the luck holds, I'll be able to deliver to you the goods you wanted. Everything is arranged. I've taken precautions. I won't put down here what they are for reasons I'm going to explain. I hope this gets to you so that you'll have an idea what kind of trouble we've run into.

"I have been followed for several days. I knew that days ago and went with care. I promise you, I did not lead them anywhere that mattered. I didn't know who they were, you understand, until last night when two of them jumped me in an alley and tried to get information by force. I had luck in the shape of some U.S. Navy personnel who came by, a little bit drunk and asking no questions.

"So I got out of that with more information than they got out of me, which I promise you, was nothing.

"One of the men is named Varney. I knew who he was. The other one I don't know by name, but he belongs to the same organization; that I know. Now first, I want to warn you, Mr. Fairchild. They knew all about the child. They knew as much as I did, when I started out. So I suggest you watch it there, because it looks as if they must have an informer close enough to you to be passing this on.

"That's one reason I'm not putting down any more than they already know. It's a big operation; there's plenty of money for payoffs. They'll go all out. I can't even be sure this letter is ever going to get to you.

"In case it does, here is what seems to be the situation. Varney works for a man named Maximilian Kootz."

"That's k-o-o-t-z," spelled Harry's daddy, and then read on.

"This Kootz (as your son can tell you) is or was one of the so-called biggest men of this generation of criminals. These big fish are usually pretty cool and aloof, but Kootz made a mistake and did his own killing for once, and they caught him cold. His case has been in and out of the courts for a couple of years, anyhow. But now it's supposed to be the end of the line. He's due to die in the gas chamber—and ask your oldest son. They convicted him in your son's own state. And that's the root of the matter.

"Here's what they have in mind. Kootz' people want to get their hands on your little girl because *you* want her. And if they get her, they'll try to pressure you and, through you, your son for a stay of execution for this Kootz. Maybe even a commutation of sentence. Or, for all I know, a full pardon. This is a wild throw on their part. They'll threaten to kill or torture her. Work on you. I don't know whether it would work or not. I don't care.

"The point is, Mr. Fairchild, I don't want those people to get their dirty hands on that little girl for any reason whatsoever.

I'm sorry now that I was smart enough to find her. She was doing okay where she was. But it's too late now, just to leave her be.

"I've made arrangements, as I said, and taken precautions. But now you understand why I don't put them in writing.

"I hope and pray you will get this, because I may need more luck than there is."

"He's scratched out a line," said Harry's daddy, on a higher pitch. Then his voice steadied lower and he went on. But Harry swallowed hard.

"Well," read his father, "I guess I can tell you a little bit about her. Her name is Barbara. (They know that much.) She is a real cute little girl, healthy and smart and very well-behaved, a daughter to be proud of. What bothers me—she's never known anything as brutal and cruel as these people who are after her. And believe me, I would do anything . . . anything . . . rather than have *her* suffer for things that haven't anything to do with her, and shouldn't have.

"For God's sakes, Mr. Fairchild, take care of your little girl."

A note had come into his father's voice that Harry had heard one time before, on the day that his mother had died.

Harry said sharply, "Varney, eh? He was in L.A. on Friday morning."

But his father was saying, "Wait. Tom's here. Here's Tom."

His brother, the governor, said, "Harry? I'll read you the postscript. 'P.S. They got her *name* out of the mother, who at least gave her a name. But they got too rough. The mother's hysterical, in a mental clinic. But they didn't get where the child was, because her mother didn't happen to know. B.' "

"Nice people," said Harry, encompassing many.

"You bet," said his brother. "And now we know, don't we?"

"That's *all* you know? No clue . . . where she is?"

"Nothing."

"There *is* this big fat criminal?"

"There is. Where have you been? Now I am, in all conscience, against capital punishment, as you may know, but if the human race needs to be rid of any one member . . ."

"He's for it, eh?" Harry cut in.

"End of the line, as your friend puts it. Oh, they've fought. I've been offered bribes. I've even been threatened already. But they couldn't touch me. Duly elected and sworn."

"Cut the political philosophy, Tom, will you please?"

"You bet I will," said his brother vigorously. "It looks to me like I'm going to resign my office."

"What!"

"All right, Harry. What else? It's a double bind, isn't it?" His brother's voice had lost its more melodious cadences. "Can't succumb to personal pressure and call myself fit to hold the office. But suppose this man goes to the gas chamber, as scheduled, and then it comes out . . . as it will . . . don't ever think it won't . . . that *I* didn't give a damn for the life and safety of a seven-year-old girl, supposed to be my own blood at that. The 'pee-pul' is a sentimental slob, old boy, and votes are ninety-eight percent emotional. So there it goes, doesn't it? Anyway"—now his brother's voice had an offhand note that snapped Harry to attention—"I can't do that to Daddy. So what's the solution? I bow out, and make it very, very public. Then what do they gain by touching this child? That'll fix it. Agreed?"

Harry was feeling stunned. He was guessing that his father must be in worse shape than could be stated in his presence.

Suddenly his brother Dick was speaking. "What a mess, eh? Now listen, Harry, have you got a glimmer at all?"

"I may have." Harry's lips felt tight.

"Then don't pay any attention to Tom. For one thing, they haven't got her yet. Or we'd have heard from them direct. Agreed?"

"Agreed."

"So before Tom starts making a noble jackass of himself, why don't you just find the kiddie? That's what you're trying to do, isn't it?"

"Agreed."

"Then *you* are our little old white hope, baby brother. Don't bother to tell me it isn't much of a hope, but tell me if it's *any*." Then the doctor added, on a different note, and there was warning again, "Daddy needs to know."

"I'd call it a hope," said Harry slowly.

"It's hope, eh? Okay. I'll give the governor tranquilizers or something, and we'll all sit still while you get on with it. Now, how will you proceed?"

"Ah, no," said Harry. "Listen, Dick, give some thought to this informer, will you?"

"You believe that?"

"Bernie told me the same thing."

"So if he said it twice, it's got to be true? I thought it took three . . ."

"Are you trying to tell me you don't believe any of it?"

"No, no. Somebody's after the kiddie. I'd as soon they didn't get her."

"What's Bernie's partner up to?" Harry was sharp. "Does *he* know enough to be careful?"

"Oh, well—seems they got him."

"GOT him?"

"Beat him up. Oh, he's okay, in a manner of speaking. Didn't know a thing to tell. Luckily for us, but not for him, I guess. Hospitalized, in Honolulu."

"What about the police?" Harry was feeling outraged by all this violence.

"What about them? We told them, here, the whole rigmarole. And it will leak. One reason Tom feels himself in a spot, you see? The cops would like to ask this Varney a few pointed questions. Wait a minute, Daddy wants you. Take it easy, Harry." There was the tag, the tip-off, the warning again. Harry knew that his father must be in a bad way.

His father said, "No description. Not the faintest clue. We don't know who's with her. How can the police find my little girl, even if they felt like trying, when she could be anywhere in the whole damn world? Where are you, Harry? Is she in Ireland?"

"No, no," said Harry. "No, no."

"Then what are you doing?"

"No, no," said Harry. "Never think it. She's *not* in Ireland." Harry was shaken by the notion that the enemy was listening in. "I'll call you back, Daddy. Same time, your time, tomorrow."

But his father said, "I put her on this spot. *I* did it. Don't you think I know that? She was doing all right where she was. But too late, now. These people . . . a little girl seven years of age."

"Listen, Daddy," said Harry. "I don't have much, but I do have something. Don't get your hopes up too high, but not all the way down, either. Let me see what I can do."

He cut the connection. His daddy was in great distress. Harry could guess that his brothers had used him and his mysterious shenanigans to temper the old man's mood of anguish and despair. A white hope, eh? Fat chance they really thought that.

But it came to him slowly that (after all) perhaps he was the best hope, of whatever color.

In Los Angeles, where it was midday, the doctor said, "Well, that's that. So I'm off again. Little cutting and sawing on my plate this afternoon. As usual. Give Harry a chance, I say. Agreed?"

Tom, sitting with his noble head resting on his hand, waved the other hand. "Over to Harry. Agreed."

Mei was weeping softly. Elaine was weeping rather more noisily.

"Shut up, Elaine," the governor said smoothly.

The old man in the bed said, "That's right. If you women can't stop bawling, go somewhere else. I am going to state that my son George is not as dumb as the rest of you think he is. Just because he's never done . . ."

"He's our baby," said Dick cheerfully. "And I'll say this—he wouldn't kid us, now. He's got a glimmer, all right."

"I'm *sure* he has," the old man said.

The doctor was watching keenly and now he flicked a glance at his brother and nodded.

"So get on with the day's work, I say," Dick continued. "Mei? How come you're not at work? Want a ride?"

"Oh, Doctor, I . . ."

"Come on," said Dick. "I went to the trouble of getting you a job and I don't approve of goofing off. So shake a leg. Half a day's work is better than none. I'll give you a ride, because I've got to go there anyway."

"Go ahead, Mei," said Paul Fairchild. "And you, Elaine, will you please—"

"Oh, Uncle Paul," wept Elaine, "it can't be the people the man says in the letter. I'm sure it must be somebody else."

"You go and boss the help, or something," said the old man sternly. "I don't have to put up with all this weeping and wailing. They haven't got her yet. *By George,* they haven't got her yet."

He was looking better.

George Fairchild, commonly known as Harry, had been calling from the hotel suite where Jean Cunliffe—for appearance's sake "assumed" by the hotel to be his sister—was tucked away in one of the bedrooms, sound asleep.

Harry began to thank his prophetic soul that he had made this arrangement. These people were not nice, too much beating up was going on. And the fact was, Jean Cunliffe had also been doing all right where she was, until Harry Fairchild had come along and put *her* on a spot. Harry was understanding how his father felt, a little bit too well. Oh, damn it.

But he had to thank his prophetic soul that he had done nothing overt, in the tag end of this long, hard day. He had been pretty sly. He had simply taken this suite, and then decreed a slow, leg-stretching ramble on the streets of the fair city, in the course of which Harry had turned, as if impulsively, into a bookstore and ordered up nearly a dozen books on the history, geography, legends and what-had-they about Ireland, both North and South. He had played the role of the scholarly tourist to perfection. In fact, it suited him, it fitted him. He had begun to suspect that perhaps he *was* a scholar, and not necessarily just an amateur. Perhaps he ought to take up a scholarly hobby rather more seriously. He was taken down with a conviction of inferiority, yet hope. And excitement.

He had even discussed it languorously during a meal of sorts, after which Jean was so groggy that he had decreed bed for her (at what was, by Los Angeles time, late morning). But, by then, the books had been delivered, and when Jean had staggered docilely off, Harry had fallen upon them like a wolf.

Muttering "The trained mind looks in the index," he had done so, and in the third volume that came to his hand there it was. "Castle Ballycoo. Modern. Ca 1700. Retaining the name of a vanished village."

Ah, but there was the name of the *new* village. So Harry had fallen upon the map and he knew where it was and how to get there. "Green. Girl. Deirdre. Irish. Ballycoo." Very simple, really, once you had the missing word. So Harry had called down and cheerfully arranged for the hotel to produce a car, at a reasonably convenient morning hour.

Then he had felt ready to call Los Angeles.

Now, having called, and having heard the news, Harry began to disrobe, being dead for sleep himself. He reflected that the pressures on him had been gaining weight rather steadily. He had begun all this pretty much for Bernie's sake, who hadn't wanted to die for nothing, who had given him the word. It had been Harry's somewhat sentimental old-school-tie fancy, which he could afford but which he needn't mention. This had been reinforced by his daddy's wish to find the child and (Harry faced it) also by his brothers' skepticism.

But it had been growing upon him for some time that perhaps he had better find the child for the child's sake. And it now appeared that he *had* better, and furthermore had better do it for his brother Tom's sake, too. Tom might not have been serious about abandoning his career for the sake of an unknown, unseen, unproven little sister. Yet . . .

The old man was in distress. And if you had to put it bluntly and crudely, they were all his loving sons, Tom, Dick and Harry. Furthermore (his brothers' wives having turned out the way they had) the old man had no grandchildren. Oh, it put the pressure on!

Damn it! Obviously Harry couldn't take up serious scholarship tomorrow. Or even the next day. Oh, no! First he had to gallop about, being the white hope of his whole family, chasing piggy banks!

"Fine thing," Harry muttered around his toothbrush.

There was absolutely nothing he could do about it anymore tonight. Best our hero rested his brain and bones. Damn it, maybe he *ought* to have walked on ledges across the faces of buildings, been bold, quick and ruthless in the cause—although there had been no sign of any followers to Dublin . . . that he had *seen,* that is.

Quick? His mind flashed back. Yah! Damn it, he had omitted to ask for the date set for the execution of this Kootz, whoever he was. Supposing that this monster perished on schedule, according to the law? Wouldn't *that* take the pressure off? "They" could scarcely expect even the government to resurrect him. Was Harry, then, working against time? No, no, what he meant was, were the villains so doing? As for old white-hope-Harry . . . *he* didn't even know what time it was.

Never mind. Go to bed. Harry resolved to lay off this bad habit of cursing himself. What did he know? Well, he knew, now, that the man in the brown suit, one Victor Varney, *was* a villain-in-chief. But wait, wasn't it odd that they had not caught one single glimpse of him since he had floated away on the moving stairs at the air terminal, years and years ago?

Could there be more than one set of villains?

Who, for instance, was Dorinda? Who was the man in the felt hat? And where the devil was the man in the brown suit?

The man was in a blue suit. He was, however, in the act of taking it off, in a hotel room across the Green.

In Los Angeles Dr. Fairchild swooped into St. Bart's parking lot and neatly into his reserved slot. Mei thanked him and walked gracefully away toward the service entrance.

She changed into her working uniform and went up to the

eighth floor. She was an aide; she fetched and carried. Mei had been fetching and carrying a large part of her life. She was glad of the work the kind doctor had found for her. She had called for help, but not charity. She would stay in that house only until the trouble was over. She went along the north wing, looking straight ahead of her. Still, the doctor was right. Best to do one's daily work.

Mei had not been weeping because she lashed herself for ever having spoken of the child. She knew she had meant no harm and could not have expected this strange trouble. She was afraid for the child, of course, but she was also afraid for the child's father. She had always thought that he had a generous heart, this vigorous, rich old man. The truth was, Mei had always been fonder of the father than of the child's mother, in those old days when she had fetched and carried in the pretty house the man had found for the pretty woman. The woman who had run away, had given her child away, had broken now, like the frail self-centered creature that she was—Mei wouldn't stain a cheek with a tear for that woman. But for the man, whose damaged heart beat strong enough to be vulnerable to suffering, for *him* Mei could not help but weep.

One of the patients, whose door was open, saw her passing by in slender grace. Miss Emaline lifted her head and said to herself, now who? Something so familiar. Brought the old days at Dolabela to her mind. But the figure was gone. Miss Emaline dropped back.

She was feeling, in the body, much better. And in her mind, she was sad, but certain. Sad because Mr. Beckenhauer, whom she had so hoped to find, was not in St. Bartholomew's anymore, or indeed on this earth, God bless his soul. Certain, because she had prayed, she had, with the Lord's help, come to a firm decision. She had been brought to see that it was a question of time. She knew there was a very wicked man who had to die. She remembered his name now. Very well. Her duty was to wait until he was dead, and the Devil himself could not make her betray her trust too soon. She had become a bulwark between Bobby and evil. She would remain so—to honor a good man's soul.

A nurse came in and pounced upon her with thermometer.

"Newspapers?" mumbled Miss Emaline.

"Oh, yes, you wanted some out-of-town papers, wasn't it? Well, I'm so sorry, Miss Hanks, I forgot to see whether . . ."

"S'all right. My sister . . . bring . . ."

"Well then, that's okay." The nurse said, holding Miss Emaline's wrist in practiced fingers. "She'll be along, I suppose? My, your sister surely has a lot of children, hasn't she?" Miss Emaline nodded mutely. "They were all in the lobby yesterday. Somebody told me they were such good children." The nurse took the thermometer out, her eyes brilliant with kindly curiosity. "How many does she have, anyway?"

"Seven," said Miss Emaline firmly.

The nurse exclaimed, flipped the mercury down expertly, and went away. Miss Emaline lay back to rest and heal and feel time passing. Nobody—nobody—knew where she was except Callie. And Callie knew nothing. And nobody knew Callie. Bobby was safe. Miss Emaline would endure. It was only until Wednesday. Unless, in the newspapers—ah, no matter. Miss Emaline knew what she ought to do.

Chapter 13

IN the morning they went winding through the Sunday-silent countryside, a little west, a little south. Jean was quietly falling in love with Eire. Quietly, because it wasn't a time for puppy-dog enthusiasm.

Harry had ordered breakfast up, and when she had come bounding, refreshed from a long sleep, and he had told her the news from Los Angeles in rather an offhand way, Jean had sensed quickly that he was more worried than he admitted. So she had kept a quietly decent outer cheer herself. Still, she couldn't help feeling *really* cheerful, because here they were, doing the best they could, and meantime . . . Oh, this green land!

Their suitcases were in the tiny car. Once they had investigated the green pig, there was no telling what their destination then might be. Harry would have to make some phone calls, whatever happened. With luck, he could tell his brothers exactly what to do. Otherwise, it all lay chancy. They would have to see, for instance, what Bonzer might know.

They had been progressing toward the green pig very slowly, what with the unfamiliar driving on the left side of the road and finding their way by map alone. They had been lost for half an hour, just getting out of the city. Then, on their way, Harry had been watching behind and after about an hour's going in the country he had taken evasive action. A car or two had seemed to him to have taken too many of the same turns. So they had ducked behind a country inn and gone inside for refreshment.

Jean had fallen in love with the Inn of the Black Dog and had wanted to know if they could come back here, supposing they were to spend another night in Eire. But Harry had said that they were not in Southern California, where the common folk drove fifty miles to dinner and back. Shannon was on the far side of *their* village; they might fly from Shannon. And even fly by night. If they needed an inn, there would be another inn. He had proved his point.

So they continued, and seeing nothing suspicious behind, they had come along as directly as they could figure how to go, but slowly, on these darling roads, with Jean eating everything with her eyes, feasting against famine, against having to leave all this too soon, alas.

They had fallen into a companionable silence. Even the fact that they had fallen into bed in the same hotel suite, but not into the same bed (on the flimsy excuse that they had been so tired) was no longer making them feel somewhat sheepishly remiss, and traitors to their generation. So they went on, rambling and winding in the green dish of the land, with Jean yearning to stop and stay there at every new curve of the road.

When, nearing noon, they were only four miles from *their* village, Harry announced that he thought they might best go to the hotel first. They had ascertained that there was one, although not called an inn, which fact Jean silently deplored. They could take rooms, whether they needed them or not, Harry said (he could afford it). He said he would need a base for telephoning. They would need a meal. They also had to find out where the castle was, and the name of the people who lived in it with their little daughter Deirdre.

So they would discover the name at the hotel, from some garrulous native, and afterwards their approach would be wide-open, quick and decisive. They would tell these parents the whole story at once, and be done with deviosity. Surely no reasonably kind person would refuse them the green pig. And speed was the thing, wasn't it?

While Jean silently deplored the need for speed, they came into wooded hills and glimpses of lakes. Now the road wound downward and there lay the tiny village. She gasped and cried, "Oh! I want to *stay here.*"

It was so tiny. There were perhaps ten buildings, all told. The buildings were tucked into the green, so strict in line, so neat, so white, stone-strict, spare, serene. There could be no such thing as speed, in this place.

Harry drove very slowly down into the cluster and, sure enough, there was the hotel (which was an inn, *de facto,* if Jean had ever seen a movie in her life). They pulled up and got out of the car. Jean was avid to get inside, but Harry touched her arm and she turned.

Behind the few buildings that were tucked against a slope at the other side of the road and above them, on a kind of high, meadowlike, green-grassy shelf, there stood a castle. It was small, as castles went. It was young, for a castle. It had stood only a few hundred years. It was a child's cardboard castle. It stood white and square, with crenelated horizontal roof lines and tiny turrets at the corners. It was too much! Jean closed her eyes to see whether it would vanish.

When she opened her eyes and it had not, she glanced up at Harry and caught him smiling at her with a certain tender amusement that vanished in an instant.

They went into the hotel.

They went through a rather narrow, darkish passage and came out at the other end into an oddly divided space where there was a man in charge. Surely they could have rooms. And a meal? Surely, said he. There to the right was a parlor, adorably ugly. A woman appeared, very small, dark-haired, pink-cheeked, and at the sound of the first word out of her mouth Jean was totally enchanted and turned to follow her like one in a trance.

The woman, in full tongue, went first up a narrow stair, Jean next, and the man after, with the suitcases. Harry let them go. Himself, he went back to the entrance. He stepped out upon the stones of the small pavement before the door and gazed up at the castle.

There was a youngish man with a pipe in his mouth, leaning against the white wall of the hotel. Harry hoped that he would prove to be the garrulous native.

He said, "Who lives in the castle?" Yon castle? he thought to himself wryly.

"Butler," said the lad, taking the pipe out of his mouth and making the mouth into a three-cornered smile.

"The *name* is Butler?"

"It is."

"Not Lord anything?"

"Mister Butler," said the lad, and said no more. Garrulous he didn't seem to be.

"They'd have a telephone? I mean, they are *on* the telephone?"

"Surely."

"How do I find . . . ?" Harry was wondering if this wee village was served by such a thing as a phone book.

"There's Miss Beale, from the castle," the lad said, "if you'll look there, and Miss Deirdre Butler going along beside her."

"Huh!" Harry's hair stood on end. He brought his gaze lower and on the opposite margin, across the street, if it could be called a street, were walking a plump woman in a tweedy costume and a little girl who was wearing a plaid skirt and a blue sweater, as a little girl should. The woman walked with a heavy lumbering, and the child tripped daintily.

What stupendous luck! Jean was upstairs. Harry couldn't wait. He took off like a rocket.

"Excuse me," he said, stepping in the path they were taking.

"What is it?" said the woman in a high sharp voice that disapproved of him at once. She was in her stout forties, her fleshy face was high-colored, she had been stopped in her tracks; her eyes flashed cold.

But Harry was staring at the child. So fair of skin was she that he could see the blood coursing, the pink coming and going. "Your name is Deirdre?" he said on a fond note, with an admiring beam in his eye. "And you were in Los Angeles, California, last Thursday evening, now weren't you, honey?"

The child's eyes were a very light blue and they widened and her face stained pink and then paled. He hadn't expected to frighten her.

"What *is* it, if you *please?*" the woman said, breasting forward protectively.

But Harry said to the little girl, "Hey, do you still have the green piggy?"

The woman said, "You are obviously an American. Perhaps you do not know that a gentleman does not stop persons and address them improperly."

"I'm sorry," said Harry, turning charm on her belatedly. "I believe you are Miss Beale?"

"I am." The woman bridled, taking, it seemed, further offense, if possible.

"And this is Miss Deirdre Butler? Hi, Deirdre." He tried again with the child.

But Miss Beale thrust the child behind her.

"If you are acquainted with Mr. Butler . . ."

"No, no," said Harry. "No, I'm not. But you see, ma'am, Miss Deirdre is in a position to do me a very great favor. And here I've come all the way from California . . ."

His worried-cherub look was having no effect.

"I suggest," said the woman, not changing her expression, which had begun with disapproval, continued with disapproval, and seemed determined to remain disapproving forever, "that you speak to Mr. Butler about whatever concerns you. Not that Miss Deirdre concerns you. I can tell you, here and now, that if you are a film person from California, Miss Deirdre is not available for vulgar exploitation."

Harry gaped.

"It is *un*thinkable," said Miss Beale.

"It sure is!" gasped Harry. "Listen. Of course I intend to

speak to her father. But it's Miss Deirdre who can do me a kindness, and I'm sure that she would."

This woman had *never* cared for cherubs. "Her father may give you permission to speak to her," she said, "but I cannot. May we pass?"

"Just a minute," said Harry, disapproving of *her* as heartily as he liked. "Could she answer that one simple question, if you don't mind?"

"Not at all. You must address yourself properly to the proper person," said Miss Beale. "I cannot stand here conversing with a stranger in the village street. May we walk on?"

"Listen, Deirdre . . ." Harry began. But the child looked as if she would burst into fragments. She was changing color so painfully that it was as if words were whips and made her cringe.

So Harry said, "Well, I'm sorry," and stepped back.

The two of them walked away. Harry stood and stared after.

Then he picked up his heels and loped across to the hotel. "So," he snapped at the lad who was leaning against the wall, "the little princess is guarded by a dragon, eh?"

"Surely." The man spit out his pipe. "That Beale!" he said with three-cornered contempt. He said no more.

So Harry dashed inside. He seemed to hear female chatter going on above him, but the hotelkeeper was there and Harry persuaded him to indicate the phone, to divulge the number, and to explain how to work the contraption.

Harry knew he had made a mistake. He ought not to have pounced upon this little girl in the village street. Go through channels, eh? Okay, channels. But Harry was smarting, just the same, not being used to having a door slammed in his wealthy young, moderately charming American face.

When a voice admitted that he was now connected with Ballycoo Castle, Harry said, "My name is Fairchild. May I speak to Mr. Butler, please? He does not know me, but this is an important matter. I came from California especially to see him."

"Beg pardon? Where is that, sir?"

"California."

"Yes, sir, but where *is* that, sir?"

"California, the United States of America," said Harry. *"Hollywood."*

"I see, sir." The voice seemed satisfied now. "I shall inquire, sir."

Harry fumed, waiting.

After long minutes the voice came back. "Mr. Butler is engaged, sir. Perhaps if you were to ring at another time."

"Now, wait a minute," said Harry. "This is an urgent matter. I would like to make an appointment to talk to Mr. Butler very soon. As soon as possible. *Now,* in fact."

"I shall inquire, sir."

More minutes.

The voice said, "Mr. Butler instructs me to say that he is engaged with guests, but perhaps in a day or two . . ."

"That won't do. I'm sorry. Can't he give me five minutes this afternoon? *Now?*"

"I believe not, sir."

"But look . . . Okay, what about Mrs. Butler?"

The voice was mute (as Harry guessed) with shock, so he said, "All right. The one I really want to talk to is Miss Deirdre. When may I come up and see *her?*"

The voice gasped. "Not at all," it said, stiff with horror. "Mr. Butler, as he has instructed me to say, will see you in a day or two."

"The hell he will!" said Harry furiously—and fortunately a little late. The voice was gone. The line was dead.

The hotelkeeper was watching him, head lowered, eyes upturned. "What's the *matter* with those people?" cried Harry.

"It happens they're busy," the man said. He, too, had a three-cornered smile. He shook his head slyly.

Harry raced down the passage to look out, but the walking figures were not to be seen. So he raced back, and up the stairs, ducking his tall head lest it be bashed on some beams, roaring around corners toward the sound of voices. There were Jean and the landlady, the woman twinkling and beaming, and Jean bouncing.

"Oh, Harry, these rooms! Oh, have *I* got things to tell *you!*"

"I," he said sourly, "just saw Deirdre."

It was as if he had hit her. "Where?"

"Oh, walking by. Attended by a dragon. Hight Miss Beale. A regular Princess Deirdre—not permitted to speak to the likes of me."

"Oh," said Jean instantly, "because you're a strange man. Oh, let *me* see her." She flew for the stairs and Harry went down behind her. But there was nobody walking in the village street.

"She's gone! Oh, I'm sorry." But Jean did not *look* sorry. In fact, her hopes had leaped higher, because Deirdre, the green-pig girl, was here and not (as she might have been) elsewhere. So Jean turned her beaming face. "But wait 'til I tell you . . . It's so darned antique and legendary you won't believe . . ."

Harry took hold of her arm and yanked her back inside. "*Will* you stop being the jolly girl tourist for two seconds," said Harry, "and shut up and listen?"

He dragged her back into the parlor. He was already contrite, as he dumped her down upon a wooden seat and made for the bar. There must be a bar. There was. Shut up tight. But deviosity was not unknown to the Irish, so Harry came back with two glasses of whiskey and put one into her hand.

He said glumly, "Okay, I apologize."

She looked up at him with a tiny frown, which changed even as he watched into lines of pure inquiry. "Tell me what happened?" she said. "I'm sorry. I just forgot and enjoyed myself again."

There were no sarcastic notes in her voice. He felt that this was not only uncanny, it was something of an insult. "Did *I* say you shouldn't enjoy yourself?" he glowered.

"No, no. Tell me about Deirdre."

So he told her. Finally he said despairingly, "Do you remember Sweet Alice, Ben Bolt? Believe me, this kid looks as if she'd jump out of her skin, if she dared to call even her soul her own, that is. What we have here is the antithesis of good old Sally Jo. So now what? Now, I got to slay dragons? Or else the hell with it . . . Be Tom, Tom, the Piper's son? At my age?"

"What *will* you do?" Jean said with a tense, controlled sweetness. When Harry got off in this vein it slew her. It really did.

"Go there. Get in. Get the damn you-know-what. *How* is what I am *trying* to discuss." Harry was very cross.

"Would you like to know," she said, "what's going on in the castle and who the guests are?"

He grunted as ungraciously as possible and sipped his whiskey while Jean's fingers slipped along the sides of her glass and she talked rapidly, and from time to time she bounced a little; she smiled a little. (She could not help it.)

"It's haunted!" she said. "The castle is. They have no less than two ghosts. No connection, either. One is a hundred years older than the other. Can you imagine? Well, it seems Mr. Butler has become a kind of ghost buff. Aficionado? So what's going on is . . . they have a medium up there, an English woman, and they also have a psychic researcher, a man, some kind of professor, suspected to be, if not English, too—at least *not Irish.* Mr. Butler would love to have an authenticated ghost, you see, and that's what *he's* after. But Mrs. Roach, who was telling me, *she* thinks that any decent Irish ghost will not oblige. And the whole village is betting on the ghosts, both of them, not to show up."

Jean bounced with delight. (She could not help it.)

"You see," she tried to simmer down, "*Mr.* Butler belongs to a branch of an Irish family, which branch went and traitorously lived in England for a while. It's his wife who belongs to the castle. I mean, the castle belonged to *her* folks. So she's okay with the villagers, but they aren't crazy about Mr. Butler, or his habit of hiring too much English help. The ghosts, you see, are only his ghosts-in-law. Oh, I think it's such a . . . I'm sorry, Harry." Jean snuffled, in order not to chortle.

"So?" said Harry. "Ghosts, is it? That's your contribution? And you're thinking, what a chance for me to dress up and go *be* a ghost, thus stealing the you-know-what, clanking chains the while."

He looked so gloomy as he spoke this nonsense that Jean thought she was going to die. She said, half strangling, "It'll have to be me. There's always a White Lady. I could make do with a sh-sheet . . ."

"Damn it," said Harry, looking around fiercely. "In broad daylight, on Sunday afternoon, they're not hunting ghosts *now*."

"The village is dying to know whether they are," said Jean, with bright moist eyes, "because it's very bad luck to poke up ghosts on Sunday. Oh, Harry, I don't mean to be so t-tickled."

"Drink your drink," he said coldly. "Ghosts-on-Sunday, hell-on-Monday. We're going up there. On business."

So Jean took a large swallow of Irish whiskey, neat, and now she thought that she *would* die.

Harry got her on her feet, pounding her back, and he took her out of the hotel, blind as she was, with streaming eyes, and held her dangling over his arm while he asked the lad for directions.

"You'll go back the way you came," the lad said in a sunny fashion, "and turn to the right, the first way you'll come upon, and you'll be brought to the gatehouse."

"So there's a gate, eh? In a fence? Or a wall? Or what? A moat, perchance?"

Jean strangled away, coughing and laughing like a madwoman.

The lad said, "Oh, they've a great fence, up there." He used his pipe for emphasis. "But not all the way around," he added merrily.

Harry took poor, helpless Jean over to the car and put her into it.

Ignoring her paroxysms, he drove back the way they'd come, took the first right turn on a road that wound charmingly through the wood and upward. When the car came out into the grassy open, there was the fence. Tall. Iron. There were the tall gates. Closed. There was a cottage that must be the gatehouse.

Harry stopped the car about fifty feet away.

Jean had not *quite* died. By opening her mouth wide, and breathing hard and achieving a kind of whoo-whooing—like a strong wind in a pine tree—that cooled, she had fought back to some semblance of control. Harry got out and stood in the road, looking gloomily at her. The gloomier he looked the more she wanted to scream with laughter. She had taken a strong hold on herself, but it couldn't last.

She said, "You'd better go by yourself. I w-wouldn't inspire much confidence."

"Not with a breath like the tongue of a dragon," said Harry, "and cackling like a little red hen, in the bargain."

She squeaked like a mouse. She *was* going to die, this time.

She breathed hard. "Whooo, whooo. Whoo-eye don't you just go? I want to admire the b-beauties of nature any . . . hoo-hoo-how." Keeping her mouth stiff, she whimpered helplessly.

So Harry took her by the chin and turned her face up and kissed her with such great and tender skill that Jean felt as if she were going to die, all right—but in quite another way.

When he let her go, he said, "All right, now? Sober?"

Oh, he knew too much. She closed her self-betraying eyes. He patted her cheek. "Find something to think about, why don't you? I'll be quick. Or holler, if I need you." Harry went loping away, onward to the gates.

Jean scrunched down in the seat and kept her eyes tight shut, to admire the beauties of nature. Because he . . . Because gosh . . . Because, what was *this,* for heaven's sakes!

Chapter 14

WITH his ego pleasantly reviving, for after all there were some areas in which Harry Fairchild could deem himself an expert, he knocked upon the gates and then upon the cottage door a second time, and finally wheedled his way into the house and finally persuaded the woman there, a thin woman who looked as if she had fed upon porridge with lumps in it ever since she had been born, to let him speak on the private telephone.

Where he wheedled and insisted until Mr. Henry Butler, pried at last away from the supernatural, came on the line.

Harry made his pitch. The man had a clipped and choppy way of speaking and a perfectly obtuse conviction that Harry could not possibly matter. Furthermore, Mr. Butler *had spoken.* He had already and, in his opinion, most graciously, agreed to see Mr. Fairchild in a day or two. Mr. Butler was not going to take this pronouncement under any kind of advisement with any notion of altering it. It was very good of him, as it stood.

At last Harry went so far as to say that all he wanted to do was buy a ceramic piggy bank. At which time Mr. Butler distinctly snorted. He said that that was an insubstantial excuse for so much argument, was it not?

"A pig is a little more substantial than a ghost, is it not?" yelled Harry.

"Good day."

Harry hung up, too, cursing his own too-short temper, and thought about making a dash, physically, and getting into the damn castle by main strength. But by now a man had appeared in the cottage, rather a large fellow, and dour, too. Harry didn't think he'd make it.

He also thought better of asking these guardians-of-the-gates, man and wife, to tell him how to break in, for the purpose of pig-snatching. No, he must retreat for the nonce, in all wisdom, and regroup himself.

He was thinking that persistence might do it, viz. little drops of water. He would phone in an hour. And then again, every hour on the hour. Wear Butler down. Meantime, consider whether a spot of burglary was feasible. After dark, of course, if it ever did get dark in this country, and if they didn't have vicious dogs, or some breed of dragon, guarding the joint.

Absorbed in the problem, he walked down the road to the car. When he was ten feet away he thought Jean must have folded over on the seat. Not asleep *again,* was she?

He hurried a little. There was no one on the seat of the car.

Harry felt annoyed. Now what? Gone after wild flowers? She certainly was nowhere on the open grass. He walked away beyond the car and began to peer into the thin fringes of the woods. He saw where the iron fence ended. Yah, not all the way around! Just a front, eh? he jeered silently. But where the devil was that girl?

He kept walking, peering as best he could down what natural vistas there were. It was green, in there. Very green—shadowed and cool. But he could not see her anywhere.

Should he wait in the car? Or look the other direction? It was true that he wouldn't have seen her, had she walked past the cottage. So Harry raced off in the other direction. The iron fence ran some distance. How could she have got this far?

From here, he could see a portion of the village. Maybe she had walked back to the hotel. Mad at him. Nonsense. If there was one thing he knew for sure, Jean Cunliffe was not *that* kind of girl.

Harry felt twinges of alarm. He seemed to have lost her. But this would not do. He hurried back to the gatehouse. The man who had arrived might have seen something as he was arriving.

The man had. He had walked past a car and it had been empty. He had seen no young woman at all. He had seen a moving car, indeed, a man driving, wavering over to the right side, the way it was dangerous, and hadn't he thought so at the time?

Harry said, "Okay. How do I get in touch with the village constabulary?"

But in the village, they told him, there was no constable. Why would there be?

Jean came to herself with a pang of pain like a drumbeat, and a continuing pounding in her head. Why was it so dark? Was she blind? No, there was a shadow, a human presence, a man. Harry?

She convulsed. There was something wrong with her body, the position of her limbs. Something must have hit her on the head. Something now stung, and stung again, the flesh of her calves and the tender area behind her knees.

She was lying on a floor, and there *was* a man who said (in a voice not Harry's), "You may as well not yell. I'll fix that, too, in a minute."

He seemed to be wrapping a length of rope around her legs, at the knees. He was tying her up. Like a package for the post. She yanked at whatever was holding her arms. Her wrists seemed to be wearing, of all things, metal bracelets. Handcuffs! Chaining her wrists together behind her back! The effect was crippling. She opened her mouth to yell as loud as she could.

The man put his hand over her mouth and squeezed her face cruelly. When he let go, she was in tears.

He finished with the rope swiftly. "Okay," he said, "open wide. I can't mess around with you, right now."

Then he was stuffing something into her mouth and she gagged and choked. But she had seen and recognized his face.

A memory of white flowers. Brown suit. Flickety little eyes. *Varney!*

After a while, when she had learned how to relax her throat and endure the loathsomeness of the gag in her mouth, everything seemed very quiet. She had governed her breathing. Now she began to be able to see all around. It was not dark where she was, only dim. Dim and quiet. She was alone, wherever she was. The man had gone.

She was lying on a floor of hard-packed earth, within walls made of great crude stones fitted together in a primitive manner. There was one tiny square, open to a greenish light. There was a broken door over there, half-closed. Over her head sagged a thatch, dusty and rusty and rotten. She was bound, gagged, handcuffed, and imprisoned within what could only be called a hut. A ruin. There was an ancient blackened fireplace, gaping cold and crawling with loathsome medieval insects, she had no doubt. Everything was too *old.* Her skin crawled. She longed for a wide, crisp, desert place. She was abruptly disenchanted with legend and antiquity.

But, in a slow dawning, she seemed to know where she was. Surely she had seen this very ruined hut from the road, along the way they had come, and feasted on the sight, too. It must be visible from the road. Otherwise, how could Varney have found it? Varney, with his American voice, as foreign here as she.

But if it was visible from the road, it was not far. Two hundred, three hundred feet? Could she roll, creep, get out of here, and to the road?

She could not. The rope was attached somewhere, like a tether.

Now that American voice played back, in her mind. She had heard, but not attended to, yet somehow had recorded this. In the midst of her choking struggles, the man had said to her, "Okay, Cunliffe. I guess you'll stay. I got a thing to do. Then we'll hear from you . . . *all about pigs.*"

He was coming back, to hear all about pigs.

So Jean lay trembling and began to think, in pain, about pain. She had never had much of it. Not yet.

Chapter 15

HARRY had roused the village. The lad with the pipe turned out to be the hotel man's son, one Johnny Roach. He took to the rousing with gusto. He had put his fingers in his mouth and emitted shrieking whistles. Seven or eight males, and as many females, were even now gathered before the hotel and a great babbling was going up, arguments about procedure, joyously joined.

Harry was inside on the phone, trying to rouse the authorities in the nearest sizable town. The man at the gatehouse had promised (providing he had Mr. Butler's consent) to rouse the outdoor staff at the castle to search the woods. Harry was afraid, however, that Jean was no longer near enough to be found by beaters on foot. He had no proof. A driver, who tended to drive on the right, was flimsy evidence of international crime. He had no powers. Except to talk fast on the phone. He was, more or less patiently, trying to convey his serious alarm into a strange ear, when he heard a feminine American voice calling his name. His heart jumped.

Dorinda said, "Oh, Harry, *there* you are! I've had the worst time finding you."

And there she was, elegant in a tawny dress, a tawny jacket, with a choker of gold-colored beads around her slender neck. Which Harry, at once, felt like wringing.

He snapped some final words into the phone and left it.

"Where is Jean Cunliffe?" he said to Dorinda, knowing now exactly what was meant by "a cold fury."

"I don't know what you mean, darling," she said. "Why did you run out on me? I wanted to talk to you, in Amsterdam. We've had the worst time. Oh, this is Vance Miller, who is with me. Here is Harry Fairchild, Vance. At last."

She was smiling. She was stripping off fawn-colored gloves. The man who was with her held his felt hat to his puny breast and nodded politely.

Harry said, "What do you want with me? What do you *want,* Dorinda?"

"Well, for pity's sake," said Dorinda, "don't bite! I want the same thing you want, of course. I want the little girl. Where is she?"

"What do you want with the little girl? What's she to you?" He *would* wring her neck in a minute.

"Why, she's my little sister," said Dorinda.

The inside of Harry's head began to roar.

The Roach boy dashed in and said, "We're off!" and dashed off.

Dorinda said, "Vance, dear, could you find us something to drink, do you suppose? Harry, now come, don't look so confounded. Sit down and tell me. What is happening here? Have you found another piggy bank? Was there a message in it?"

Harry went into the parlor and sat down. The fact was, he didn't know what else to do. She followed him and sat down, too, with grace. Her face had become grave.

"I'm afraid it's getting serious. Don't you think so? Go ahead. I'm listening."

He said, "It's getting serious, all right. Where is Jean Cunliffe?"

"Your little friend? That's what is troubling everybody?" She looked around as if to say, but should it, really?

Harry said, savagely, "I'll listen to *you,* for five minutes. Or less—if it isn't fascinating."

"Oh, Harry," Dorinda sighed, "why so grim?" The little man came in his shadowy way and, evidently having prevailed upon the hotelkeeper's natural instinct to be hospitable, gave them whiskey. Dorinda thanked him. Then he too sat down, and where he sat, although it was in the middle of the room, became mysteriously a corner.

"I had thought, you see," said Dorinda, "that you and I were on opposite sides. But now I'm sure we had better join forces, at least for the time being. My poor little stepmother is in a hospital. Did you know that? Some people . . . Well, it just isn't the time for fun and games." She smiled and sipped. Expert and dainty.

Harry didn't open his mouth. He was listening. His very pores were open to receive the truth about Dorinda.

"To begin at the beginning," sighed Dorinda, "and, Harry, you *mustn't* look so dense, my father married a wife. Five years ago, I think. She's rather a cuddly little creature, Marybelle. *I* didn't mind, you see. I'm not at home very much anymore. And after all, one's father has his needs."

Harry glanced at his wristwatch and Dorinda went faster.

"But then this man, this Beckenhauer, he came and all the trouble began. My father hadn't known a thing about Marybelle's marriage to *your* father. Nor, of course, about a child. Well, it all came out. It had to. The point is, my father is a man of some . . . status. He doesn't care for the idea of bigamy. So there was a period of . . . well, call it confusion. But Marybelle has her little ways, and he began to think that she must have her child—or lose her mind." Dorinda made a moue. "He's fond of her. But naturally, although he wants to find the child, for her sake, for both their sakes, he wants to do it without publicity, if possible. And since I happen to be fond of my father, I thought . . ."

"That you would see what you could do," barked Harry. "So you nipped yourself to Los Angeles and picked *me* up."

"Well," said Dorinda, with her gentle smile, "the Fairchilds were a jump ahead. Father, of course, had hired people. But I thought I might find out just how far ahead the Fairchilds were."

(And chose the weak spot, thought Harry. Shooo-er you did!

He didn't know what else to believe—but *this* he believed.)

"By following me, you'd get ahead?" he snapped. "Why didn't you tell me, ask me?"

"It was fun while it lasted," she said wistfully. "But we can't have that sort of thing anymore, can we? They'll fight out custody. So now, Harry, darling, please? Tell me all about it?"

She seemed to think that now he would.

"How did you follow me *here?*" said Harry coldly.

"Oh, Vance, you see . . ."

"Who is he?"

The little man said apologetically, "Vance Miller. Private investigator."

"Vance was able to guess—once we knew you were after piggy banks—that there was one in Ireland," said Dorinda calmly. "He called airlines. In Dublin, we called hotels. We found the car-hire place. *They* said you had gone west and south."

"They did!" Harry flew an eyebrow. Oh, she was a liar, Dorinda was. He simply knew this. He had better pull his wits together.

"They guessed?" she shrugged. "But we stumbled upon . . ." She leaned toward him, smiling and smiling. "In the Inn of the Black Dog, you asked about a hotel, here."

Harry thought, damn it, so I did.

"After that, we just came along. What does it matter? Here we are. Harry, do you *know* where the child is?"

"What child?" he said glumly.

"Why, our little sister," purred Dorinda. "Barbara is her name. Where is she, Harry, please?"

"I don't know."

"But have you got hold of another pig?" Dorinda frowned.

Harry began to rub his forehead. "That's going to take about a week of hard labor."

She said, "That's too long." She said it hard and fast—too fast.

Harry had sense enough to keep on rubbing his forehead. He didn't look at her. But he thought, and what's your hurry,

Dorinda, darling? He said, as if he hadn't noticed, "There's not much point in it, anyway."

"What do you mean?" She had reestablished control. This was sweet inquiry.

"No point, until I find Jean Cunliffe."

"But why? What has she . . . ? I don't see why that's important." Now she was plaintive.

His wits were racing now. He lifted his head. "Do you think," he said cuttingly, "that I would have dragged *her* along, if I hadn't had to have her?"

"But I don't understand, Harry, darling."

"Then you don't, Dorinda, darling," growled Harry, "and I couldn't care less, whether you do or not. But believe me, if Jean Cunliffe isn't with me—pig or no pig—I *cannot* find the child. And neither can you, by the way."

"But surely she's already told you whatever it is that she knows."

"Suppose it can't *be* told? Suppose she has to see with her eyes and be there in person?"

"Harry, I don't . . ."

"So, if you'll excuse me, I'd better get on with finding her. Since it's all so serious." He got up. "By the way, Dorinda, do you happen to know a man named Varney?"

Dorinda was looking at him as if to see right through him. She said quietly, in a moment, "I think Vance does."

"Or a man named Kootz?"

"What a miserable name," she said. "Vance?"

The little man said, "Know who they are, sure."

"You know that Varney murdered Bernie Beckenhauer?"

"Wasn't our concern," said Vance. He had a mild and colorless voice. "It's what Beckenhauer did with the child."

"But, Harry," burst Dorinda, "some terrible thugs did get after Marybelle. I called home last night. There *are* criminals. That's exactly why I say that you and I . . ."

"Who left a trail for these criminals?" said Harry. "Could *they* guess Ireland? Or did they just follow?"

"Follow *here?*"

"Where's Jean Cunliffe?"

"Follow *me?* Oh, Harry, is *that* what's making you so antagonistic? But how could they have followed me? Wasn't she gone, before I ever got here?"

"I guess so," said Harry slowly.

"And mustn't we work together, now? The child is my little stepsister. She's your little half sister. Shouldn't we work together against 'them'—whoever 'they' are?"

"Maybe."

"Well, then, tell me. Beckenhauer put a message in a pig, didn't he? And the pig is here? In this village? Were there only two?"

Harry swung around. "I told you," he roared, "until I find Jean Cunliffe, I can't be bothered with pigs."

"But I can't *see,*" cried Dorinda, and for a flash her face was full of anger. "You don't make sense, Harry."

Harry said, "Okay. While it's been nice, Dorinda, darling, I mustn't sit and chat. Especially senselessly."

He went out into the air. He looked up at the castle, at the green hills. He was thinking, so I goofed at the Black Dog. But she never *stumbled* in there. I was followed that far. So she's a liar *and* in a hurry. And somebody's got Jean, so I need a reason. Give me a reason for saying what I said. Give me a reason that she'll believe. On the chance. On the chance that *Dorinda* has got Jean. Or knows who has. There's a chance, isn't there? Just as every little girl might *not* be seven years old?

In a moment Dorinda came up behind him. "Harry," she said softly, touching his tense shoulder. "Please, aren't we friends? At least, aren't we on the same side? Don't be huffy, just because I tried to use you. Of course I did. But things begin . . . and then they turn out—differently."

"Oh, they surely do," he said morosely. He turned and looked down and was able to smile. "I'm just upset," he said gently.

"About this Jean? Well, I know you're fond of her."

"Sure. Sure," he said. "But if *they've* got her and if, in their foolishness they're trying to force Jean to tell them something, *she can't do that.* And what if they go too far, and she can never . . . ? Well, there goes the only chance I know of, to find our little sister."

"Why must *she* see? I don't understand. Why must she be there?"

"Because," said Harry slowly, "and I may as well tell you, if we're on the same side, Bernie Beckenhauer gave her a part of the message orally."

"Yes?"

"Poor kid, she can't remember it," said Harry. "But she may. She thinks she's bound to, when and if she sees the other part. But without her, pig or no pig, end of the line."

There was silence.

"How do you know all this, Mr. Fairchild?" said Vance, who seemed to be there. His question was mild, but (alas) it was reasonable.

"Know?" sneered Harry, his wits racing around in his skull.

"But this is *stupid,*" cried Dorinda.

"How so?" flared Harry. "You forget that Varney was on that plane. You think Bernie was stupid enough to write down a message in the clear? The whole clue? When, for all he knew at the time, *Varney* would be reading the message?"

Harry thought, that's good. He fell silent.

"She can't remember?" said Dorinda with a hint of sullenness. "That's what's ridiculous, Harry."

(So it is, he thought, but it must serve.)

"The human mind?" he said. "Agreed."

"Why can't she say what he told her?"

"Chow-ee! If she could have *said,* I wouldn't have had to bother with her. *I* could have written it down. Don't argue, Dorinda. Half the clue is in Jean Cunliffe's head, and if I don't have her head along when I find the other half, I can't get it *out* of her head. So where is Jean? That's my problem, and if you don't want it, leave it alone." He turned his back and looked at the hills.

Dorinda laughed.

He tried not to wince. He thought, didn't work, I guess.

"Darling, you are just a wee bit . . . well . . . gullible?

Why, the crafty little wretch! She wanted the free ride, don't you suppose?"

He clamped his jaws together.

"Don't you suppose?" purred Dorinda.

"If so, the ride is over—the minute I put her in front of the message. But when will that be?" He was muttering.

"She knows where all the pigs *are,*" said Dorinda musingly.

"Nope," said Harry, in a flash, "she does not. Neither do I, yet."

"But Harry . . ."

"People are working on it. I *will* know where the other pig is, but Jean doesn't know." (Maybe he was talking too much.) "So where is she? Damn it, I'm paralyzed." He shut himself up.

In a moment Vance said, "Miss Bowie, shouldn't I run over to the nearest big place and see what I can do to lay on a search for this . . . uh . . . Jean?"

"Oh, yes," said Dorinda. She began to run her hand along Harry's shoulder as if to pet and comfort him. "Don't you think so, Harry? And you and I can hunt for her, too. We can take your car. Maybe she is simply lost in the hills. Maybe nobody's 'got' her. I can't believe that, you know. How could *they* find their way here?"

"Maybe I'm looking on the dark side, do you think?" he murmured.

"Where was she last seen?" said Dorinda in an energetic way.

But Harry watched the little man slip along to a car and he thought, she's believing. So he took Dorinda's arm and said, "You know, you seem to be cheering me up, Dorinda, darling."

"Well, you mustn't fret," she said. "Women *are* devious. But we can't have you paralyzed."

Varney had returned, walking softly. He pulled the broken door as nearly closed as it would go. He listened. It seemed for a long time.

Then he came, decisively, and ripped the gag away. When Jean stopped retching and had succeeded in bringing a little moisture back into her mouth his big cruel hand was poised to punish her face again, so she did not yell.

"Okay," he said briskly. "The yokels are going to be stirring any minute. So we'll make this fast. What about pigs?"

She stalled. She kept working her mouth.

"Come on." He hit her face, hard. "Beckenhauer put something in a piggy bank, eh? *I* didn't see him do it. But *you* saw him."

"No."

"Yes, you did. Quit with the lies." He slapped her. "*What* did he put?"

"We guess it's a message." (They knew this anyway.)

"You're not telling much, are you?" He hit her again. "And the pigs got sold, like to the kid in Amsterdam. And you know where."

"No."

"Come on. You missed in Amsterdam. There's one here. Up in the castle, naturally. That'll be taken care of. What I want from you is how many more pigs and where are they?"

"We don't know where."

"Yeah? You're chasing around the whole damn world and you don't know where? How many pigs? Where? And hurry up." He hit her again. It hurt.

Jean said with sudden spunk, "If you hit me once more, I won't say anything."

"That so?" He put a cruel hand on her and it hurt terribly. When he let her go, she was sobbing. She struggled to stop it. It was degrading. It was shameful. He knew how to hurt and shame a woman. He chose to wait her struggle out. He knew what he had done to her. Finally he said, "Seeing the light?"

She said, "Oh, I certainly do see the light. There's no *use* in this. I tell you the truth. You just hit me again. So there's *nothing* in this."

"Nuts to that stuff." He hit her face angrily and then his hand was poised to hurt.

"*I* can't win," she gasped. "But neither can you. So do what you'll do. I can't stop you. That's what I see."

Oh, she had seen through to the whole truth about this torture business. There was no such thing as "instant safety." There was *no* kind of safety. Only pain. Therefore there was no pressure whatsoever. So she waited for the inevitable pain, hearing her own frightened heart, remembering mercy, in the form of fainting, that *would* come and could be trusted.

She seemed to hear a sound. A syllable? A voice?

He had heard it, too, because his hand froze. His head turned. He shifted his legs, preparing the spring in his knees. Something rustled, very softly. Something clicked. A fingernail on stone?

Jean wasn't breathing. The man rose. He was powerful enough, the big body under the civilized blue suit was animal-strong enough, to do this slowly and silently. He went away from her, across the dirt floor to the broken door. He listened there. Then she heard the door protest as he widened its gap. He went outside.

She turned her cheek to the packed dirt. Ought she to scream now? Would it be any use?

But he was back swiftly. He was standing over her, still for a second of time. "Nuts," he muttered. He crouched and she cringed and tried to brace for pain.

But he began to work at the rope around her knees. He was taking it away. Well, then he would drag her off somewhere else and no difference to her.

He put his arm under her torso and lifted her roughly and flipped her over. Her chin struck the hard ground and she yipped. "Oh, shut up," he said. Then he was using a key on the handcuffs and then they were off. Her shoulders screamed with the pain of release, but she rolled to her side. He was standing high again and looking down. His face was in shadow.

"So you lied to me, in Los Angeles," he said savagely. "You little twerp!" And he lifted his foot and with his hard shoe he kicked her thigh. She screamed a reaction, but he didn't touch her again. Swiftly he was gone.

She didn't believe it. She lay still, waiting for more pain. In a little while she began to cry. Very quietly her tears ran down her dirty, swollen face.

Chapter 16

DORINDA and Harry coursed the roads in Harry's rented car. She, keen as a hawk, analyzed and advised. Harry was running on a perverse kind of faith. In deviosity? He listened. His ears ached with taking every slightest hint she gave him. She was being very careful. Or else he was all wrong.

Jean, very wobbly on her feet, staggered to the broken door and found it heavy. The sag of it was digging into the ground. She leaned; it groaned, and yielded at the top, and she skinned through the opening. One shoe came off.

She was in a wood. Not far from the road. She could see where the road must run. But she dared not go there. She still couldn't believe in freedom. But as long as it felt like freedom, she would choose.

So she went reeling off the other way, deeper among the trees, into the green gloom. Her arms ached; her breast ached; her face was still stinging. Her head hurt. The spot on her thigh, where he had kicked her, was painful, and she limped on one shoe, but went reeling and staggering as fast as she could, just away.

After a while, she looked behind and could no longer see the hut or any suggestion of a road. She did not seem to have broken any trail. She sank down on the ground. There was moss. She stared at its dainty beauty, its tiny perfection, for a long time.

It was very quiet in the wood. She heard him coming. She couldn't run. It would only be degrading, if she tried. So Jean simply toppled over and put her cheek on the moss and breathed in the emerald delicious smell—as long as she could choose at all.

Harry, tugging at the broken door to open it wider, heard Dorinda, calling out behind him, "Is she there?"

When he could see inside, he breathed deeply a moment before he called, "You were right."

"Oh? What? Oh! She *is* there!" Dorinda came, in a pretty female tripping on her high heels, down the remainder of the slope from the road. She leaned upon his shoulder to look in.

"Rope," said Harry. "See. Cut." He stooped to pick up something. "Shoe."

He stuck to monosyllables. He felt like falling down. It was relief from doubt. *He* had been right. Dorinda had guided him here. He'd taken great pains to let her do it. So now he knew, didn't he?

"She must have *been* here," said Dorinda. "Oh, wonderful! But where is she now? Perhaps she's frightened." Dorinda was looking into the woods. "Call to her, Harry, why don't you?"

"They've only taken her somewhere else," said Harry, gruffly. "That's all this means."

"Oh, but maybe not," said Dorinda hopefully. "Call her name, why don't you, Harry?"

Harry pretended to be peering off into the woods, but he was seeing the lift of Dorinda's chin and her look of haughty displeasure.

He knew, now. *Dorinda was on the other side.*

She said impatiently, "She has to be around. She can't be far. Find her." She looked as if the trees must bow, the hills must shift.

So he knew that somebody did not have Jean, anymore. *Dorinda knew that Jean was free.*

"What shall I do now, Dorinda, darling?" he said pathetically, succeeding in keeping any faintest note of joyous sarcasm out of his voice.

But after a moment, when he began, in earnest, to range and shout among the trees, no one answered.

If it was a kitchen, it was the largest kitchen Jean had ever seen in her life. She didn't care what it was, except that it was warm, and she had been so chilly; clean, and she had felt so grubby; inhabited, and she had felt so lonely.

She hadn't said much yet. No quickly plausible explanation of her plight had occurred to her. Furthermore the strange, strong, man had not asked her any questions. He had simply picked her up from her bed of moss and carried her, crooning comforts, all the way here.

And now she was comforted. They had put her in the easiest chair, a wickerish affair, worn to a pleasant hollow, and there was a round table, wearing a long cloth, drawn to her right side and on it a sewing basket, only recently abandoned, and her cup of tea.

They had stripped her feet bare and put them into a basin of clean water, her cold hands were around the warm cup, and while the man still marveled (as far as Jean could understand his jabbering) at how he had found her in the wood, the woman, with many exclamations, was very gently, and with blessed warm water, washing the traces of tears and the dirt from Jean's face.

The woman stood back finally and spoke more slowly. "How pretty she is—hurt and all. Miss Deirdre, love, come look! She'll do very well."

Jean popped her eyes wide and peered and saw that there *was* a little girl, sitting silently over there in a wooden chair, her child's legs dangling, her small face drawn long and full of woe.

I am in the castle! Jean thought. Harry may even be here, too!

"I am so grateful," she burst to her benefactors, "to you for finding me." And while the man and the woman began the rapid jabber (that was English of a sort but hard to hear), Jean smiled radiantly at the child.

But now came a high, quite intelligible, but very demanding voice. "Who is she? Why was she trespassing?"

The man was abruptly still. "Ah, Miss Beale," said the Irish woman, changing her manner to a kind of subservience that was also curiously contemptuous, "Fogarty found her in the wood and in such a state, poor soul, she hasn't told us a bit of it."

"Let her say, Margaret."

Jean looked up at a high-colored face, a pair of cold eyes, a thin mouth, and a total hostility.

"Can't you speak, young woman? What is your name, if you please?"

"My name is Jean Cunliffe. Does Mr. Harry Fairchild happen to be here, now?"

"Ah, the American." Miss Beale looked more disapproving than before. "The young man who made such a disgraceful scene at the gates. *You* are the missing American girl? I see. We shall soon have you where you belong."

"Let her be," said the Irish woman softly. "She's had a fright."

Miss Beale said, "Not at all."

The man, who was watching, made a soft sound in his throat and Miss Beale said sharply, "Go about your business, Fogarty. For some reason these Americans are determined to intrude here. But *this* trick will not succeed. I shall speak to them at the gate. They know, I believe, what is to be done with her."

The man (he wouldn't trouble himself to contend with the likes of Miss Beale, his look said) retreated toward some far corner where there seemed to be an exit. The Irish woman wore a self-contradicting look, a respectful sneer.

Jean said, loudly, "Thank you. But I would like to speak to Mr. Butler before I go, if I may."

"You may not," said Miss Beale.

"Ah, Miss Beale," said the Irish woman in wheedling tones, "would you look at her poor feet? Would you look at the great bruise on the side of her poor leg?"

"I am quite sure that her friends will attend to her injuries," said Miss Beale sternly, "if, indeed, she has any injuries. I shall attend to having them notified at once."

She turned and walked, putting her feet down heavily, as if to tread upon all opposition.

"And how is it in the house?" said the Irish woman, slyly.

"It is all nonsense," said Miss Beale. "And mind you keep Miss Deirdre here. We don't want ideas in her head."

She tossed her own head and went away.

Fogarty had vanished. The Irish woman rolled her eyes and possibly implored some saints, but so rapidly as to seem, again, to be speaking a foreign tongue.

Jean looked at the little girl, who stared back rather blankly. What ideas? Jean wondered. She told herself that it is not a child's fault if she is born with pale watery eyes. "Do you remember me, Deirdre?" she asked softly.

The child looked suddenly reassured; she wiggled from the chair and came nearer.

"Did you like flying?" said Jean.

"It was lovely," said the child, her color changing.

"Think of it!" said the woman, suspiciously.

Jean bent her head suddenly and said, "Oh, would you look, please?" She parted her hair with her fingers. "Margaret? I don't know any other name."

The woman accepted "Margaret," looked, and cried woe, and rushed to produce from somewhere a cold compress for the great lump that was there.

The child said, "Is it painful?" She spoke very well for one so young. She could not be older than seven, perhaps she was not yet that old.

"Oh, it doesn't hurt, anymore," Jean lied cheerfully. In fact, Jean's aches and pains were receding from the forefront of her consciousness. She knew now that Harry had not gotten in, did not have the pig. But here was Jean, inside, and something should be done. Miss Beale seemed to be the rock in their path. Jean sensed that although she surely wasn't popular, she had power. Jean didn't know *what* to make of the Irish woman. So she smiled at the child, with whom she had just contrived to be alone.

"I was sorry you didn't get the pink pig, Deirdre."

"It doesn't matter, you know," Deirdre said.

"Are you very fond of your green pig?" Jean hurried on. "Or would you give it to me?"

The child blushed and paled.

"I'll tell you a secret," said Jean. "There is a little girl you've never seen. I need a certain something that may be inside *your* pig, so that I can help her. Wouldn't you help her? I'd send you a pink pig, for yourself. Would you mind very much?"

She could see the swallowing in the child's thin throat.

"We'll have to break it. You could have back everything that is your own." The same old pitch, thought Jean. But doesn't she understand me?

The child said, "There's not very much in it," and Jean caught a shadow of sullenness. Come, this was an improvement.

"Do you think you could go and fetch it and give it to me now," said Jean, "because I'll have to go away?"

"I am not to leave here," said Deirdre, in an explanatory way.

"Oh." Jean had no trouble sounding disappointed.

"If my father says that I may give it to you, I don't mind," said Deirdre.

"Oh, good! Would you run and ask your father now?"

"I am not to disturb him." This was simple explanation, again.

"I see," said Jean. She heard the woman coming. "Don't your things *belong* to you?" she asked the child, curiously.

"One doesn't give one's things away without permission," said Deirdre, staring with pale eyes.

Margaret came with a cold cloth and applied it with soft cries. The child withdrew a little.

Jean was feeling stymied. This child wasn't in the least concerned to keep the pig, but she wasn't a child who could *do* anything. Yet here was Jean, inside the castle and obliged to try. She had an intuition that Margaret would not help her make off with a family pig. How was she going to get to talk to the father or the mother?

"What in the world are they doing," she said suddenly, "in the house? If it's all right to ask."

The child answered, quite vigorously, "Oh, Madame Grace is in the library asking the spirits to write on a slate."

"Oh, they'll never be writing on a slate, not they," muttered Margaret. "Is that better, my dear?"

"Oh, much better," said Jean holding the cloth to her head by herself now. "Are you on the spirits' side?" she asked boldly. "You're not afraid of them, I see."

"Not I." Margaret's eyes were bright.

"Not I," Deirdre echoed with a sigh. "Miss Beale is afraid, you know." A sly glance went between the two of them.

Jean thought, what's this? Am I on to something?

"I would so like to see them," sighed Deirdre. "Mother says that they are not unkind."

"Why should they be unkind?" muttered Margaret. "Unless *driven*. Now, love, Miss Beale will have the hair off my head." She was gently urging the child away.

"Oh, my *hair!*" Jean cried. "Please, is there a comb?"

"There is," said Margaret approvingly. "Now, will I pour you a drop more of the tea?" She fussed awhile and was gone.

So Jean said to the child, "Quick, before anybody comes. What can we do, Deirdre? I must have the pig and you don't mind. But they won't let either of us speak to your father. Is the pig in your room? Where is your room?"

The child was looking much distressed. Or was she?

Jean took her bare feet out of the water and bent to dry them, lacking a towel, ruthlessly on the long tablecloth. "You just tell me one thing," she said, her exasperation showing. "Have I *your* permission?" When the child didn't answer, Jean said, "Where I come from, the children own things. But I see you can't help me, can you? All right. Who can? Would Margaret help me?"

The child bent her head and looked owly and then, like a draft of cold air, Miss Beale was back.

"Miss Deirdre, what *are* you about? Sit in your chair, if you please." The child scrambled to obey.

"A message has been telephoned to the hotel," said Miss Beale to Jean. "Either you will be sent for, or I shall see that you are taken there. Drink your tea, Miss. You do *not* feel ill, do you? I thought not."

Jean straightened slowly. She took up the tea and drank all of it, thirstily. "What strange people you are?" she said. "You won't let me speak to Mr. Butler?"

"It is not necessary," said Miss Beale.

"Is he a sensitive?" said Jean, looking around the room. "Are you, Miss Beale?"

Miss Beale snorted.

"I am," said Jean casually.

Miss Beale bridled at once. "You will not," she said, "achieve whatever it is you wish to achieve, by talking nonsense. And not, if you please, before the child. We've enough nonsense in the house, as it is." She turned and began to walk away in her heavy tread.

"Oh, Deirdre's not afraid of kindly spirits," said Jean gaily. "Why"—she took up her cup and sailed it high into the kitchen air—"should she be?"

The cup crashed. Miss Beale leapt and whirled.

"Oh," said Jean, after a second's staring, both hands to her head. "I *see*."

Margaret was back, bearing a comb and a hand mirror. She froze and stared at the broken cup.

"They are only playful," said Jean. "Children, I believe, aren't they?"

Miss Beale's thin mouth was opening and closing; her meaty skin was scarlet.

"You have a poltergeist," said Jean, with an air of bright patience. "Didn't you know?"

Margaret was imploring saints. Miss Beale shrilled, "Don't be absurd! *You* did that. With your own hand."

"I broke your china?" said Jean. "When you have been so

good? You're not *afraid?* I'm sure you're not. A poltergeist is only a little spirit that would like to have some fun."

"It's not Irish, that," said Margaret, darkly.

But Deirdre said complacently, "It was only a kitchen cup."

"Deirdre, come hold my hand," said Jean. "I know . . . I sense . . . There *is* a child's spirit, here. It wants to show me something."

"You are . . . You are *pitifully* transparent." Miss Beale became hoarse in her rage. "You are a complete fraud! Margaret, take up those pieces and we'll hear no more of this."

But Jean with her bare toes had taken hold of the tablecloth on the far side of the table. Bland in the face, she yanked with her foot. The sewing basket tumbled with great dignity to the floor.

Miss Beale lost color. A spool of thread rolled slowly toward her and she backed away with her large feet shuffling.

Jean, having quickly restored the cloth to balance, said chattily, "I do love children, you know. They seem to like me, too. This has happened to me before."

Margaret, fearless though she might be, was consulting saints in the corner, but Deirdre had wiggled to her feet and was drawing near.

"It's only a child," said Jean, smiling and gay. "Isn't it, Deirdre?"

"Hadn't we best tell Father?" said Deirdre, blushing and paling. "He wouldn't like not having been told."

Good for you, thought Jean. She wanted to wink but dared not, under Miss Beale's hostile glare. She took the little girl's hand, however, and dared to squeeze it.

Miss Beale said abruptly, "Not at all." Then she said, "Very well. Leave it. We shall see." With her head very high on a stiff neck, she began to walk. She turned and said, "An arrant fraud will be very refreshing *and* salutary, I'm sure." She lumbered away.

Jean beckoned the comb from Margaret, who rolled her eyes and slipped quickly away again. Jean kept smiling at the child as she combed her hair, going gingerly around the lump at the back. Well, she thought, I've lied myself at least a pale and watery blue in the face, but now, by gosh, I'll get to talk to Mr. Butler, before they throw me out of here.

Deirdre said, "Is it a girl spirit, please?"

"A little girl, of course," said Jean gently. "She only wants to have some fun, *sometimes*. Don't you think so?"

The pale eyes were intent. Jean looked into them as deep as she could look and said, "Maybe we can help her?"

But Margaret came and took the child by her shoulders and put her back into her far chair. Jean realized that Margaret didn't know *what* to make of this American woman.

Chapter 17

HARRY, with Dorinda beside him, drove up to the iron gates and leaned on his horn. The gateman sprang to open. "She's found," shouted Harry. "Is she all right?"

"She is. If you'll take a turn to your left, sir, around to the kitchen?"

Harry saluted and roared along the castle's drive, which ran straight the two or three hundred feet to the front of the building.

"Not us," he said. "The main entrance for us, although commoners. We don't know any better, do we?" He screeched to a halt and got out, and Dorinda got out quickly and hurried beside him. He was in high spirits and so seemed she.

Harry assaulted the door with sound, using whatever implements came to hand, including his pounding fist, and a manservant opened it with a look of consternation.

But Harry brushed him aside. "Where is Jean Cunliffe?" he shouted and, taking Dorinda by the hand (for, in a cock-eyed way, he was feeling grateful to her), Harry burst through into a large room where a dapper smallish man with a reddish beard lifted a hushing hand and hissed, "Silence, please."

They had come upon a tableau.

The room was of noble proportions and had a staircase at one side. It was furnished with every evidence of moneyed elegance;

the taste was ornate and there was (although on a large scale) clutter.

In the very center of the space stood Jean Cunliffe on her bare feet. She was holding little Deirdre by her hand. She did not turn to greet them, but kept her head tilted as if she were listening to something no one else could hear. Her face was lopsided; one cheek seemed very pink and somewhat swollen. But she seemed intact, and she was holding the center of the stage.

Her audience consisted of two men and three women. The red-bearded man was nearest Harry; nearest Jean there was a short man with a high-domed forehead and a small but perfect Roman nose. He turned now, cast a sharp look, and gestured imperiously for quiet. Beside him, a slender woman with a faded face, and fair hair limp on her head, was drooping in a limp blue dress. Apart, there was a large woman with a moustache, arrayed in a gown of whispy gray stuff, rather floaty, and trimmed here and there with steel beads. Last, stood none other than Miss Beale, in a flowered frock, looking as stern and outraged as before.

It was Dorinda who called out, "Oh, Jean! Darling, are you all right?" And the man with the red beard looked at her with popping eyes. "Don't speak to her, please," he said, but in tones of awe, because Dorinda had just bowled him over.

The dome-headed man came toward them now, in a brisk, exasperated trot. He said in his choppy manner, "Fairchild? She is quite all right. Bear with this, won't you, please? Very interesting."

"He ought," Miss Beale bleated, "to have gone round to the kitchen."

The dome-headed one said, "We must have silence."

Jean said, in a droning way, "Not here. But somewhere . . ."

"Let yourself be led," said Mr. Butler encouragingly. "Simply follow." He was a man with an obsession. He zeroed his attention in on Jean, who now tilted her head the other way and walked slowly toward the wall, missing the staircase, and tending toward a row of pedestals that bore assorted ornaments. The child went beside her, seeming content.

The woman in gray said, "An Ameddican. After all—" in a throaty, indignant way.

"Hush, Madame," said the red-bearded man, whose accent was neither here nor there, but a kind of global English. "Tell me." He sidled closer to Dorinda, whispering. "You are her friends? This young woman is a medium, is she?"

Harry felt a kind of boom of understanding that seemed to take place in his breast. "I . . . uh . . ."—He put on his worried-cherub look—"don't think she has wanted it known." He was whispering, too.

Miss Beale drew nearer and put her head with theirs. "So unfortunate for Miss Deirdre, Professor. Very unwise. I should not have thought . . ."

Jean, whose ears felt two feet high, and whose bare toes were tense on the rug, said, "Deirdre mustn't leave me. I hear through her."

"Hear! Hear!" cried the gray woman, who just might have been released from some spell by the new arrivals. "Mr. Butler, this *must* be a joke or a hoax of some kind. I cannot—"

"You needn't follow, Madame Grace," said Butler frostily. "Please remain quiet."

But Madame Grace, fluttering her smoky panels, continued to protest. "There has never been any manifestation sensed by anyone in this place that has ever been suspected to be a child. *Or* a poltergeist, for that matter. And if you have observed—"

A large vase fell off a pedestal with a mighty crash.

"The little child's spirit"—Jean spoke dreamily in the ensuing silence, while holding tight to Deirdre's startled little hand—"says that you have never really liked it."

"I have never really liked it, very much," said the slender woman in blue, in a sweet and languid voice. "Fancy a little spirit knowing so, Henry?"

"Splendid," said Henry Butler.

Jean, feeling the little hand curl closer into hers, thought, Oh boy! But now what?

She had not dared to turn and look at Harry Fairchild. In her concentration, Dorinda's voice had not even surprised her. No time to think, except about what in the world to do next. How to keep on pig-hunting, with this particular mad deviosity.

Her first sight of Henry Butler had made her certain that he was in no mood to discuss giving or selling a child's piggy bank to some crazy Americans. So she had continued to dwell on the subject that did interest him. As long as she interested *him,* she could continue. But Jean didn't think the professor (professor of what, from where, she knew not) was being fooled very much, and there was the outraged hostility of Miss Beale, and Madame Grace, the medium, had by no means taken kindly to the eruption of a rival.

"Now, *she* did that," cried Madame, in the moment. "She is playing tricks. You must have noticed that nothing at all happens, unless *she* is very near. Professor, surely *you* saw how that was done? She wasn't even subtle." Madame seemed outraged as much by professional ineptitude, as by anything else.

"Very interesting," said the red-bearded professor, who had been staring at Dorinda and hadn't seen another thing. "Don't you agree, Miss . . . er . . . ?"

"Dorinda Bowie," said Dorinda, smiling at him. "May we follow too, please?"

Jean had taken the opportunity to sail halfway up the first flight of the staircase.

"Of course. Of course. Of course," said the professor gladly, offering his arm.

Mr. Butler had his wife on his arm, and the two of them were a few steps behind Jean and the child. The professor now led Dorinda to the stairs.

The gray-clad woman stood abandoned. "Don't be such b——— fools!" shrieked Madame Grace, casting aside all tact, in her defeat.

Mr. Butler looked down and said, "Will you be good enough to wait in the library, Madame?"

He had spoken. She flounced around and set her shoulders.

Meantime Harry (who was feeling tickled to pieces) had kept his eyes busy. He slipped toward Miss Beale, who had been drawn by a fearful fascination to stare at the shards on the rug.

"Come on," he said. "Mustn't miss the fun, dear lady." He had a long and limber leg, and as he turned her and her startled face away from the wall, Harry tried a quick kick behind her back.

Another vase, pedestal and all, came crashing down.

Mr. Butler said with enormous satisfaction, "Ah . . ."

Jean squeezed, with a startled hand, the child's hand and looked behind. She could see them below, foreshortened, Miss Beale staggering on Harry's arm and Harry looking upward with such a look of pure but troubled innocence that she had to cough. She bent and put a light and joyous kiss on Deirdre's brow. "It's all right," she said.

Her confidence had surged to a sudden peak. She turned and looked into the eyes of Deirdre's mother. Jean could only vaguely remember this woman's face, and had had no sign that the woman remembered hers. Now she said, boldly, "But I'm sorry for the mischief. Shall I continue, Mrs. Butler? Or would you rather not have things broken?"

"I haven't cared for that piece, either," said Mrs. Butler, in her languid way. "Who was it gave us that, Henry, do you recall?"

And the Master said, "No matter. No matter, at all. Go on. Go on." He had a glassy look. He called behind him, "Coming along, Professor? Are you watching closely?"

"Oh, certainly," said the professor, blinking.

"But this is so fascinating!" breathed Dorinda, firmly refascinating him.

And Jean was hit suddenly. *Is that Dorinda?*

But she went on. In the upper spaces, she halted. "There is something—" she intoned, feeling Mr. Butler's hot breath on her very neck. "In a child's room?" she inquired of the air.

She felt the faint tugging of the little hand she held. "Ah, this way, then?" said Jean. She seemed to lead where she was being led, but her bare feet were beginning to feel rather cold.

Surely, all this would soon be *too* ridiculous!

But the ridiculous procession followed her. Deirdre's parents, in solemn silence. Dorinda and the professor, murmuring next.

And finally Harry Fairchild, bearing a good deal of Miss Beale's weight, but hurrying to catch up and be helpful, when he could.

"Not the child's room," moaned Miss Beale.

"Why not?" he whispered. "Walk faster."

"But my room is the very next room to the child's room." Miss Beale's voice moaned dismally around on the vowel.

"Afraid of children?" said Harry carelessly. "A big girl like you?"

"Not at all," said Miss Beale. She braced up and her eye flashed cold.

"Well, never mind," said Harry dragging her. "We don't want to miss this."

When the little hand signaled "stop," Jean heard the mother sigh, "It *is* Deirdre's room, then."

So Jean reached and opened the door herself. It was a handsome room, very large, with many many objects in it. It was also very bright. Jean's head began to spin. How to spot a small green pig among so many small and many-colored things! Harry would help her spot the pig. What was Dorinda doing here? No time for that. Where was the little green pig, in all this array? She couldn't see it anywhere. And what would she do, when she did?

Jean found herself in the center of the room, where she had stopped. Now she released the child to put both her own hands to her face and hide, behind slitted fingers, the swift run of her eyes over every nook and niche and shelf. Deirdre seemed to drift away. A tableau arranged itself.

Mrs. Butler sighed, and sat down in a chair near the door. She was a woman without energy. To climb, and come as far as this, seemed to have exhausted her, but she hadn't the force to complain.

Mr. Butler was full of energy, which he compressed into a tense and waiting stance.

The professor led Dorinda just within the door and shifted them to the left. Miss Beale did not wish to enter here, at all, but Harry dragged her in, and they shifted to the other side. All now became silent spectators.

Dead-center-stage stood Jean Cunliffe, and there she was stuck. In the middle of an upper room in a castle in Eire. Hunting a pig!

Nothing happened. How could it?

Finally, Mr. Butler cleared his throat, and Mrs. Butler sighed and her chair creaked slightly.

Harry, who was hunting the pig as thoroughly as he could, by eye alone, began to think the fun was over. And wondered, what now?

The professor said, "Oh, I say, have you lost touch? But are you quite sure this is the right room? Now, you were never in a true trance, were you Miss—er—Cunliffe?" He seemed to have suddenly realized that he had a fee to earn.

Jean said, "Wait." She took down her hands and stared before her, hoping to seem entranced, at least a little. She couldn't think what they were to wait for. "There is something . . ." But the word "pig" was, she realized, what you might call unsuitable. She couldn't say "pig." "Something—we must do—to help her," she droned.

There was silence.

Until the professor cleared his throat in a way that suggested that the jig was up, and Miss Beale, who could no longer endure, cried out in her high-pitched voice, "I am very sorry, but I do not think that Miss Deirdre ought to be a part of this sort of thing, very much longer. As long as I am responsible, I do feel . . ." She was working herself up. "Surely, Mr. Butler, you must realize that the child is being terribly frightened. We shall, at the very least, have to move her to another wing?" This last was hopeful.

"Please ask that woman to be quiet," said Jean loudly. "She is terrified, herself, and it disturbs us."

Mr. Butler said at once, "Be quiet, Miss Beale, if you please. And if you cannot be quiet, leave the room."

Miss Beale turned scarlet.

"Deirdre is not in the least afraid, and never has been," said Deirdre's father. "That is nonsense."

Jean was astonished by the heartiness and even the pride, in the father's voice. She looked for the child. Deirdre was over there, near a window, with the light behind her. Her face was in shadow.

Jean thought, well, she helped as much as she could. So the time had come to give up the act? It had gone about as far as it could go? She debated casting herself on somebody's mercy, but Mr. Butler's personality exuded no promises of mercy. Whose mercy, then? The mother's?

Mrs. Butler was looking at Jean with watery pale blue eyes. "The little spirit is unhappy?" she said much as one would say, but the mail has come, hasn't it?

Was this a communication? Had the woman seen through the whole charade, long ago? Jean took in a breath. Well, she thought, here goes!

Harry thought, oh, oh, and began to wonder how a man who had been fooled was now going to be charmed.

But the red-bearded one spoke up, in a tone that was very dry indeed. "It *is* difficult, isn't it? Perhaps there is an explanation?"

"You see," Jean began. But her heart was sinking. They *wouldn't* see. Or else they *would,* which might be worse.

"I *beg* your pardon." Suddenly Madame Grace was a large and agitated gray flutter in the open doorway. "Mr. Butler," she said in a glad cry, "I can't help thinking that you ought to be informed. Two strange men have just entered the house, through the dining-room window, and are doubtless ransacking the silver cabinets, at this very moment."

"What? What?" said Butler.

Harry saw Dorinda swing around and caught the flash of fury across her face. The professor's brows were very high and his beard jutted.

"What has been done about it?" the Master barked.

"I have rung," said Madame, with dignity.

There was a shout below.

Now Miss Beale was rallying completely. She burst into triumphant speech. "An explanation, indeed! A simple plot! American gangsters! There must be several of them. This young woman was merely keeping our attention while her confederates . . . You know very well"—she was worked up, and her shrill voice pierced the ear—"that this man"—she pointed at Harry—"has already attempted to enter the castle with wild inventions. Ah, but he *is* inside and his other . . . his other"—Miss Beale was about to pop—"his other moll, as well—" She exploded. "And as for that one"— She pointed a shaking finger at Jean, and a little green pig sailed past her ear and crashed to the floor.

Miss Beale screamed, hoarse as a crow, and staggered against Harry, who was forced to hold her up. Deirdre shifted like smoke to the other window. Dorinda moved gracefully and crouched to touch the pig's fragments and the few coins that lay on the carpet. But Jean looked across at Harry Fairchild and shook her head very slightly and sadly.

All this then had been for nothing?

Furthermore, how were they going to get out of here?

So Jean began to rub her eyes and said, in as phony a voice as she had ever heard from her own throat, "Oh! Where am I?"

Mr. Butler cast one glance around and torn between passion and duty, he angrily chose duty, and dived through the doorway, parting people with his hands as if they had been draperies. The professor said, "I say," and went darting after. But he was torn, too—and he put his red beard back around the doorjamb for a last look at Dorinda's handsome contours, where she crouched, before he vanished.

Male shouts, female screams, and assorted bangs were arising from below.

Harry propped Miss Beale against the wall and came to Jean and held her. She didn't know whether to laugh or cry.

Feet were running in the house afar. A dog bayed outside. Deirdre was looking out the window.

Madame Grace said, "Stand where you are," in a voice of menace, and then she vanished.

Now were left in this room only the three Americans, Miss Beale (in a paralyzed state), the child, and the pallid woman in the chair.

"Mrs. Butler," said Jean, "please believe me. Whatever is going on down there has nothing to do with us."

The woman looked at Jean, and Harry, too, with her lack-lustre eyes and said, "I don't suppose that you are thieves, really. But I do think we have had enough, for one afternoon."

"I agree," said Jean. "We'll just go. Thank you for being so kind. We really ought to pay."

But Harry was pinching her hard, and she stopped speaking.

Mrs. Butler said, "Not at all. It was interesting, I suppose. Henry was pleased." She sighed. "Miss Beale, perhaps you will be good enough to see that our guests are served whatever they will have? That is, of course, once the burglars have been routed." Mrs. Butler put a boneless hand to her brow.

Deirdre was standing beside her mother now. "They're gone, Mother," she said, as if one said, the mail has come.

"Oh, Deirdre, thank you very—" Jean began.

But the mother cut this short. "If you will excuse us? I'm sure Miss Beale will look after you." Her swan neck bent in a dismissing bow.

Miss Beale broke away from the wall convulsively, and went staggering. Dorinda now arose from where she was crouching, and quietly put all the coins from the piggy bank into her own handbag. "Goodbye," she said sweetly, and walked out of the room.

Harry said, "Come on, honey."

But Jean lingered. "Deirdre," she said impulsively, "someday you must come to California to visit. I wish . . ." Something stopped her.

"I should like to very much, thank you," said Deirdre primly. "One day, perhaps."

"Perhaps," said her mother. "Goodbye." Two pairs of pale eyes were saying, *and that will do.* Two pairs of watery blue eyes were saying, *but what strange people you are, really.*

Harry took Jean out of the room.

At the top of the staircase, Miss Beale hung, frozen. They went silently by.

At the landing, Madame Grace stood sternly. They went silently by, on Dorinda's heels now.

At the bottom of the stairs was the professor. "Decamped," he announced. "Nothing taken. Er . . . Miss Bowie, this *has* been interesting. I wonder whether I might call . . ."

Dorinda said, coolly, "I think not."

"I mean to say . . ." Rebuffed, he veered. "Miss . . . er . . . Cunliffe?"

"She doesn't believe in ghosts," said Harry, solemnly. "But *they* believe in *her*, you see? So it *is* difficult, isn't it? Goodbye." And they went on.

There was no one to let them out, so they went out by themselves, but now Mr. Butler appeared on the paving stones and began to talk very fast.

The intruders had been routed, he told them, and he was, of course, quite sure the incident had no connection with them. Would they accept his apologies for the outburst of a member of his staff who had so unfortunately—er—burst out? Would they not stay for tea? No? But would Miss Cunliffe consent to come again, since he would like very much to pursue the matter? Perhaps on another and better occasion?

Harry told him, with quiet relish, that perhaps there would be another occasion, perhaps when Miss Cunliffe again visited this part of the world—perhaps in a year or two? But they must beg to be excused, having certain concerns of their own. Mr. Butler would—perhaps—understand?

Inside the castle, Miss Beale said to the females of the staff, assembled, that she was very much afraid that she would be leaving this post. She could not, she said, *quite* understand so superstitious a people.

The staff said nothing—except to certain saints who understood them perfectly.

Upstairs, Mrs. Butler said to herself, aloud, "The American girl was very nearly impertinent. No bringing up, I imagine."

She sighed and said to Deirdre, "One ought to pity poor Beale. But your father will soon find someone else to look after you."

"Lovely," said Deirdre, her color changing.

Elsewhere, Vance and Varney raced out of the woods, tumbled each into a car, and tore off in different directions. The dogs bayed mournfully. But the males of the staff joined joyously and argued together.

Chapter 18

HARRY put Jean into the rented car and Dorinda slipped in at the outside, crushing all three of them together in the tiny vehicle. They drove off, in yet another direction.

And Harry said fiercely, "Jean, did they hurt you?"

Jean said, "Yes. He did."

"Who did?"

"Varney."

Dorinda said, "Oh, the criminal! Oh, poor *child!* But you're all right, now?"

Am I? thought Jean. She was feeling all her aches and pains back again, and there had been no message in the green pig either, and what was Dorinda doing here anyway, and how come she and Harry were together? When Jean had been (all by herself) very ingenious, in spite of many handicaps, and her feet were freezing.

Harry said, "Better get her to a doctor. Hey, Dorinda, you were great. You kept the professor's mind off, all right. Good going."

Then Dorinda had to be the one to say, "Oh, but Jean was so clever! Wasn't she marvelous?"

"She sure was," said Harry.

"Now we'll all go after the other pig, won't we?" said Dorinda gaily.

"Oh, we sure will," said Harry. "All us good guys."

"How *can* we when we don't even *know* yet—" Jean clapped her hands to her head (as best she could in the cramped middle). It hurt, and perhaps it was out of order. She held it and muttered, "Wait a minute."

"Oh, Jean, honey," said Dorinda, purring on, "you *will* be able to remember. I'm sure you will."

"Remember what?" groaned Jean. "I hope you realize that *I* don't know what you're *talking* about."

Silence.

"But how odd," said Dorinda, "that she doesn't remember what to remember! Isn't that odd, Harry, darling?" Her voice was a blade, with edges.

Harry said nothing.

"I *wish*—" burst Jean.

But now Harry cut her off. "Hey, honey, how did you manage to get away from Varney?"

"He just suddenly let me go. And don't call me—"

"He did, eh? Odd," drawled Harry. "Wasn't that odd, Dorinda, darling?"

Dorinda said nothing.

"Little-old-honey here," said Jean angrily, in a moment, "can't *understand* you darling, darling people."

After that, nobody said anything.

Harry simply whizzed them, at a perilous pace, back to the hotel, and as he pulled up, Johnny Roach leaped joyously upon them. Dorinda got out, with her usual grace, and walked immediately toward the hotel entrance.

Jean, who was mad as a hornet by now, suddenly bent double.

"What's wrong?" said Harry in alarm.

"Oh, not a thing! I was bashed in the head, hit in the face, kicked *and* tortured. Handcuffed *and* tied up like a—like a chicken. But why do you ask?"

"What hurts you now?" He was bent over her.

"Oh, not a *thing!*" she said. "Why should it? For pity's sakes, you idiot. I'm only fishing for my purse, which is under this *darling* seat, someplace." She couldn't see, she was so mad.

He said in her ear, "Is your passport in your purse?"

"Of course, stupid." She bit his head off.

Harry sat up and said loudly, "Johnny Roach? Get in, will you? Show me the way to a doctor, for this poor unfortunate girl."

"Surely," said the lad, and he got in with spry goodwill.

As Harry took off like a rocket, Dorinda did not even turn her head.

When they had whipped around a couple of curves, the lad said mildly, "If it's the doctor you want, do you think I ought to say he lives the other direction?"

"Never mind *him*." Harry braked and stopped the car with a coy skid. "Listen to me. Here. Take this." Harry was pulling out money. "Send our bags here." He slapped a card on top of the money and thrust all into the lad's hands. "And let it be assumed that we are at the doctor's. Give us a start. I'm getting her out of here. Don't *talk*."

"Roger. Wilco," said the garrulous native, quaintly, and got out.

Harry roared them off along the winding roads of the green land. "Tied up like a chicken, eh? O.K. So we've just flown the coop." (Jean was not amused.) So he said, "We'll fly home. From Shannon. Get out the map."

"In my bare feet, I'm flying home?"

"Listen, honey," said Harry, steering like mad, "we'll find you a doctor, in the first biggish town. Shoes, too."

"I don't want a doctor," shouted Jean. "I'm not interested in shoes. I want to know what's going on. And if you don't tell me, I'm going to drop dead, here and now, in a rented car, and you'll be sorry."

"I would, surely," said Harry, and then before she could hit him, as her whole mien threatened to do, he began to tell her.

In Los Angeles, it was visiting hours at St. Bart's Hospital. "You're looking pretty good, Em," Callie said, thrusting some dilapidated flowers into a vase.

"Oh, I'm better, much better. And how is . . . everyone?"

"Fine. All fine. Well . . ." Callie surveyed her bouquet. "Like I always say. Choose one. The kids *or* the flowerbed."

"Are the children with you today? Downstairs?"

"Not today. Hey, Em, relax. Rex is home. One of us is always with them. You know that. Say, I probably won't come tomorrow. Rex thinks he'll drop by. Make a change for you, too."

"Very nice," said Miss Emaline vaguely. "It's just 'til . . . Wednesday."

"Ho, they're letting you out Wednesday? Good."

"No, no. I mean—I don't know. I wasn't—thinking of that." Miss Emaline stirred and tried to smile at her sister.

"If something's bothering you, Em," said Callie, "what can I do?"

"Well, it's nothing much. Just . . . There is a woman here. She seems to work here. I believe I know her, Callie. She's from Dolabela."

Miss Emaline had been worrying about Mei Fong all day. She knew that Mei couldn't possibly stumble upon the name Dolabela—even by accident—in the records, because Miss Emaline had taken care to give Honolulu as her home address. So that if Mei just did not happen to come into this room. . . .

But here was Callie saying happily, "What do you know? Old-home week, eh? Do you good to swap a few yarns?"

"No, no," said Emaline. "She hasn't seen me."

"Well, then, listen," said Callie, "why don't I go see if I can find her? What's her name?"

"I'd rather you didn't. I'd rather not, Callie. Please. Callie, you *won't* . . ." Emaline rose from her pillow accusingly.

"Sure, I won't, if you don't want me to," said Callie, and she sat down and did not ask the obvious question.

"Because I am so much better off," said Miss Emaline weakly, answering the question just the same, "just being quiet." (And safe, she thought.)

But her conscience winced. She must not lie to her sister. "Oh, Callie, you know I can't tell you everything. Yes, she worries me, a little, but I can't tell you why. You know I can't burden you. This is for me to bear."

"Whatever you say," said Callie, amiably. Then in a moment she added gently, "You always did go for bearing burdens, Em. I wouldn't take them from you, unless you'd ask. You know that." Then she grinned. "It's sure awful quiet around here. Too quiet for *me*."

It was eight o'clock in the evening, over the Atlantic, where they were. Jean, who had been mulling and musing, said softly, "I blew it, didn't I, Harry? About that remembering?"

He had learned something about this girl. So he said, "True. And *I* blew it when I used the singular. *I* said to Dorinda, *the* other pig. So now she knows there's just one more. What a goof, eh? Never mind. We're for the waiting game. How is your head?"

"O.K. Although not as clear as it's been cracked up to be."

"Comes of being hit on it?" He mumbled this. This had frightened him out of some of *his* wits, he felt.

"I don't *understand* the Butlers," she mourned.

"Honey, they don't understand you, either, believe me."

"O.K." Jean sighed and slipped her other foot out of her other new shoe.

They had shopped frantically, in the duty-free shops at Shannon Airport, Harry spending money like water, babbling nonsense, and looking over his shoulder constantly. Jean was now wearing her new suit of Irish wool, and her new Irish linen blouse, and her head was not aching anymore, and the bruise on her thigh was passive, unless touched, and they were going home, and all they had to do was wait, and yet . . .

The trouble was they had boarded in such high spirits. In the first place, they felt they had got away. In the second place, Harry had phoned Bonzer, from the airport, with Jean on guard against any and all eavesdroppers, and Bonzer had said in calm accents that, having reason to suspect this phone of being tapped, he, Bonzer, would not go into detail about how things were. He would certainly inform Mr. Fairchild's father of Mr. Fairchild's impending arrival, and would, of course, meet the plane. And felt that Mr. Fairchild would be glad to be done with long and arduous journeying, and he, Bonzer, would be glad to see him, and Miss Cunliffe, too.

So concluding gleefully that Bonzer knew something, they had boarded, tourist-class this time, and, going jauntily down the aisle of the plane, had seen a little man, huddled by a window, meek as a mouse.

So Harry had fallen into the upholstery of his own seat and held his head.

After takeoff, recovering somewhat, he had gone to pounce upon Vance Miller and had demanded to know where Dorinda Bowie was now.

"I really couldn't tell you, Mr. Fairchild," Vance had said apologetically, as if he didn't know.

Well, she wasn't on *this* plane. Harry had made sure of that, and come back to hold his head some more.

Still, they mustn't be too cast down. Harry had pointed out that his brother, the governor, could always resign. More hopeful, if the good guys couldn't find what they were all after, neither could the bad guys, since it must be noted that, if the bad guys knew any other way to go, then why were they following? Always following?

Therefore, the thing for Jean and Harry to do (even if Bonzer had the third pig located) was to lie low and refuse to go anywhere. How, then, could they be followed?

And after all (although the Fairchilds did not have the child safe or Bonzer would have said so) there could be better news at home than they could guess.

They had spoken thus, wisely, and fallen silent. Now they fell silent again, and, time having jumbled into such confusion that there was no longer any pattern of night and day, they dozed, keeping each to himself any qualms, any memories, and any anticipations, as the plane carried them steadily toward the city of New York, the United States of America.

Varney said, "Quit fooling with those damn things, Dorinda. Not going to be a message on metal."

"I suppose not," she sighed, jingling the coins in her restless hand. "All there was, I took. Nobody seemed to care."

"There was a diversion, right?" said Varney, sullenly.

"How come you and Vance had that *brilliant* idea?" Her tone was not praise.

"Pig had to be in the castle. Who else, in that hole, would have been just going through Los Angeles?"

"Johnny Roach?" she said casually.

"Who's he?"

"One of the peasants. Did postgraduate work at Berkeley, so they say. All kinds of people are traveled, these days. As well as my father's daughter." She sounded bitter.

"Hell," said Varney, "it *was* in the castle. Listen, when I stopped you to tell you where I had her, you figured to con it out of Fairchild. But when Vance showed up at the hut, he said Fairchild hadn't even got into the castle, so . . ."

"*I* got in," she shrugged. "And as long as you got out, skip it. Wrong pig. There's one more. Somewhere."

"You should have let me alone," he growled. "How come you fell for that nutty bit about she couldn't remember?"

"I didn't, for long. The fact is, she doesn't know where the other pig is."

"So?"

"So you tend to get a little rough, Vic. Harry wouldn't have *moved*."

"No?" He was skeptical.

"Some people take time out, to bury their dead," she snarled at him. "You messed things up once already, didn't you, Vic? I seem to have heard, somewhere, that it's not easy to get a dead man to tell you where things are." Her profile seemed as hard and as sharp as a knife. Her whole face menaced.

"Beckenhauer made a stupid move." Varney sank back into his seat. "So it happened. So lay off, will you? Nobody will prove it."

"Where?" she said between her teeth. "*Where?*"

"The Fairchilds haven't got the kid yet," he said, pretending to be drowsy. "We got eyes on all of *them*."

"We've got eyes in the operating room?" she blazed. "How do you know what the doctor says to his patients?"

"I'd agree, the doc's a daisy. But you're forgetting, Dorie. Our line into the house, she says this Harry is the Fairchilds' only hope." Varney sank deeper. "Him and his pigs."

"How is the governor?" she asked shortly.

"On a spot. We get the kid, he can't resign."

"But it narrows," she said and looked down at the Atlantic Ocean.

"Why not grab both of them, say in New York? Vance is on the plane with them. We're only an hour and a half behind."

"Because they don't know, yet, where the other pig is. The *right* one. The *one* other. And we don't know how they expect to get to know. Unless . . ." Dorinda smoldered. "How long would it take to get that information out of them? Then get the location of the pig, from whoever has it?"

Varney stirred uneasily. "Yeah, and then get the pig. Then get the kid. Forget it," he advised. "Quicker to let them find the damned pig and then, zingo! So try and take it easy, Dor."

"But it narrows," she said. "I wish there was another way."

"Maybe there'll be news," he consoled her.

Chapter 19

PAUL Fairchild was holding court from one of the big chairs in his bedroom, late as it was (and still Sunday night in Los Angeles!), when they arrived. The old man seemed alert and more vigorous, more like his old self, than he had been in months. He hung on Harry's first words, accepted them, and did not appear to be crushed by them.

So Harry felt that the decision he had made in the car, on the way here, had been the right one.

Dick, the doctor, wanted to know if this was an Irish lassie, and if so—good for Harry. So Harry introduced Jean Cunliffe. Tom, the governor, who had flown over for the night, became courtly and put her into a ringside seat, while Harry greeted the woman called Mei, who seemed to be staying in the house, and Cousin Elaine Fairchild.

Cousin Elaine seemed subdued.

All Harry had said, in the first place, was that they had run down a couple of places where a clue might have been, but it hadn't been in either of them. Now, he said, there was a third possibility, but a winding way to go, before they could find out exactly *where,* and it would take too much time.

This was a falsehood.

Harry had been nervous as a cat, going through Customs, boarding another plane, in New York (where Vance Miller had seemed to vanish). And nervous as a very nervous cat at International, in Los Angeles. But Bonzer had met them, and brought the car to them, without anything happening.

Once on the freeway, it had seemed safe to speak, if safe anywhere, so Bonzer had spoken.

The admirable Bonzer had proceeded as instructed in the matter of the traveler's check and all had gone as Mr. Fairchild had hoped it would go. There had been only one ten-dollar check. Bernie's associates, although in great distress—what with one partner dead of a knife wound and the other hospitalized—had most efficiently (and even on a Saturday) secured the home address of the signer of the check.

The yellow pig had been purchased by a man named Michael Mizer, who had a ranch, not too far from Anza, California, which ranch was, as Bonzer had taken pains to discover, one hundred and fifty odd miles away from here, and seemingly in, or beyond, some mountains. Bonzer had done nothing more about the yellow pig, pending instructions. For one reason, he had sensed that he was sometimes being followed. For another, he had felt sure that Mr. Fairchild would wish to go himself.

But Harry wasn't going, or even telling that they knew where to go.

He had been horrified, even terrified, by what had happened to Jean Cunliffe in Ireland. He wasn't going to let it happen again. The child might or might not be safe where she was. Harry didn't know where she was, or whether safe, but he did know where Jean Cunliffe safely was now, and he said as much and added that he was going to see to it that she was kept safe, because a bird in the hand and so on.

There was, he had said, a spy in his father's house and no such spy was going to be told where the right pig could be found. Therefore, he was not even going to admit that he knew. No, not even to his father. His father was a big boy now, and he could take it. He'd have to, Harry said, and that was that.

Jean had been somewhat startled to hear all this about herself. She hadn't argued with him.

Now she was absorbed in a study of this house and these people. As for the house, she would have called it a castle, had she not so recently (today!) been in a real one. The women in the room she glanced at curiously, and dismissed. The governor, she thought, was charming, in looks and manner. The doctor she liked very much, for his blunt good cheer. But almost at once, she began, without analysis, to fall for Harry's daddy.

Paul Fairchild was telling *them* the news, now.

The Honolulu police had tracked down the missionaries from Dolabela, what few of them had collected in that city. There was their leader, a Reverend Mr. Webb, recently widowed, and there had been four devoted women besides, each earning a living as best she could and all living humbly. But at the moment, there were only three devoted women. The fourth one, a Miss Hanks, was on the Mainland, attempting to contact some churches, so it was said. It was not known in exactly what city, or even in what state, she was now. It was not known exactly how she had traveled, whether by ship or plane, or on what day, or at what hour.

But she had taken with her the Webbs' foster daughter, a little girl named Barbara.

The police would trace this Miss Hanks, sooner or later, whatever way she had taken, said Harry's daddy. And what did Harry think of that?

Harry winced a little and caught the warning in his brother's eyes.

"We think she's in Los Angeles," his father went on. "My little girl."

"Yep," said Dick. "If you look closely at Bernie's letter, you'll see that's implied. So Daddy's got a small army roaming the streets, checking hotels, motels, boarding houses, and ringing every doorbell with the name of Hanks on it."

And who else, thought Harry in dismay, has a small army doing the same?

"But no luck yet," said Dick cheerfully. "Biggish place, Los Angeles and environs."

Tom said, "In effect, impossible. We can't wait for luck. So I've got an interview with the press, set up for the morning. Going to be taped and broadcast. Nationwide. See, I haven't quit, and I'm not going to quit. The execution date is Wednesday, at 8 A.M."

"Too bad," said Dick, "we can't shove it ahead a little, like tomorrow morning?"

Tom said cuttingly, "That's impossible. But I figure to get it into their heads that I am not a private party. That their plot won't work. *Can't* work."

"Right," said the old man.

Harry found himself whistling without sound.

"I put my neck right out on the chopping block," said the governor. "Fix it so that whole population knows I can't and I won't. That ought to make them stop and think."

"Damn right," said the old man.

"Well, well," said Harry, in admiring tones.

"Good move," said Dick.

"Smart," said Harry, quickly.

He and his brothers were in good rapport. He was no longer the odd one out. They were all the old man's sons, Harry, Dick and Tom. The old man looked fond, and said nothing.

Harry appeared to relax. "So I shall now my tale unfold." Then he stiffened and cast a stern eye around the room. "Mei, I don't remember the rest of your name, excuse me, please?"

"Certainly, Mr. Fairchild."

"Would you leave this room, please?"

"Certainly." The woman rose. She looked momentarily recovered her natural dignity and moved gracefully toward the stricken and her eyes, on the old man, were revealing, but she door.

"And Cousin Elaine," said Harry, "would you please leave us together, just the immediate family?"

The other woman began to remind Jean of Miss Beale. She was not as plump, and a sandier, drier, paler-looking creature, but she looked now as if she would pop. And in her own way, she did. "I am very sorry," she said in a dreary whine, "if you feel that I don't belong. I have been here so many years and taken care of your father so very very intimately I should have thought that I was one of the family. The fact is . . ."

"Just go," said Harry, blandly. "Because the fact is, I don't intend to say another word, until you do."

He sat down beside Jean.

Paul Fairchild said, "Go ahead, Elaine. Indulge him."

"You'll indulge him, Uncle Paul?" the woman flared. "That's what you think of *my* devotion?"

"Just run along, damn it," said Harry's daddy. "He's got a reason, I imagine."

"Toot off, Elaine," said Dick. "What do you care?"

"And is *she* tooting off?" cried Elaine, her eyes on Jean.

"No, no," said Harry.

"Why not?"

"Because I need her," said Harry, flatly.

The doctor had Elaine by the shoulders. "You are being put out," he said, "and Harry's got us dying of curiosity, so you just go be mad at Harry somewhere else."

Elaine was looking wild, but the doctor put her out.

Mei, standing in the hall, bent her head and walked away. She had walked warily in this house, where this woman had never welcomed her. Mei had no comfort to give, nothing to say. But Elaine raised her fists as if to pound on the door that had just closed in her face. She did not pound. But neither did she unclench her pale and anguished fists.

Inside the room, Harry said, "Cousin Elaine may be the spy, Daddy, and if not, I'd be sorry for wronging her, if I had time, but not now."

"Well," said his father, "whether she is or not (and I can't believe it), you've got her insulted to the bone, so's she'll never get over it. But done is done. So come on. Tell us what you've been up to."

So Harry began to tell the tale of the pig hunt, with Jean chiming in, now and then. She began to enjoy herself, very much. She could *not* help it. They were wonderful listeners, they laughed in the right places, they caught every single point so quickly, the doctor was so keen, the governor was so kind, but the old man was just tickled to pieces and his white hair stood up on his head and his eyes shone and Jean got the feeling that the two brothers were sympathetic listeners, yes, but the old man would have gone right along with them through the whole idiotic sequence.

When it had all been told, Harry glossed over the question of the third pig, giving no details, only saying falsely that the weekend had interfered with investigative processes. Then he stated his decision not to move at all.

Now *he* demanded answers. "What's the man's name, in New Zealand?" They told him. Hightower. "Has he a grownup daughter, by some other wife?"

Not that they knew, they told him.

"O.K. Has this Kootz got a grown-up daughter?"

"Who?" said Tom.

"Who!" Harry was agog.

"Oh, you mean Cuts."

"I thought his name was . . ."

"Well, that's the way *he* pronounces it," said his brother. "Yes, he's got a daughter. Had one, at least. I've studied the story of his life, believe me. I've got clemency, you know, and I went into the whole thing pretty carefully. Daughter hasn't lived with him since early childhood. He sends money, we presume. She may not know where it comes from. Or else she uses another name, not to be embarrassed by his fame." The governor bit on the word.

"*What* other name?"

Tom shrugged.

"Maximilian Cuts," said Harry, in sober awe. "Otherwise known as Max-the-Knife?"

"How did you know?" said the governor wearily. "That was years and years ago."

"And from 'Knife' comes Bowie." Harry held his head. Jean Cunliffe strangled her credulous laughter.

The governor said, "It's not frantically funny. Our Max has caused more dirty corruption and human misery in one lifetime than I am going into. Which is neither here nor there, legally speaking. The issue is a first-degree murder. Conviction and sentence. Fair trial. Appeals. The law scrupulously cherishing *his* rights. But the law says that he dies on Wednesday." The governor sounded noble and sad.

"So now we know," said Harry, "who and what Dorinda Bowie is. Well, well, well. But she's not stupid, Tom. Does his daughter really think she can get him *off?* With *these* monkeyshines?"

"I think I told you," Tom said, "that I've been pressured ever since the Warden fixed the date. Maybe there's been a little more pressure than I've let on. But they couldn't touch me. For one thing, I don't even *need* money. Then, no kids. And for some reason," Tom rubbed his face, "they've shied off Pat. Pat's my wife," he said, aside to Jean. "But this . . . They've glommed onto this pressure, because . . ."

Tom didn't finish the thought but the knowledge was in the room. Tom was vulnerable, if at all, through his father.

"What they want," the governor said, "is simply time. I wouldn't be surprised if they haven't found new hopes of buying up, oh . . . one or two bits and pieces of somebody's conscience—somewhere along the line. They must think, that if I will only give them a little longer, they might now get back on the legal merry-go-round. But you see, if I do not . . . Well, that's the way it is, I guess. It can't be anything else." There was an electric silence, crackling with the knowledge that the governor had the power to grant a stay.

Harry broke it, saying, "Yep, I guess that must be the way it is. But they haven't got our little sister. So they still can't touch us. Hey, Daddy, you should be in bed. Come on, Jean."

Now there was a hot discussion about what was to be done with Jean Cunliffe for the next two days. Paul Fairchild wanted her to stay right here in his house. But Harry said no. All right, then his daddy would put guards on wherever she was going to be, and nobody had better argue with that, damn it. Harry said, fine, she'd be in his apartment.

Jean said no, she could go to her own apartment, but to this they all said no.

So Harry got up and went with his brother Dick to phone and fix it from downstairs, and in a moment the governor thought of something he had meant to mention, and went after them.

The old man, who knew very well why all his sons had gone off by themselves, smiled at Jean Cunliffe.

"This whole damn house could be bugged, for all we know," said Harry to his brothers in the upstairs hall. "And Cousin Elaine insulted to the bone, for nothing. So where?"

So they chose to confer together while sitting on the middle stair of the staircase, neither up nor down.

"I'm making this statement tomorrow," said Tom, in a low voice, "because it's too late to drift. The story is creeping out, for one thing. Two columnists have called me on it already. I can't quit. I won't put the onus on a successor. And I won't chicken out, especially since it would obviously be either unnecessary or futile. And *that's* the way it is. They haven't got her, yet. But they had better not get her."

"Story got out through the cops, eh?"

"Oh, sure."

"Then it must be out that you're looking for a woman named Hanks, in Los Angeles?"

"Don't doubt it."

"Yep," said Dick, "but if we can't find her, and the cops can't find her, the chances are *they* can't find her. The *chances,* I say."

"If they do," said Tom, "and Kootz goes—has it occurred to you, Harry, that there is such a thing as revenge?"

"I hoped I was only being sentimental," groaned Harry.

"No, no," said the governor. "Hope they don't get the child. Don't hope for anything, after they do. And hope, by the way, that this hasn't occurred to Daddy."

"Don't bet on that," said Dick. "Has it occurred to you, Harry, that the Hanks woman might turn up on the front lawn, at any moment and walk right into one of 'them'?"

"Occurred to you," said Tom, "that she could start asking around?"

"Occurred to you," said Dick, "that if some columnist prints himself a little item, people who know where Hanks is may read it, and seek a little fleeting fame?"

"Chow-ee!" said Harry, holding his head.

"Sure you shouldn't go after information about this yellow pig?" said Tom. "Quick? And go after it? Taking an army? Cops, maybe?"

"Ah, no," groaned Harry. "To tell the cops is telling them, as you've just agreed. How can we know they won't leap-frog? And if I go by myself, I *know* they're following me."

"Why not hole up here?" Tom asked. "Worried about Elaine? What could she do?"

Harry said, "I'm worried about somebody in this house. Maybe it's this Mei. I'd rather you laid on protection for my place."

"Don't blame you," said Dick, with a brotherly leer, "but this Mei seems like a good kid. Nuts about Daddy, of course. I got her a job. She works hard." Dick had betrayed his scheme of values. "She stays in the house, waiting it out. But she's a hell of a lot better for Daddy than old sourpuss Elaine ever was, I can tell you that."

"Daddy looks good," said Harry cautiously.

"He does," the doctor agreed. "He looks better. Well, he's got a living-tension on."

Tom said, "He'll never hold it against me."

"We don't have to get sloppy," Dick said.

The Fairchild boys were silent, a moment.

"Sum it up," said Harry. "There is a little girl named Barbara. Somebody named Hanks has got her. We guess she's hereabouts. We know Daddy's army is looking. We can be pretty damn sure that so is theirs. And one of 'them' had Jean tied up like a chicken and I don't like any part of it. And maybe Daddy can take it, but . . ."

(He thought, I don't care so much about some little girl having to take it. *Any* little girl, damn it.)

"God help our little sister," Tom said, "if such she be."

"Or even if she isn't," Dick finished briskly. "I sure wish

to God I could think of somewhere brilliant to look. Pull her out of a hat like a rabbit. But if *I* can't, the chances are, they can't. So it's the tightrope, for two days. Daddy can take it."

"You understand," said Tom, "this statement might not do a thing for us? They'll want to hurt. They'll know what would hurt."

"Unless," said Dick quickly, "after Kootz has bit the dust, there's a cooling-off period. Power structures do change. Sentiment does give way to business-as-usual."

The governor nodded.

"So," Dick continued, "I think you're right. Harry, wait out Kootz' span. Get the child later on. Via pig, if necessary and/or possible."

"So I figured," said Harry.

"Agreed," said Tom. "Best we can see to do."

The Fairchild boys sat, a moment more in silent communion.

Chapter 20

THE old man was explaining to Jean how come he had no grandchildren. Tom's wife and Tom didn't really like each other very much. It was well known that they lived together, but apart, she settling for the status and the money, and Tom for the smooth surfaces necessary to his career. Patricia Fairchild, said her father-in-law, was ambitious, but not for offspring. Dick's wife, Diane, she had up and died. And Dick and his colleagues hadn't been able to save her. So Dick was a wounded man. From this stemmed his jolly insouciance about death; meantime, he knocked himself out, every day, to keep folks from dying too soon. *He* wouldn't marry again, for a while. As for George, he was young . . .

"George?" Jean wondered. She'd never heard of a George.

"I give you my word," said the old man solemnly, "my wife and I, when we named the first two boys, never thought of such a thing."

"Oh. *Harry!*" said Jean and bit on her laughter until she caught his eye and then they both laughed.

"Oh, Harry may be the baby," said his daddy, "and not—uh—quite so *pushing*. But he's smart in his own way. Now, you take pigs." He went on to speculate that his elder sons might not have taken pigs that seriously.

Jean said she thought it showed imagination and intelligence to have taken pigs so seriously. And the old man beamed upon her.

Jean asked if Harry's daddy realized how Harry had saved her from a whole lot of mess and bother in that hut. And maybe he had even saved her life. She said she'd like somebody to know that she appreciated this. She couldn't say so to Harry.

"Well, Harry's shy, you know," said Harry's daddy, twinkling. "Scared to death somebody might catch him admitting that he's just as human as anybody else. He *may* turn out to be the smartest of the lot."

They were having a lovely time.

"I think you have remarkable sons, Mr. Fairchild."

"Boys are fine," he said, "fine. But girls I've kinda missed out on. I always did want a little girl, *too*."

"It'll turn out all right," she said. "I can't help believing that it will."

He patted her hand. But he let her see his toughness. "It may be that my little daughter will just vanish away from me. I'd settle for that, of course, rather than have her hurt. Be no different for me than it was . . . before I knew about a little girl named Barbara, seven years of age, with flaxen hair. *I'd* be the same old fella . . ."

"But not quite," she burst.

"Not quite, honey," he said. And he let her see what she had already seen. He wasn't all that tough. "Oh, we've got good hopes," he went on robustly. "First, the police will trace the Hanks woman, as a part of the Beckenhauer case. And we'll be led safely to her. Second, the woman herself knows what's up and is just lying low, and she'll bring my little girl to me, when it is safer."

"I hadn't thought of that. I'll bet she will!"

"We don't know what kind of woman she is," the old man went on. "She could be so scared she'll never come out of whatever hole she's holed up in."

"But then," said Jean, "we can go after the pig, and find her."

"That's right."

"There must be something in it that will help. I believe in the pig, don't you?"

"Absolutely. I'm very high on pigs. That's if you're sure you can surely find the third one."

"I'm sure." She began to twinkle at him.

And he flew one eyebrow. It went up just the way that Harry's did. So she leaned very close and said, "Don't say I said so, but we already know." Then she added quickly, "Don't blame Harry. He doesn't want the spy to know where it is. He believes in the spy. He said *you* were a big boy, now. *You* could take it. He's awfully fond of you."

The old man blinked. "I appreciate . . ."

"And he's right," she went on. "It's safer not to try for it now. I won't tell you where. But oh, you should hear how he found out."

"Now that I'm a big boy," said Harry's daddy, looking cherubic, "couldn't I keep a secret?"

"Oh, of course, you can. Listen." So Jean poured into his ear all about the traveler's check and Harry's tale to the bank. "And Bonzer," she said, "was just wonderful. I won't tell you the address. I better not, honestly. But you see, there's a *lot* of hope that you will find your little girl, once we wait this out."

He patted her hand. "You do me good," he said. "Now, you let us Fairchilds take very good care of you. Yes, that gives me better hope. And mum's the word."

There came a knock on the door.

"We've been having a hot discussion of the weather," he said and called, "Come in."

Elaine came in. She was looking very sour. "Since your immediate family is no longer with you, Uncle Paul," she said bitterly, "I thought perhaps you were ready to be helped to bed, by the help? Oh, I'm sorry. I see you've got the girl."

"I certainly do hope," said Paul Fairchild, "that my little girl grows up to be a whole lot like this one. Goodnight, Jean, honey."

"Goodnight, Mr. Fairchild," said Jean, who was dying to

smack him a daughterly kiss. But it was just as if she had done so, since he knew all about that.

So Jean said goodnight to Elaine and went floating out of the room, feeling for a reason she didn't analyze as happy as she had ever felt in her life.

"Don't say it," said the old man to Elaine. "I don't want a word said. Puts a hex on. By George, George is turning out the way I'd want a son of mine . . ." For some reason he seemed as happy as he could be. "Oh, *he's* the smart one!"

"I'm sure," said Elaine grimly. She shut her mouth tight again, and attacked the bed to whip it into readiness.

"And you know," the old man said, as he rose, "we should have taken notice, long ago. You take a man like Bonzer. Very good man, Bonzer. Knows how to do what he is told, and do it damned well. *Devoted* to my son George and always has been. Goes to show."

"I suppose your smart son George has found the child?" said Elaine haughtily.

"No, no. No, no." The old man chuckled. "I can't help taking pleasure in my boys, you know. I can't help that."

"You've had too much excitement," she said. "Much too much excitement."

"And tomorrow's going to be a doozy, too," the old man said, not without grim relish. "And all the way to Wednesday."

Then his boys were at his door, for a brief goodnight.

Harry took Jean under his wing and summoned Bonzer from the back regions of the house and off they went, Harry driving, Bonzer watching on all sides and making sure that the carload of hired guards was on their heels.

Dick, the doctor, roared off, separately.

Tom, the governor, went upstairs to a guest room.

Mei had already retired, and was saying her prayers.

Elaine, having seen Paul Fairchild to his couch, and darkened his room, and closed his door, went to a telephone.

"What?" The voice was sharp.

"George Fairchild, (that is, *Harry*) and the girl, have gone to his apartment, with guards all over the place." She spoke in the monotonous manner of one making a report. "I must leave here." Suddenly Elaine began to weep. "I can't *take* this. You better pay me what you said. I've got to start a new life. I'm not as young as I . . . There is nothing you can do now, but *I* did the best I could, even after I found out you had lied to me. Don't forget you owe me . . ."

"Where is the kid? Where is the Hanks woman?"

"I don't know. They don't know. You've got to listen—"

"Anything about a pig?"

"A what?"

"A *pig?*"

"Well, they must know something. They told Uncle Paul something that's made him lively as a cricket. The old fool! I—"

"Get him to tell you."

"I can't. He's gone to bed."

"There's no time. How did they find out what they told him? Where did they go for information?"

"Oh, it was Bonzer, I think. He did something he was told to do. I'm only guessing."

"*What* did Bonzer do?"

"I don't know."

"Guards on that apartment, eh?"

"Oh yes. You see it's hopeless. The governor isn't going to—"

"They put guards on whoever told Bonzer what Bonzer found out?"

"How do I know? Please, I'm going to need . . ."

"We've had an eye on Bonzer. We'll check back over his tracks. We'll see . . ."

"Oh, no, it's all over. Not my fault. I can't stay here and be treated. . . . So when can I get . . . ?"

The phone was dead. So Elaine went weeping up to her room. They'd said it was the child's own mother, after her. Well, if they'd lied, that wasn't *Elaine's* fault. Everybody misunderstood. She was much put upon, and maybe even cheated in the bargain. When she hadn't meant . . . She had only . . .

It was all just a fairy tale, anyhow. There *was* no daughter of this house, except herself, who had earned it. Uncle Paul was foolish. Old. He ought to have died soon after Aunt Beatrice, as would have been respectful and convenient. All these years! But now . . .

Oh, that George, that *Harry,* and that new girl. She hoped *they'd* find out what it felt like to be lied to, and put upon, and cheated, and unappreciated, and all your plans, your whole vision of your future just whimsically spoiled and ruined, for nothing. For *nothing!* For somebody's faceless child.

Harry was nervous as a cat until they had made it safely to his apartment. Then he sagged physically, but in his mind he began to go around and around the possibilities. The truth was, anything could happen.

He found himself going all the way back to the beginning, thinking of Bernie Beckenhauer, who ought not to have died in vain. And where was the murderer, Varney, now? And how, on top of everything else, were they going to get *him* and bring *him* to the hour of his execution? Harry felt that the human race could do without Varney, and was a little shocked by the violence of his own feelings.

He looked at Jean, the victim of Varney's violence.

Well, look at her! She had gone to curl up on his couch, as if she had come home, and she was just sitting there in her very becoming Irish clothing, gazing at his view, smiling to herself, as relaxed and complacent and carefree . . . as a . . . as a *cat!*

Bonzer had gone off, probably to make up beds, discreetly. Harry got up and mixed drinks, and sat down to brood some more. She didn't want the drink; she only sipped. She didn't need a drink, apparently, and she didn't even have the decency to *look* worried.

He said, "You're safe. You'll stay right here. A prisoner of fate, or something."

She smiled, but not as if she saw him. "I haven't any clothes."

"You won't need clothes."

She looked a little startled at *that,* and he was glad.

"Bedtime? You'll take my room. I'll take the den."

She looked a little puzzled.

"Some things I . . . uh . . . don't ask Bonzer to put up with."

Her mouth dropped open. Ah ha, now she was paying attention, eh?

Harry hid behind his worried-cherub look. "It's only fair to tell you, isn't it? I can't very well take you to my other place, what with the retinue *we* have. No offense?"

Then this unpredictable girl rocked and fell over on the couch. "That's O.K." She was choking? "I wouldn't want to upset B-Bonzer, either." She muffled herself in a pillow.

"What's the matter with you?" he growled.

"Oh, I don't know, Harry," she gasped. "There's a way you look, sometimes." She took a good hold on herself. "Oh, I'm sorry. I'm light-headed, or lighthearted, or something." Her face, drawn serious, was ready to dive back into the pillow, in case this didn't last. "Well, I *enjoyed* meeting your family," she said defiantly. "I liked them. I'm afraid I had an awfully good time. I can't always help it. Look"—she sat straight but her eyes were brimming—"I'll sleep in the den. I'd just as soon. Well, I mean, I'll sleep wherever Bonzer th-thinks I ought. But I'm not very sleepy. It doesn't seem like night. Harry, may I please just sit here? There's nothing we are going to *do* . . . I mean about the pig and all." She threatened to giggle but controlled it. "So, please may I enjoy myself, if I do it very quietly?"

He said, "Sometimes, you know, I could sock you one."

"I know," she said meekly, and snuffled.

"Well, I'm glad you're taking no offense." He made a good recovery. "So you liked my family, eh?"

"Oh, I sure did!" Her sigh was ecstatic.

"Got on with Daddy?" For some reason, Harry resented all this.

"Harry, why do you all call him Daddy, like very *small* boys?"

"I don't know. We always have."

"Well, he's a doll. He's a love," she cried. "And he's made me feel like a Princess in a Castle, with moats and everything."

"Oh, Daddy's taking care," said Harry glumly, "and hang the expense. He always spends a lot of money, when he's not quite sure what else to do."

"So do you," she said dreamily.

Harry felt shock. "You don't want to underestimate my daddy," he said darkly. "He can be a charmer, but he's nobody fool."

"Neither are you. Oh, Harry, your daddy's awfully fond of you."

Harry was literally squirming now. These things were *not said.* "Oh, Daddy's a bit of a corn-ball," he began. *"And so am I?"* he thundered, before she could say a word.

"Listen," he said, when it became apparent that she wasn't going to agree—aloud, anyway, "I'm going into the den, maybe to bed. I've got worrying to do, and I can see *you're* not in the mood."

"Well, no," she said seriously. "I'm not, really. All those guards and police and money and all. Well, then, for *me,* it's just about all over. I can keep hoping, like everything, on your daddy's side. But this is like Cinderella's last dance. Well, did *she* worry?"

"Wait 'til midnight," he grumped.

"Yes, I'm pretty close to a pumpkin," Jean said. "Midnight comes on Wednesday."

Bonzer trotted through, and beamed on Jean, saying that all was in order and goodnight. Jean beamed on Bonzer. The adoration seemed mutual.

So when Bonzer had gone, Harry bent, with every intention of kissing some sense of who was supposed to be adored around here, into this maddening girl, but Jean said, "Don't do it." Her blue eyes gave real warning.

"You're thinking of Bonzer? Honey, I . . ."

"I'm thinking of *me,*" she said honestly. "I don't know when I've felt so . . . just plain silly happy. I don't want you to upset me. If you wouldn't mind, Harry?"

So he didn't. How could he, after that?

But . . . damn it!

Chapter 21

SOMEBODY was shaking her by the shoulder. Somebody was barking out her name. She came wide-awake. She was in Harry Fairchild's apartment, in Harry Fairchild's bedroom, in Harry Fairchild's bed, in Harry Fairchild's pajamas.

"Oh," she said, "Harry?"

"I'm going," he said fiercely, with his dark hair on end. "After the yellow pig. *Got to. Now.*"

"Then, I'm coming, too." She rolled out of his bed and to her bare feet in one swift motion.

"No, no. I'm taking Bonzer."

"You're not dressed. I'll be dressed as soon as you are. What's the matter?"

"Hell's loose," he said. "They called Bonzer from Bernie's office. Somebody burglarized. In the night. Got his file."

"File?"

"Bonzer's. The thing they handled, as far as they knew, for *him*. Somebody's got that name and address."

"Where the pig is!" Jean was horrified.

"Right. They could have been there, already."

Bonzer was thrusting cups of coffee into their hands. Harry sipped and talked. "I phoned this Mizer. No answer. Maybe the pig's alone in the place. Maybe it was broken, long ago. We've got to know. So we're *going*. Driving. Plane won't save time.

Country place. Hurry up," he said crossly because (no use) he couldn't imagine going without her.

Bonzer fielded the coffee cups. Jean flew into the bathroom, and she flew into her Irish clothes, and she flew to stand beside him, down in the elevator, into his car. Bonzer wasn't going, after all.

"We'll call, if we need the troops," Harry explained. "But we won't. If the worst is true, then Bonzer and my brothers and the troops will have to see what they can do, right in this town."

He was a Fairchild. He brushed off the guards.

"We're shaking off any and all followers," he explained, as they popped into the street. "If, by chance, it wasn't Vance and Varney and Dorinda and company, I'm not leading *them,* with a parade. I'm getting us there, as fast as I can go, which is going to be pretty damned fast *and* devious, so hold onto your head."

Jean did. It was nine-thirty in the morning, past the peak of early traffic. Harry, a modern centaur, half-man-half-automobile, turned and twisted. He nipped down side streets, he made U-turns where he shouldn't, he whisked up freeway ramps and down the next ones, while Jean watched on all sides.

Then they were out of the maze and running (as far as they could tell) free to the east.

"Enjoying yourself?" He grinned at her. His own skill had cheered him up.

"No," said Jean, "I am not. This is my fault."

"Can't be."

"Yes, it can be, and it is."

"Why?"

"Because I told your daddy last night . . . not where, but that we knew where. And that Bonzer found out for us. So somehow . . . somehow . . . *that's* how."

Harry whistled. He said nothing. He didn't reproach her. He didn't comfort her, either, saying "maybe not." He just drove swiftly on. (He'd learned things about her, this ordinary girl.)

Jean sat, and let the tears pour down her face, but made no sound. True was true. Done was done. That was that.

And this was this. Now, and only now, was she absolutely sure that she had up and gone and fallen in love with Harry Fairchild. Fine thing! Oh, a *fine* thing! Her heart was breaking.

Miss Emaline had turned her head as far as she could, the other way, and she kept her eyes closed and tried to breathe without any slightest commotion, but it was no use.

The woman gasped. "Miss. . . . *Hanks!*"

So Miss Emaline tried to look coldly at her face, the snub nose, the high cheekbones, the bright brown eyes.

"Yes?" she said.

"But, Miss Hanks! But, Miss Hanks!" Mei put the trash basket down on the bed itself and clasped her hands. "Everybody is looking for you. Even the police . . . Where is the little girl, oh please?"

"I don't know what you mean. I don't know you." Miss Emaline equivocated, adding to herself, "Know you very well."

"Yes, you do. Yes. You remember me. Miss Hanks! Miss Hanks! Please tell me where? Mr. Fairchild will send people . . . Oh, he will be so happy."

No, no, thought Miss Emaline. No, I mustn't believe her. And a nurse came in.

"Nurse," said Miss Emaline, "tell this woman to go away, please. She's bothering me."

"Oh?" The nurse picked up Miss Emaline's wrist, and looked with stern disapproval at the position of the wastebasket.

Mei snatched it up and babbled, "But it's very important. She has to *tell* me . . ."

The nurse frowned. She said, "Just out of the room, please."

Miss Emaline's pulse was very fast.

"I would like to leave here," said Miss Emaline, thinking, but where shall I go?

The nurse said, "We'll ask the doctor, shall we? Now, you just rest. You won't be bothered."

If so, I must endure, thought Miss Emaline. It is my penance and my glory.

The nurse went swiftly out into the corridor, looking for the woman Mei to question her and tell her off. But Mei was scooting along toward a phone booth, giving thanks in all simplicity.

She dialed. She said to the answerer, "Miss Elaine! Oh, Miss Elaine!"

Mike Mizer had brought his visitor into the one room that retained intact the personality of the woman who had decorated his whole house, while she was alive. He and Tony tended not to come in here, very much. But it seemed only right that this lady be ushered to the most formal of his many rooms, the one at (what he thought of as) the back of the house, Edna's parlor.

He didn't know a thing about her, this visitor, except that she was damned good-looking. When she had turned up at his gate, in that cool blue Continental, driven by a man who seemed to be a chauffeur, although he wore an ordinary felt hat, Mike hadn't needed a lot of persuasion to jump into the jeep with Tony (because she had asked for Tony, too) and lead the way into his little kingdom, and the low-lying, long and narrow house.

He had been right there, at the gate, because this was the day that they had decided to repair his gateposts, rehang his gate, and while they were at it, rebuild the small bridge over the ditch. They'd been there since dawn.

The sleek car had pussyfooted over the temporary planks successfully, and it was now parked in the shade of the eucalyptus hedge, out at the back, with the manservant-chauffeur waiting in it.

So here they sat, he and seven-year-old Tony, and this Miss Bowie, in Edna's parlor, and Mike was trying to figure out what to offer her. Trouble was, the time of day. Just about noon. And Jim and Mabel, the couple who took care of the house and the meals for him, were out at the gate now, serving the noon meal from what would have been called the chuckwagon in olden days.

Mike couldn't very well ask her to lunch here. And he couldn't figure how to get her to wait, while he changed out of his working clothes, so that he could take her to lunch in town. And there again, the nearest town with a halfway decent restaurant was forty miles, and "halfway decent" might not be the thing, either. Mike was a man of substance and didn't mind the expense, but where could he take this bird of paradise?

So, with his mind racing around among all these considerations, he was listening with less than perfect concentration to her words.

"I've had such a time finding you, Mr. Mizer," Dorinda was saying. "Do you remember buying a little pig, a child's bank, at the airport in Los Angeles? For this little man, I suppose." Dorinda smiled at Tony. But (as a part of his father's mind, which was constantly father, noted) Tony wasn't having any.

Oh well . . . kids resent . . . Mike let the thought float through and disappear. "Say," he said, "I guess that's right. We'd been on a little trip. We got kinda pushed into that store. Somebody got hurt, as I remember. So I told Tony he could have a present if he'd grab it quick, while I nipped into the bar. Guess it was a pig, at that. Huh, Tony?"

"And he still has it?" said Dorinda.

"How about it, Tony?"

The little boy said, "Yes, ma'am."

"Oh, I'm so glad," she sighed. "I did such a silly thing. You see, I bought a little pig, too, that very same evening."

"I didn't see you there." Mike thought that if he had, he sure wouldn't have forgotten, but he didn't think he ought to say this out loud. It was a little soon.

"I saw her," said Tony. He was sitting on a footstool, behaving himself well enough, his father thought, and yet not being . . . something . . . what? As hospitable as he ought to be?

"You did?" said Dorinda, in a purring way that some people use on kids, as if to admire them for seeing at all.

"Yes, ma'am," said Tony. (Oh, he remembered her 'cause she'd been mean. Wasn't *his* fault. *She'd* bumped into *him.*)

"You see," Dorinda turned her lovely face to the man, "I bought a little piggy bank for my niece, for her birthday. And I had the impulse to put something in it, for her. So I dropped a thin little old locket, that used to be my mother's, into the slot, you know? Thinking that she should have it, someday. And one day, when the little bank was broken . . . But"—Dorinda straightened her back—"the stupid girl in the gift shop wrapped the wrong pig."

"Hah! Now I get it, ma'am. So you think the whatchama-callit is in Tony's pig? That it?"

"That's right."

" 'Tisn't," said Tony.

"Hold on," said his father. "How do you know?"

" 'Cause nothing rattled," said the boy.

"Oh, but I . . . Oh, but it *must* be," said Dorinda.

"No harm in making sure," said the father, genially. "Say—uh—Miss Bowie, maybe you'd like a cup of coffee?"

"That's very kind of you," said Dorinda. She was slipping the string from a cardboard cube and opening the box. "But do you think I could have the little pig, please? I've brought another one. I hope it's an even better one. See?" She acted as if Tony were about *three* years old.

Now she took out of tissue paper a piggy bank that Mike looked at with a leery eye. It was pretty fancy. All gussied up. Sequins?

"Or," she said, quickly sensing this, "if there's anything else your . . . Tony, is it, dear? . . . anything else you would rather have?" She was purring again. There was a phony sound to it that Edna had never used to their sturdy little son.

"That's O.K.," said Tony gruffly, and his father said quickly, "Say, Tony's glad to do a lady a favor. Eh, Tony?"

"Sure, Pa."

"Well, aren't you a darling!" said Dorinda, who just didn't seem to know any better. Tony looked disgusted and his father thought, well, she's good-looking, anyhow.

"That was easy," he said to his visitor. "I'm sorry you had to go to so much trouble. Well, no, I guess I'm not, either. We don't get too many visiting ladies. Let me fix that cup of coffee? I can do that much in the kitchen. See, my cook . . ."

Dorinda seemed a little tense. "Oh, no," she said, "you're busy. Please don't take the time, Mr. Mizer." But she read his disappointment, evidently, because she relaxed just a little and looked around. "What a lovely place you have," she said. "So spacious. Perhaps I could see a little bit of it, while Tony fetches me the pig?"

"Why, sure," Mike got up, relieved to be moving. "Be glad to show you around a little bit. I—uh—wish I could ask you to take a bite of lunch—"

"Oh, no," she said. "You are being very good to me, as it is." She had risen, seeming glad to move, herself. Tony hadn't moved at all.

"Up," said his father sharply. "Don't you see the lady?"

So Tony dragged himself up on his short little legs and his father said to the visitor, "Kinda tough putting his manners into him, all by myself."

"Why, he's an adorable little boy," said Dorinda, hitting wrong again. "Could you please bring me the little pig, dear?"

"He'd be glad to," said his father.

"I'd be glad to, ma'am," said the little boy. "But, Pa. . . . what about Rocket?"

"Oh, oh," said his father.

The head nurse said to Dr. Fairchild, "Are you quite sure this is necessary, Doctor? I really don't know . . ."

"Just take my word for it," said Dick Fairchild.

"I've put in a call for Dr. Perkins," she said. "I'm afraid I had to do that."

"Glad you did. Maybe he can put some sense into her."

"But these men? Really—with guns, Doctor? The patients are going to be terribly concerned."

"I'm putting two of them outside her door, and one in the next room, watching out the window. Believe me, it's necessary. Now, my father, Paul Fairchild, will be coming along, any minute now. He's to be let in to talk to her."

"I don't know. I wish Dr. Perkins . . ."

"We've been looking for this woman all over the damn city and here she is practically under my nose. There's something she is going to have to tell us, fanatic or not."

"She's Dr. Perkins' patient, Doctor."

"Well, get him here," said Dr. Fairchild.

"Show you something," Mike Mizer had said to Dorinda, and she had let him lead her through the ranch house, the narrow way, and out on the veranda, where his own bright narrow valley could be seen rolling away pleasantly on either side, and briefly to the sharp hills, straight across.

"Now there's what we call the home corral," said Mike, "and that's Rocket. See him?"

"I beg your pardon?" Dorinda shaded her eyes.

"I'm selling him to a fellow. He's going to be picked up in the morning. But right now, Miss Bowie, nobody's going to cross the home corral."

The bull was angry at being where he was and alert to their presence. He was cutting up, some. Mike Mizer dwelt fondly on his prize, the fine creature, raging and romping there.

"I don't understand," Dorinda said with faint exasperation. "It is a bull, isn't it? What has that to do . . ."

"Oh, well, see those rocks? Straight across? See where they go up, real steep? See the shadow, down a little bit to your left? Well, that's Tony's cave, that is. His own private personal cave."

"Oh?"

"And that's where he's got the little old piggy bank stashed. Eh, Tony?"

"That's right, Pa."

"So you see, we can't hardly go fetch it, until . . . lemmee see. We'll be loading Rocket up real early tomorrow morning."

"That's too late," said Dorinda, not pleasantly at all. She pulled on sweetness like a veil. "Oh, couldn't you . . . Perhaps my driver could go and get it."

"He better not try," said Mike. "Rocket's nothing to fool with, ma'am."

"But couldn't he get down from the top, so that the animal couldn't reach him?"

"Doubt it," Mike shook his head. "That's a bad enough climb, without Rocket waiting on a fall."

"But this is . . . Surely," she said, "there's some way."

"Well, I'll tell you," said Mike, "when the help comes off the job at the gate, I guess we could shoo Rocket into the next corral."

"Oh then, please? Would you do that?"

"Anything for a lady," the rancher said gallantly. "Let me fix you some coffee while we're waiting."

"How soon?"

"Pretty soon," he said soothingly. "Cooler in the house."

"But I'm afraid . . . I haven't too much time." She was very tense.

"Well, I've thought of something else," Mike said. "A good idea to be sure. So, Tony, suppose you go look around your room and you might just take a good look in the shed, while you're at it. No use going to a lot of trouble, moving Rocket, if the piggy don't happen to *be* in your cave, after all."

"Oh, please," Dorinda said. "Do that. Will you, dear?"

"O.K." said Tony stoically.

"Now you just rest your mind, ma'am," said Mike. "Don't you worry. You want that little pig? It's yours. Our pleasure. That right, Tony?"

"Sure, Pa."

"You're very kind," said Dorinda and let him lead her back into the house, as Tony scampered off across the bright space toward some outbuildings.

Harry had made excellent time, considering that, once off the freeway, they had been winding, with inevitable uncertainty, on mountain roads, having to match the map and their choices very carefully, and stop to ask, besides. Still it wasn't much after noon when they came to a gate, and a sign with two large M's leaning away from each other like dancers.

There were several men and one woman gathered there. There was a small concrete mixer and two dusty old cars and one station wagon, on the tailboard of which there seemed to have been set forth a picnic lunch. The gate proper was off its moorings, leaning on the fence. A narrow ditch, just inside the gate, was gaping open and seemed impassable.

Harry called out the window and one of the men came forward. He was an Indian, in jeans. "Michael Mizer?" asked Harry.

"This is his place, sure." The Indian was cheerful.

"Can we get through?"

"Well . . ."

"How far to walk?"

"Mile and a half, maybe. To the house, you mean?"

"If that's where Mr. Mizer is."

"Yep."

"Well, it's pretty important."

The man grinned, shrugged, turned, and shouted. They saw that the men were going to place some heavy planks across the ditch. Jean viewed this with alarm.

"Say," yelled Harry, "excuse me. Did—uh—anybody else show up, looking for Mr. Mizer?"

"You mean the lady?"

"Oh, oh," said Harry under his breath. "That's right," he yelled.

"Yeah, she's still there," the man said.

"Anybody with her?"

"Fella doing the driving, is all."

"Thanks. Sorry for the trouble."

" 's O.K."

There was no comment to make, so they waited silently until the planks were in place and then, gingerly proceeding, they negotiated the crossing. Now a private road went curling around a small lump on the land and began to go downward into the banana-shaped little valley that was neatly cut into rectangles by white fences, and they soon saw the house, brownish and blending, low and long.

They saw the sleek blue car in the shade of a tall eucalyptus hedge. And a man at the wheel. He had on a felt hat.

Then they saw the little boy in jeans, scampering. He stopped and looked.

So Harry pulled off the narrow road and stopped. Jean got out and ran toward the child, who began to walk slowly to meet her.

"Hi," said Jean. "You're the boy who brought the yellow pig. My name is Jean Cunliffe. I'm the one who sold it to you."

"Hi," said the little boy.

Harry came up behind Jean. "Hi," he said, man-to-man.

"Hi," said Tony.

There was paralysis in the sun.

Over in the shade, the small man slipped out of the Continental and went toward the house.

"Well," said Jean flatly, "we're here and we've found you. And I bet somebody else has already asked you for the pig. That's what *we* want."

The little boy said, "Pa and me told her she could have it."

Harry turned to look at the house. "Vance went in, I think. We'd better go talk to the father. Maybe we can get him to be on our side."

"We promised her," said the boy.

"Sure," said Harry, "and if you promised, then you promised. But *we* can't let her get away with it, that's all."

"For your information," said Jean brightly, "we are the good guys. Has she broken it yet?"

"She hasn't got it, yet," said Tony with a touch of mischief. " 'Cause it's in my cave."

So he explained. He pointed. They saw the brown field and the dark, fierce body, rampant on it. The bull was snorting and tossing his head.

"It's in your cave, eh?" said Harry. "And your cave is over there, and you're sure, eh?" (Harry's prophetic soul could sometimes be a nuisance.)

"Oh, sure, *I'm* sure," said the boy. "Pa told me to go look around, but he just wants to talk to *her,* some more." He kicked at the ground with his small boot. His thumbs were tucked into the top of his jeans. His brown little face was still and wise.

Harry said, "How about *down* that rock? You ever get to your cave that way?"

"No, sir. My pa says it's dangerous."

"Which is one of the *good* things about your cave, eh?" said Harry with understanding. "Still, you could do it?"

"Well . . ." The boy looked up at the tall man. "Pa says don't try."

"You know, I think I'll try," said Harry, "large and clumsy as I am."

"Oh, Harry." Jean didn't like the look of that beast.

"All right," said Harry, "talk is talk and brains are brains and deviosity is deviosity but there comes a time, you just gotta go. Our friend here, *he* knows that. Say, how do I get around to the top of that rock? There must be a way."

It had to be from the top because the whole base of the small cliff lay within the field where the bull was running.

"There's a way," said the boy, gazing up at Harry. "It's not steep, on the other side."

"O.K." said Harry. "I'm going to go and steal the yellow pig. But not from you, you know. *You* gave it to the lady. You promised, so it is hers, right now. Have I got that straight?"

"That's right." The boy's eyes were bright.

"O.K. Now, we happen to know that she doesn't want the pig. She wants what's in it. But what's in it happens to belong to Harry Fairchild. And that's who I am."

"Harry, if you should fall . . ." Jean wasn't enjoying this.

"I've thought of that, myself," said Harry. "That animal doesn't look much like Ferdinand."

"Oh, he'd toss you," said the boy, rather merrily.

"I'll bet he would. But not if I *don't* fall."

"I guess not." The boy was studying Harry closely.

Harry wasn't crazy about his project. "What's the plan," he asked, "your Pa has, for getting the pig for the lady?"

"Oh, Pa says when the men come back, he'll have them turn Rocket into the next corral."

"I see. We-ell, what with one thing and another, I don't think I'll wait. Jean,"—he had her arm tight—"watch from here. Try and make a diversion, if that gets to seem like a good idea. I've got a head start, which I am going to lose, if I don't get going."

So Harry let go of her, and went racing along the white fence until he came to the place where another fence went off at a right angle and enclosed the bull. He climbed over.

The animal raced beside him, twenty feet away, beyond a fence but breathing fire. Harry was no matador. No track man, either. It was very hot. The sun beat down. The ground was rough. His shoes were slippery. His suit felt cumbersome. Cloth stuck to his limbs. But Harry ran.

It was no time to be clever. It was time to take your physical advantage while you had it. With every scissoring of his legs he became, in fact, in time, in space, closer to the yellow pig than "they" were. Very simple, really.

Jean, standing in the fierce sunlight, in her Irish wool, felt nervously chilly. She turned to look at the ranch house.

Tony said suddenly, "Pa's not going to like it. This is my Pa's place. It's not yours."

"I know," she said, "I know." She searched his face. But there was nothing to say to this child. He wasn't Sally Jo. Or Deirdre, either. What could she say that would bring him to the side of thieves and strangers and trespassers, no matter how charming? This boy, according to his lights, which were clear and bright, was discounting the pleasure he had taken in Harry Fairchild, and sticking to his primary good and loving loyalty. He went (and who could say he must not?) scampering toward the house to tell his father.

Miss Emaline lay rigid. Dr. Perkins stood beside the head of the bed. Paul Fairchild stood at the foot. He said, "Please let me take my little girl. I'm asking, I'm begging."

Miss Emaline's mouth kept a tight hold on silence. How

did she know he was who he said he was? When she was well, and the evil man was dead, *then* she would take quiet, sensible steps. But not now.

"You don't know the problems," he said, "or the power of the ones who are after her. Please let me take care of her. I am a very wealthy man, Miss Hanks. I've hired many many people, just to take care. Please? Tell me where she is?"

"Daddy," said Dick in warning. He was at the other side of the bed. He wasn't liking his father's look.

Dr. Perkins said, "I can't have her harassed, gentlemen."

"You do know, Miss Hanks," said the governor, who stood beside his brother, "that the execution of Max Kootz is set for Wednesday morning?"

Miss Emaline's eyes flashed. Of course, she knew that!

So the governor said to her, "I can understand that you feel obliged to protect her, and that you are not sure, you don't know, you dare not believe, that we only want to protect her, too."

She thought, he's a smooth one.

"Surely you can tell us this much," the governor went on. "Can anyone else find out where the child is?"

"No," she said, loosening her mouth for the first time. "No. No. No."

"But you won't trust me?" said the old man.

"I trust in the Lord," she said. "I have prayed and I have been answered."

(Oh, they could torture her and she wouldn't tell too soon. The evil man must die and go to hell; then would her bonds loosen, her penance be done.)

(It was also true that Miss Emaline had never had so many handsome worldly men around a bed of hers, before.)

She said, "Doctor, will you tell them to come back on Wednesday?"

"Wednesday, gentlemen," her doctor said.

Meanwhile, back at the ranch house, Vance had come sidling through the screen door. "Miss Bowie."

"Yes, Vance?"

"Fairchild and the girl." He jerked his head.

"What's that?" said Mike, pleasantly.

Dorinda turned to her host and said, "Mr. Mizer, you say you are selling that animal to someone? Would you let *me* buy him, please?"

"I don't know what you mean, ma'am." Mike was startled.

"I'll buy him from you, at whatever price you say."

"Look, Miss, I'm very sorry . . ."

"I'll pay you double."

"I—uh—promised him to this fellow." (She couldn't think . . . !)

"But I'll pay you more," she insisted, "and right now."

(She *did* think he'd break his word, for money!)

"Then, you see," she smiled, daintily, "we can kill him, can't we? And cross the field?"

Now Mike Mizer's insides turned all the way over. What the hell kind of woman was this? He said, "I don't think you understand, ma'am. That's a fine bull, and he's promised, and my friend is counting on him."

"But I must," she cried, "have that pig. Right now. There's so little time. What difference does it make to you?"

"You don't find an animal like that on a tree, ma'am. I took a lot of pains with him. And I think you must be a little crazy. Rocket's not going to be killed. I'll tell you that."

Dorinda had a small gun in her right hand. "Yes, he is," she said. "Sit still. Vance?"

Vance had a handgun too.

The rancher leaned back and smiled broadly. "Well, I'll be damned," he said. "What is this? A Western? What are you going to do with those little tin toys, may I ask? Shoot *Rocket!*" He laughed at them.

Dorinda said, "Vance, I saw a gun case. That way. Go find something you can use to kill that animal. And then go kill him. And go get the pig. And if anything gets in your way, you know what to do. I can't fool around anymore. I'll keep this one quiet."

Vance went obediently into another room.

Mike Mizer was grinning, even wider. "I guess you've been telling me a story, Miss," he said. "What *is* in that pig?"

"No matter to you."

"Watch it," he teased. "That silly little gadget might go off. Make you jump."

"It might," she said, and Mike suddenly wasn't so sure it might not.

"Good shot, are you?" Mike had seen the shadow on the screen of the door. "Watch it!" he said, speaking louder. "Steady." Then he wheedled, "Don't be a damn fool, ma'am, if you'll pardon the expression. You're not going to hurt me. Or Rocket, either. What are you going to do when half a dozen of my hired hands show up? Shoot them *all?* Help's around."

So the little boy shifted silently away from the screen door, where he had been listening. He began to run. Jean saw him, and catching his urgency, she ran toward him.

Harry's head had just appeared at the top of the rock.

The boy said, "That lady's holding a gun on Pa."

"Oh!"

"So I'm going to get the help."

"Oh, yes—"

"Don't worry." The child grinned at her and began to scamper up along the road.

But Jean thought, despairingly, that his little legs must run a mile and a half, and she didn't have the car keys, and it was going to take too long to get the help, and what could *she* do, in the meantime, here at the ranch?

She looked fearfully at the ranch house, which seemed to lie baking there, as it had been baking. She could hear the bull ranting and raving, in his fashion, at the far side of the corral Now she looked his way, and saw the spread-eagled body on the rock face, and the animal ranging to and fro beneath, and she had to go and think of rattlesnakes and sunstrokes, besides, and she thought, this is not good. I don't *like* this.

She moved toward the shade. The eucalyptus leaves were crisp and they whispered harshly under her feet. So she moved close to the house wall and began to creep along beside it. Now she couldn't see Harry. But why was Dorinda holding a gun? And where was Vance?

Harry wished he'd had sense enough to take his jacket off. The rock was not quite as perpendicular as it had looked. He was finding hand- and footholds. But he was steaming with sweat already and how the devil he was going to swing into the cave, he did not know. He hoped for the best. The going was not all that good. He had to be cautious; he had to be slow, and the animal, down there, wasn't helping his morale, much.

So here he was, in effect crossing a façade; in effect, acting like the muscled hero, the bold one, and maybe it was about time. Or maybe it was late in life, for Harry Fairchild.

He wished he had taken off his shoes. No, no, any shoe was better than none, he guessed. He gouged a long wound into fine leather with a fierce thrust, and found another foothold. O.K. So he had to do this, had he? So he'd just do it. He would get the pig, get the message, read it, and (lest afterward he were to be set upon by them) he would *eat* the message. But for now, he'd think no more about it. A journey of a thousand miles begins with a single step. So where was he going to put his left foot?

Jean had reached a window, and she was suddenly able to see all the way through the narrow house and out a window, at the other side. From here she could even see that dark eagle, plastered on the rock. It did not seem to move at all. Her heart thumped in her throat.

Then she saw another figure. It had moved into the bright frame of the opposite window. It was outside, on the other side of the house. A silhouette. A man. With a hat. With a diagonal shadow, crossing his outline. A man with a gun!

She scurried back the way she had come, to the corner of the building. What was he going to *do?*

She saw him run to the white fence. She saw him rest the long gun. She saw that he was sighting. At *what?* At *what?*

Harry felt a sting on his cheek, a fleck, glinting off the basic rock, sharp, cutting his flesh. He couldn't let go, to feel of his face with his hand. He could turn his head.

So he looked behind him. There was a man on the far side of the corral, a man with a gun. And the man was shooting bullets at Harry Fairchild, who was plastered helplessly against the face of the rock and could neither duck nor run or take any cover at all. Nor drop.

Below the bull roared.

Jean went running back along the house wall. She'd have to get somebody to help. The blue car stood empty. But she could *hear* something. The car seemed to buzz at her. Twice. Was it going to blow up? She didn't care if it did. But then it came to her what the sound had been. How ridiculous! How supercivilized, in so primitive a situation! How mad! There was a *telephone* in that car.

But she had now come to a screen door, the way into another room. She heard voices.

Dorinda's, saying, "Oh, shut up. You don't know what this is about and you don't need to know."

Jean heard a man say angrily, "What's he doing?"

"What I told him to do."

"Fun's fun, but if he shoots Rocket, it's not going to be a whole lot of fun for him. Or you, young lady."

"Oh, shut up, or I'll see you do."

Jean had her eyes and nose against the edge of the screen now. She could see Dorinda, who had a gun in her hand, sure enough!

The man said, "Go ahead. Try it. You better know exactly where to put a bullet. Because if not, you're dead, lady."

Dorinda was going to shoot the man. Jean didn't have time to worry about this, because Vance was out there shooting at

Harry! So Jean grabbed the doorhandle and yanked it and sang out (of all absurd things in the world) the first sentence that came into her head.

"Telephone for you, Dorinda."

"What!" Dorinda jumped and turned.

And Mike Mizer leapt.

Chapter 22

VERY quickly, and without any particular mercy, he twisted the gun out of Dorinda's hand, bending her arm as cruelly as was necessary. Then he had her threshing, but imprisoned, and he had her moving, and he had her out of Edna's parlor and out of his house.

"Now git!" he said, "you fool woman!" and sent her sprawling into the dust.

"Who are you?" he said to Jean. "Say, I've seen you someplace . . ."

"But he's shooting!" cried Jean. "The man is! He's shooting at *Harry!*"

"Where?"

"On the rock. The cave. The boy went for help but it's so far—"

"No, no," said Mike. "Tony's only up on the hill, where he can signal. Come on. I'll get me a better gun than this piece of junk."

Mike Mizer went racing into his house and Jean after him.

Harry heard another bullet strike the rock. He, however, had found another toehold. He descended. It was very simple, really. There was, at the moment, nothing else for him to do, but continue intrepidly.

Dorinda picked herself up and went to the car. She got in, stared at the light that was still lit, and then she took up the telephone.

The little boy came sifting, like a ray of darkness, down into the row of eucalyptus. He could see the man at the fence and that wasn't so good. But he could see the woman in the car, and that might be good. And help was coming. He'd signaled from the hill and seen them start.

Inside the house, Jean's teeth chattered. Mike was loading.

On the rock face, Harry's left foot dangled before the mouth of the cave, in thin air.

Dorinda said, "I need . . ."

But the voice said, "Hey, Dorinda! News! The Hanks woman is found!"

"Good."

"She's in St. Bart's. The Fairchilds got guards on her."

"They've got the child?"

"Not yet. They're not moving. Listen, we bought a look at the admitting records. Find out where Hanks was staying. Kid's got to be there."

"Right," said Dorinda. "Good. *Get her*. And I'm coming."

Mike Mizer was out on the veranda, with a long gun trained on Vance, and he was shouting.

Jean, behind him, shaded her eyes and strained to see. She saw Harry Fairchild, hanging by both hands somehow, with the rest of him swinging, swinging—and while she watched he got his momentum and at the top of the outward swing, just as he heaved to throw inward, he let go.

The bull raced in a wild circle.

At the fence, Vance lowered the gun.

Harry Fairchild had vanished.

The blue car came softly around the house corner. Dorinda shouted. Vance dropped the gun, lowered his head, and ran. Mike Mizer, with his sights on the running, living, human being, could not pull the trigger. He was too civilized.

Jean sat down.

The Continental whipped up the road. It took a swift swerve, to avoid the old car that was coming down.

At the gate, the planks were still in place. The blue car hit them accurately, and raced away.

Back at the ranch, his father yelled with his heart in his mouth, "Tony! Where's Tony?"

The little boy came scampering around the house corner. The car full of men came down the road. Everybody shouted.

In the cave, it was very dim, and much cooler. There was a pallet; there were wooden boxes; here were the boy's treasures; this was his lair.

And there stood a little yellow piggy bank.

Harry sighed. He wiped blood from his cheek with his handkerchief and took up the pig in his other hand. He tapped the pig on the rocky floor until it broke open. Among the coins, there was a tightly folded piece of paper.

So he wiped the blood from his lacerated hands, and then he very slowly unfolded the paper, and leaned toward the cave's mouth, for the light.

Mizer was shouting. His men were running. A gate was opening. The bull was being dared and bullied. The sport was dangerous. But Jean Cunliffe sat in a leather-thonged rocking chair, on the ranch veranda, and rocked slowly . . . rocked gently and slowly, in the lovely shade.

After a while, Harry was there, in the house, washing out the cut on his cheek, drinking coffee, gulping a sandwich, and at the same time telling Mike Mizer enough about it so that the man could protect himself and his son. "Call the police," Harry advised. "Tell them it's the Fairchild business. The Beckenhauer case. She might be back. I'm not letting you read the note. Then you *can't* talk. Not that the note"—his voice was tense—"means such an awful lot, that I can see."

Jean had it in her hands. She could hardly read it. It was written in pencil, legibly enough, but her eyes weren't focusing yet.

"Dorinda went away pigless," said Harry, "and, believe me, that isn't like her. She'll be back with troops, I'm betting. Or they'll waylay us. We better—"

Mizer said, "We'll get set for her." He began to chuckle. "Hey, you know what this young lady did, don't you? Strikes me pretty funny, now. Here's your friend—Dorinda, eh?—in a fit state to shoot anybody or anything. So comes this one and says—" Mike mimicked, " 'Telephone for you,' she says."

Harry grinned and flew his eyebrow.

Jean said, "It just came to me because there was a telephone in that car."

"Worked fine," said Mizer. "Fine."

"She was talking on the telephone in her car," said little Tony.

"Oh?"

"Sure. I heard her."

"Did you happen to hear what she said, podner?" asked Harry.

"Well, let's see. She said 'Good.' And she said 'Good' *two* times. And she said—I think she said—'Get her' . . . And she said, 'I'm coming.' "

Jean said to Harry's stricken face. "But we've got the pig. The message."

"Doesn't make a lot of sense," said Harry, "does it? Listen, I think we"—Oh, this was a reversal!—"we'd better follow them."

"Go ahead," said the rancher. "Get on it. Here. Stick up that cheek. Go ahead, and good luck. Damn fool woman! Going to kill a fine animal."

"I didn't like *her,*" said Tony. "You guys hurry up!"

So suddenly they were in the car and racing for the city. It was going to be quick. They knew the way back.

"Nobody following *us,* eh?" Harry said, a little bitterly. "They don't need the pig, anymore. Or so I'm gathering. Aren't you? We should have called Bonzer."

But it was no good calling Bonzer. *They* had nothing to tell him. If the villains got the little girl, the troops would know that, before Harry-the-white-hope could hear about it, where *he* was.

"Oh, we can worry just fine, on our own," said Jean. "I'm *pondering* this message."

"Some message," said Harry, gloomily. "For this we flew, spent money, played ghost, annoyed wild beasts . . ."

"Tell you what," said Jean. "You just drive like the wind. I'm in a worrying mood, and I'm going to *worry* at this."

She had the little piece of paper and she read what was written there, slowly, aloud.

> "One of them's on this plane. Don't talk to me. Take him to your sister's. Lie low. I'll send, soonest. B.B."

(Bernie from his grave.)

"All right." Jean scrunched down on the lovely black leather, well out of the breeze. "We shall attack, systematically."

Harry, driving like the wind and not forgetting he was in the mountains, let the corner of his mouth begin to think about smiling.

" 'One of them's on this plane.' O.K. That was Varney."

"Right."

" 'Don't talk to me.' Now, who was Bernie warning off? Miss Hanks, don't you think?"

"Could be."

"Hah, but he says 'this plane.' So. Miss Hanks was on the *same plane as he was.*"

"Yep," said Harry. His heart leapt up.

"This message," Jean said, "wasn't written to you, at all. It must have been written to *her*. But he didn't get it to her. He still had it on him, when he got off the plane. He just happened to see those pigs."

"So?"

"Naturally, he thought of you. He trusted you to figure it out."

"I am not worthy," said Harry solemnly. "Go on."

"So, the child was taken to this Hanks woman's sister's."

"And who is her sister?"

"Well, we don't know, but maybe we can find out."

"Maybe."

"Wait a minute." Jean sat up. " 'Him.' Look, it doesn't say 'take her.' It says 'take *him.*' "

"Odd."

"No, it isn't. No, it isn't. No, it isn't," she cried. "Harry, I *saw* your little sister. She was dressed like a boy, hair cut like a boy. 'With flaxen hair.' Your daddy said so. Why, I saw Miss Hanks, myself. Of course, I did. And I remember, at the time, I noticed that she told a lie."

"A lie?"

"Oh, sure. Sure. And she told it to *Varney*. Oh, listen, Harry. He came into the shop, you see . . ."

"Bernie did?"

"Yes, and he must have put this into the pig," (Jean was living it all over again) "and he asked me that silly question and then she came in. But later on, Varney asked her whether Bernie had spoken to her. And she *lied!* She said he hadn't. But he *had.* I heard him. Bernie said to the woman with the little boy . . . he said, 'Get out of the way, sister, will you please?' "

"Sister!"

"Uh-huh. Telling her to go to her sister's."

"So, the child is at her sister's."

"Of course."

"Well," Harry hated to dash her down, "we'd kinda guessed that already. We have to find the sister eh?"

They raced on for a mile or two.

"We can't find Miss Hanks, you know," said Harry. "Should a sister, whose name we don't even know, be easier to find?"

But Jean said slowly, "I saw her sister."

"Hanks' sister?"

"I also saw her sister's husband."

"Huh?"

"Oh, I sure did," said Jean, "and all those children. They called him 'Papa.' Oh, and they called the child, the one who was with Hanks, they called him-her 'Bobby.' I remember that."

"Bobby, for Barbara?"

"Uh-huh. Uh-huh. And they said 'Aunt Emaline' was here. So Miss Hanks was their aunt. So the other woman was her *sister.*"

"Surely was, you think?"

"Must have been. Must have been."

"So. All we have to do is find the sister." Harry said this, as if it were new.

"Well," said Jean, "I betcha I know how we can find her sister's husband. And if we find the husband, can the wife be far behind? They might live in the same house, for instance."

"How?" he snapped.

"He's a musician. Oh, Harry, listen. He had a bald head, and a beard, and a fat stomach, and black pants, and an orange shirt, and a guitar, and half a dozen kids of all colors—and you can't tell me that *that's* a run-of-the-mill description!"

"Maybe not," said Harry. "Maybe so." (He was thinking, Oh, my prophetic soul! I was right, in Ireland. She *didn't* know what to remember, until she saw the message.) He was agog.

"Oh, *maybe* . . ." Jean was bouncing.

"So whatever *they've* got," said Harry, "maybe we can leapfrog?"

"Oh, Harry."

"Honey," he said, "feel free to enjoy yourself, a little bit, would you, please?"

"You know," said Jean, "I do feel better."

And Harry Fairchild with a pang, a boom in his breast, thought to himself, my God, I adore this girl! I love her! I love her!

Vance was driving now. Dorinda was on the telephone. "That's ridiculous!" she fumed.

Varney said, "Only address given was in Honolulu. She didn't put anything local down."

"But somebody's got to know what she did with the child."

"She's got a sister, is all we could gather."

"Then the sister's got the child."

"But I can't get the name."

"Get it."

"They don't *know* it, at the hospital."

"Get it out of Hanks, then. *She* knows it, doesn't she?"

"Can't get at her, Dor, I'm telling you."

"You'd better, Vic. We've got to get her, anyhow. Somebody to prove it, when we've got the child."

"Well—there's this chance. I'm going back, myself. Could be, the sister will show, when it's visiting hours. She'd do, to prove it."

"Right. Stick on it, then," said Dorinda. "I'll get to that Hanks woman, myself. We're coming in. Fast as we can."

She hung up the instrument and said to Vance, "Go faster."

Miss Emaline had had a shot to calm her down, but she wasn't asleep. Her room was quiet now; she was alone. The doctor wouldn't let her leave. No matter. Where could she have gone? Not to Callie's. Not today. Not yet. And she didn't have the strength to go to some hotel. These guards would have followed her. Well, she couldn't hide. She kept thinking of Mr. Beckenhauer. Who had left her a duty. Keep Bobby safe. Just do not tell, until the wicked man is dead. Then, and only then, the danger would be over. For the wicked shall be slain; the righteous shall remain. It was a question of enduring. Yes, Lord. Monday, Tuesday. Monday was wearing along.

Only one thing to worry about, on this day. Callie wasn't

coming. She wouldn't come and bring the children. Not today. But Rex was supposed to be coming.

Well, Miss Emaline had fixed that. She had told the nurses, and begged the doctor to reinforce her request. No visitors. "Turn my visitors away."

So Rex wouldn't come up to this room, and be caught by those guards or that Dr. Fairchild—if that was really his name—and be pressed to tell.

Bobby was safe where she was. Miss Emaline would be firm in the right, faithful to the end. She would not speak. No, though they burned her at the stake! Until, on Wednesday, all those men would return—as Miss Emaline had powerfully decreed.

Chapter 23

THEY came tearing in on the freeway. Jean had suggested her place, her telephone. It was just enough handier so that Harry agreed. The time was 4:28 P.M., when she used her key and they came into the airlessness, the shabby little abandoned cell where somebody named Jean Cunliffe had used to live.

Harry grabbed the phone and Jean grabbed clothing, from her drawers and closet, and nipped into the bathroom to wash and change and get out of the Irish suit, at last. She knew how to be very quick. She wouldn't hold him up, never, not she!

When she came out, fresh and proudly smiling, Harry was looking wild. He had tried Bonzer with no luck, no answer. But he had just talked to his brother, the governor, who was about to leave his daddy's house, to fly back to his post and his duty. There was news all right, but whether good or bad, Harry wasn't sure.

Miss Hanks was in St. Bart's Hospital, recovering from something like pneumonia. The Fairchilds had her under guard. The villains couldn't get at her. But she was idiotically and stubbornly refusing to talk to the Fairchilds. Which was infuriating! Oh, she had a sister. This was known. But not the sister's name or address. No record of it, either. Miss Hanks had signed herself in. Address given was in Honolulu. A staff doctor had taken care of her; *he* didn't know the sister. The sister had children, but nobody knew a thing about a little girl, brought along from the Islands. No one had heard one breath of such a child.

Well, this was not to be borne. They were going to St. Bart's, right now, and Harry would make this Hanks talk, all right. He was wild to get at her.

But Jean held back. "Harry, shouldn't one of us try to find the sister's husband? It could be, you know, our one and only advantage. You go to the hospital. I'd better stay here and see what I can find out on the phone."

He didn't like it. "How will we be in touch?" he said rather pathetically.

"Through Bonzer? I'll call Bonzer? You call Bonzer?" Jean didn't like this either. But she was right. And he knew it.

"How about money?" He was giving her money. "To bribe people, and all. Who knows? Take a cab to my place. Don't walk around exposed."

"I'm all right," she said. "They're not after me, anymore." She sounded wistful.

"They better not be." But he believed this. She was right. "Take care. If you find out, call Bonzer."

"If *you* find out, call Bonzer."

"If I find out, I may just go there." (Without you? he thought.) He didn't like it.

"I know," she said. (Without me? she thought sadly.)

"Good luck, soldier."

"Good luck."

He kissed her goodbye, the most natural thing in the world, and then she had to listen to his car take off, strain to hear it slip away, that fine, fast, gay-sweet car, in which she had had her own place.

But Jean pulled herself sternly together and made plans. First, she phoned for a cab to be sent. It must wait. Her own ancient vehicle was, for heaven's sakes, not reliable enough. She wanted transportation ready and waiting. Who knew where she might have to go? She had *plenty* of money. It was a strange feeling.

Then she called a girl acquaintance, who followed folk singers, in a passionate way.

"Hey! Hi, Jeanie," said Julie. "How've you been, dove?"

Jean couldn't go into *this*. She asked questions.

"You mean you don't know? You're talking about Rex Julian."

"I am?"

"Well, he's one of the *greatest!* Everybody *knows*."

"Where does he live?" Jean couldn't wait out any ravings.

"Heck, I dunno," said Julie. "How should I know where he lives? You mean when he's home? Listen, what's the scoop?"

But Jean hung up. As quickly and as easily as this, she had the name. Her spirits zoomed. But no such name was in the phone book. Oh well. She took a firm grip on the telephone.

There was a man, and he was neither Vance nor Varney, sitting in the lobby at St. Bart's, behind a huge rubber plant through which he was able to see the indicators at the tops of the elevators.

When Harry Fairchild came swinging along the corridor from the parking lot, to inquire at the information table, and then to push an elevator button with ferocious impatience, the man watched carefully. Yah, Fairchild! Harry got into an elevator. Eighth floor. The man twitched.

Three minutes later, Rex Julian came along the same corridor, oddly attired, ambling, not seeming to know quite where he was. He finally drifted toward the information lady. The watching man twitched and stirred. And rose. And listened.

Rex accepted what he was told, looked around in his lazy hazy fashion, turned and ambled off again. The man skipped after, in a quick-step along the long corridor and said, "Excuse me, mister?" Rex looked at him. "You know Miss Hanks?"

"No visitors today," Rex said. He had eyes of a very light brown color, strange eyes, that seemed to look with great attention, and yet not see.

Rex pushed outside and the man took advantage of the

same wag of the door. Behind that wide back, the man made a signal to another man and then, himself, seeped backward into the building.

Rex, in the open air, looked around as if he had forgotten where he had left his car. At last, he started down one of the aisles. Varney went striding down another, in parallel. The parking lot was well filled during visiting hours. Rex made a turn toward his dusty station wagon, in a far lane. Varney made a turn toward Rex.

Varney was keyed up. And down, in alternation. In Los Angeles, he was a wanted man. He had felt uneasy, hanging around in the open air. He had been swinging from tense anxiety to spells of numbness, and back again. A signal to act was most welcome. Now, who was this bird, and what did he know?

"Just a minute, mister," said Varney.

Harry stood at the foot of Miss Emaline's bed, with one of the guards hanging onto his arm. He had proved to them that he was a Fairchild. He had, then, stormed in here. He didn't realize how he looked—unshaven, with the plaster on his cheek, his hair on end, his clothing soiled, his hands so cut and torn, and his anger showing.

He said, "These people knifed Bernie Beckenhauer. Beat up his partner. Sent the child's mother out of her mind. Kidnapped and tortured a girl who was helping us. Pulled guns on a man who had nothing to do with this. Shot at me. They don't give much of a damn what they do, to anybody. So you had better tell me, Miss Hanks, before they get that little girl. Now, damn it, you have *got* to see that."

Miss Hanks was like a board in the bed. No, no, the more reason not to tell. She didn't recognize this angry young man, who looked so fierce and spoke profanely.

A nurse said, "If you please," in shocked tones.

"And if you think the minute Kootz is dead, that she'll be safe," shouted Harry, "you're damn wrong."

Miss Emaline braced herself against this wild tough person.

Ah no, *that* wasn't true. She knew better. The wicked shall be destroyed; then the innocent shall be saved. Miss Emaline had the Lord's word for it.

Dick came in. All the nurses were in a terrible twit. Harry was breaking rules and Dick, after all, was a doctor. But Harry didn't even look at his brother, the doctor. He was concentrated on this woman, this stubborn *fool* of a woman. Dick held his peace, to give Harry one minute more.

"Beckenhauer wrote you a note on the plane. He hid it in the gift shop. He phoned me and told me how to find it. Because I was his friend."

She blinked. She didn't believe it. Mr. Beckenhauer had been a kind and quiet gentleman.

"Do you know his handwriting?"

Miss Emaline took the bit of paper. Her hand was trembling but her will was steady on its righteous course.

"He says that he will send," said Harry. "Do you see that? All right, *I'm* the one he sent."

"Mr. Beckenhauer was a good man," she quavered. "The Lord receive his soul."

"He told me that he didn't think so much about getting himself dead—for nothing."

Her mouth tightened to a hard line. She thought, that's why. That's exactly why.

"You had our little sister dressed like a boy," Harry pressed on. "You took her to *your* sister's. I want to know your sister's name and where she lives."

"I don't know you," said Miss Emaline. "My sister is a good woman."

"Good people can get *killed*. Like Bernie Beckenhauer. What's the *matter* with you?"

But Miss Emaline thought, this is torture. I must endure.

"For God's sake!" Harry felt wild.

No, she thought, I must not now weakly give over my proper burden to strange men who curse me, and persecute me, and seek to play upon my human fears.

Dick said, "Harry, get out of here. You can't do a thing and I can't let you stay."

In the corridor, Dick said, "Vain as hell. Only one that God will speak to."

Harry said, "Well, I blew that."

"You look," said his brother, kindly, "like the devil."

"So the Hanks woman is your wife's sister, eh?" said Varney. "O.K. So where is the kid? Come on."

This man was driving Varney nuts. He had funny eyes and he didn't seem to hear words very well.

"The kid? The kid this Hanks had with her? Now come on, big fat buddy. You better give."

Rex had not yet glanced down at the gun in Varney's hand. He kept looking into Varney's little shifting eyes, with an air of listening, *listening* to his *look,* which was nutty.

"Come on. What's wrong with you? Are you stupid or something? Where is the little girl?"

Rex had full lips and, in the midst of his beard, they began to shape into a tender smile. For some reason, this sent Varney berserk. He hit the man.

Rex staggered against the side of a car, recovered balance, and looked down curiously at his own hands.

Varney hit him again, a hard swipe against the bald head with the gun. Rex slithered down the metal and became a heap on the ground.

Varney looked all around. Nothing. He crouched over the big flaccid body and began to tug and tear at the very tight hip pockets. He'd have got the name and address from the car, but he didn't know which car. Never mind. This bird would have a wallet. Had to have. *Did* have. Ah.

"Thank you so much," Jean cried into the telephone, and hung up. It had taken a lot of telephoning but she had finally reached the right agent. In her head, engraved forever, was the address where the little girl, Harry's little sister, must now be. Here in Los Angeles. Not awfully far, either.

Her cab was waiting, out there. But she held on to herself and called Harry's number. Bonzer didn't answer.

Shall I call the hospital? She wondered. No, it would take a year to find Harry. And he may have the address. He may even be there. So shall I call Harry's daddy? No, I'd get that Elaine. I can always try Bonzer, again, from somewhere else.

So she ran out to the cab and got in and gave the driver the precious address. Or was it?

Nobody had paid any attention to her, here. Nobody had been hanging around. Nobody was following. She sat in the cab very tensely, hugging herself. She was exultant. And she was not. She let her doubts appear and looked them over.

It was possible that she had figured it out all wrong. Maybe the big bald guitarist had nothing to do with any of it. And it was *his* address that she had. Maybe she had read things into the events at the airport, so long ago, so long ago, only last Thursday. Maybe she had wanted too desperately to be clever, to use her head for what it was cracked up to be, to earn her salary—oh well, to earn Harry Fairchild's esteem. She might have strained—womped the facts around, just to figure it out *somehow*.

She could be on a false trail entirely. She thought she'd have to go and see. Oh, she'd be careful.

Dick, in the eighth-floor corridor, had his brother by the arm, again. "All right. All right, Harry. But *they* can't get at her, don't forget. It's a hell of a lot better that *we've* got her under guard, don't forget that. You say she came in on Bernie's plane? Then we'll send somebody to the terminal, see who met her."

"Way ahead of you," said Harry. "I'd better call Bonzer. Maybe Jean's got something."

"O.K. But stay out of that room, Harry. If her so-called mind changes, the guards are there, don't forget."

"Dr. Richard Fairchild," said the speaker. "Dr. Richard Fairchild, please. Emergency room."

Dick darted off. Harry went down to the lobby and found a phone booth. He called his own number. Bonzer didn't answer. He called Jean's number. He let it ring a long time. Nobody answered there, either.

So he came out of the booth and stood still. At a standstill. Stopped. Cold. Nowhere. And alone.

An aide, a young girl, came up to him breathlessly. "Are you Harry Fairchild? Please, your brother wants you. Right away. In the emergency room. This way."

Dick met him in a kind of anteroom. "Spot of violence in the parking lot," he said grimly. "Called *me,* because somebody said this chap was asking for Emaline Hanks."

"Let's see him."

The big bearded man, with the wound on his bare scalp, was unconscious and breathing in a poor rhythm. He was wearing tight black trousers, and an orange knitted shirt, and no jacket. Harry said, "Jean saw this man. This is the one."

"Rex Julian," said Dick. "That's the name on his watchband. But look here." The man's hip pockets had been turned inside out. "Robbery?" said Dick, skeptically.

"They've got the address!" Harry was as nervous as a racehorse at the starting gate. But where would he run?

"Hold on." His brother held on to Harry's arm, gave some swift instructions, then turned, and the two of them went racing to the elevators, shoulder to shoulder, and on the eighth floor they went racing to the room. Dick silenced the twittering nurses, brushed aside the guards. Harry was at her, first.

"Rex Julian," he said, to the woman on the bed. "Found unconscious. Knocked out. Wallet gone. So they've got his address. Is he your sister's husband? Is the little girl *there? Where?*"

"Rex?" she croaked. (Papa? she thought.)

Dr. Fairchild said sharply, "We'll do all we can for him, but I don't guarantee a thing. Will *you* give me permission to operate? Where is his *wife?*"

Harry said, "How much do you want on your precious soul? Your sister, too?"

She said, "Callie?" (A terrible truth came to Miss Emaline. She didn't really care for children, never had. Not since her little sister, Callie, had been born. Because a god named Daniel Hanks had tumbled in a bed . . . Oh, god! *Oh, God!*)

"Pigeon Street," she burst. "Can't think . . . number . . . tore it up. Old house, looks like falling down. Big, used to be white. The children . . . Bobby's there. A grocery store, on the corner, where we turned to the right. The house sits under a hill . . . backyard . . ."

"From what street did you turn to the right?" asked Harry quietly, and his brother glanced at him with respect.

"Beachwood Drive," said Miss Emaline. "I know I thought of chewing gum, but it wasn't quite . . ."

Dick put his hand on her trembling shoulder. "Better not take these guards off," he said to Harry. "I'll call up Daddy's army."

"I'll go," said Harry.

Chapter 24

IT was an old house, with many gables. It seemed to sit peacefully, there. The cab driver didn't seem to think that Jean, in her own blue cotton, could afford to have him wait, while she went into this broken-down old house. So she gave him money. He settled. Nobody was around. Jean, feeling the cab driver's gaze upon her as a comfort and a backstop, went up on the narrow old-fashioned low porch. She couldn't find a doorbell, so she knocked. Waiting, she looked around the neighborhood.

This block was the flat entrance to a side road that went on to curl up over the hills, where the "view sites" were. Just along here, there seemed to be a blight. There was a vacant lot, behind the small grocery store on the pinched corner; then came this house, which must once have been somebody's fine country estate, before there were any roads over the hills. On the other side of this house, there was an abandoned cottage and a lot-for-sale sign. Across the street, there were no dwellings at all, just a narrow strip of weeds at the base of the weed-grown slope. Behind this house, there must be a yard that ran all the way back to the other beetling hill.

Jean thought, what isolation. Nobody near to be annoyed by music. Or children.

She knocked again.

The door seemed to open itself. She had to look down to

discover that two short children were tugging at it. One was a little boy who might be an Indian, and the other was the red-headed lass whom Jean remembered.

"Who is it?" sang out a woman's voice, from within. "I'm kinda stuck, so come on in. O.K.?"

So Jean went in, and through a spacious hallway from which the stairs ascended, and through an arch to a very large sitting room, with windows toward the yard at the back. It wasn't the neatest sitting room in the world. It looked more like a hobby shop, after a hard day. There were no curtains at the back windows.

The woman, whom Jean remembered, was sitting in the midst of yards and yards of flowered material, sewing by hand. "Hi," she said. "Excuse me, but I don't want to lose track of this hem. Boy, am I lousy with a needle. New curtains. How are you going to like them?"

Jean had to answer, helplessly, that she liked them. She was struck by the busy peace, here. There were children hanging over a big table spread with scraps of colored paper. There were children on the floor. The woman said, yes, she was Callie Julian. Jean was asked to sit down, which she helplessly did, while the children seemed to shift to pay hospitable attention. From every nook and corner, there seemed to be a child, watching, listening, smiling.

But for some reason, Jean's heart had begun to pound. She said, "Mrs. Julian, your sister is in St. Bart's Hospital, isn't she?" Callie showed no surprise, so Jean rushed on. "Well, I . . . I've come from the Fairchilds. I want you to let me take the little girl, Barbara Fairchild, to her own father. It's very important. Do you *know* anything about it?"

Callie, who was using a very long thread and taking enormous stitches, smiled and said, "I know one thing. None of my kids is going away from me, not just like that. Look, they live here. That's a kind of funny thing to come and say."

"I've got a cab waiting," said Jean. "There's been so much trouble. I don't know how to explain it all to you. I don't want to—scare anybody. But if you won't let me take her, right now, quickly, then I'll have to find a phone and call somebody. Maybe the police. I mean it, Mrs. Julian. I see you *don't* know. There isn't time. She's got to be protected. Where is she?"

Jean looked around the room. The children now seemed to have drawn together, as if the very idea of removing one of them had caused them to cohere. They were all standing over there. In the middle of the pack, Jean saw a flaxen head. "Oh, I see her," she said. "Hi, Bobby."

The little girl's hair was cut like a boy's; she was wearing shorts, as they all were. All the little legs—the black, the brown, the white, the pink, the tanned—and all the little knobby knees were bare. All the pairs of eyes—the dark, the blue, the green, the gray—were watching solemnly. The group was like a huge sensitive flower whose petals had curled to protect its heart.

No child answered her.

Callie glanced at the pack of them. "Don't worry, mob," she said, lightly.

"Mrs. Julian," cried Jean, "you have *got* to worry. If you won't let me take her, and I see you won't . . . then I had better make that call." Jean stood up. "Where is the nearest . . ." she began.

Somebody was knocking on the front door.

Jean said, "Oh, wait! Please!" She was afraid.

But Bobby detached herself, and so did one of the little boys, the one with the huge black eyes. It was evidently their turn to do the honors. The other children shifted and loosened, as if they became spectators, watching, listening, smiling as before. But Callie put down the billowing cotton fabric. She was frowning slightly.

Jean thought, maybe it's Harry. But oh, her prophetic soul!

It was Dorinda.

She came in, moving fast, with a sweeping air of command. "Ah, look who's here," she said at once. "This is *it,* then." She looked at the children.

Callie stood up. "Excuse me. Who—"

The children had drawn together into their knot. A man

appeared behind Dorinda. He had a child by the arm, on either side, and he seemed to toss them into the group. "Better get rid of the cab," he said. "Right?" He disappeared.

Another man now appeared, from another doorway at the far end of the room. "Nobody out there," said he.

And the head of a man appeared at the back windows, looking in. "All clear," he boomed against the glass. He was Varney.

Jean had braced and thought of dashing. But which way? The house swarmed with them.

Dorinda said, "All right. I want the Fairchild girl. Which one is she?"

Callie said, "I'll thank the whole lot of you to get right out of my house and leave me and my kids alone."

"Don't be silly," said Dorinda.

Callie said, "Now see here . . ."

But Varney had come into the room. He walked ponderously to Callie and pulled her arms behind her. Jean knew what he was doing. He was a fancier of handcuffs, Varney was. He was not only handcuffing Callie but he ran the chain around the rail on the back of the chair. Then he shoved her down into it, with a thud.

The children surged, in a shrill and single-impulsed mass, toward Callie. But the strange man grabbed at as many as he could, and Dorinda grabbed, and Varney helped. The little black boy evaded them all, and dashed for the front door. But he reappeared, in the embrace of Vance Miller.

Jean could see no way, no hope of escape. They swarmed. And it was her turn, now. Varney said to her, "Hiya, baby?" Her arms were being wrenched behind her and the handcuffs were going on. He let the corner of his mouth slobber just a little and he slapped her hard, on her right cheek. "Sit down." Jean sat down.

(Well, she'd been here before. Now, we go round again, she thought.)

She said to Callie, loudly, because of the noise here, "Just don't tell them *anything*. Because it doesn't *matter*."

Varney hit her again. "You see?" said Jean. "No matter what, they hit you, anyway."

Callie, chained to her chair, and trampling her new curtains, had lost every bit of color from her face. Vance and the strange man had all the children herded into a corner now. They were howling and shrilling. The noise was frightful.

"Shut them up," yelled Dorinda.

Varney went to slap one or two, but this only increased the din.

Dorinda was in a flaming rage. Her face, in fury, was another face. "Get the one we want," she shouted, "and we'll get out of here."

"Which one?" yelled Varney.

"Which one?" shouted Dorinda, standing over Callie, who simply stared at her, stunned to silence.

"Come on. Come on. Which one is the Fairchilds' precious brat?" Dorinda whirled on Jean. "Do you know?"

But Jean said coolly, "Supposing I knew? How would *you* know, if I lied?"

Varney came and cursed at her, but he didn't touch her, this time.

"Separate the girls," ordered Dorinda. The children tightened together; the noise was even worse. Dorinda looked murderous. "Shut them up, *somebody,*" she shrieked.

The other strange man now reappeared, the one who had gone to send the cab away. He had evidently been snooping through the whole house. "Hey, there's a pretty deep cellar, with no windows."

"Then, for God's sakes," howled Dorinda, "put some of these damned screeching brats down there. Put the *boys.* Get rid of them, anyhow."

So the men, all four, attacked the mass. The children squealed and wiggled. There was a pulling of limbs.

But Callie spoke up. She didn't scream, but at the first sound from her throat the children began to shush each other. "Just go on down cellar," she said, "Joe, Lenny, Carl." She did *not* say "Bobby." "Do what they want, for now. Just wait. Papa will be coming."

So the men began to be able to separate from the rest one little black boy, one little white boy, and one little Red Indian, who were taken away.

Four little girls were left in a row, including the one with the boy's haircut. They stood silently. The silence was terrible.

Varney returned and stared at them sourly. "I got a hunch we'd better hurry," he muttered.

Dorinda said to Callie, "Which one of these? Which one? What do you care? She isn't yours."

(And Jean thought, with wonder, she really doesn't know. All that stuff about her stepmother was just lies. She doesn't even know what *color* woman Marybelle is. She doesn't know which child is Bobby.)

"I won't tell you one word, to hurt any one of them," said Callie. "They are all mine."

So Dorinda slapped her, rather gaily, and went to loom over the children. "Now, listen," she said, "I won't touch three of you. There's only one I want. We'll just take that one, and go away. Now, which one of you just came from Hawaii? Which one is Barbara?"

Four pairs of eyes stared. "What are your names? You." Dorinda grabbed the redhead. "Who is she?" She pointed at the little towhead.

"She's my sister," said the redhead.

Then they all began to chime. They pointed fingers at each other. They jumped up and down. They cried, "She's my sister! She's my sister! She's my sister." All of them, the redhead, the towhead, the brown-haired one, and the little Oriental, too.

Dorinda changed tactics. "Darlings," she cooed.

But the four little females were not fooled. This female couldn't fool them.

Varney said, "Nuts!"

But Dorinda said, "Well, we've got her. We've got them all, and so we've got her. Bring the car around back, Vance. I'm getting on the phone."

The girls began to scream again, rather cheerfully.

Varney was trying to say to Dorinda that they ought not to take so long, but the noise was frightful.

"Put the whole damn lot of them down cellar," yelled Dorinda over the noise, "and if they won't shut up, then shut them up. I don't care how."

"I can quiet them," said Callie, "if I'm with them."

"Take the old bag down cellar, too," said Dorinda, contemptuously.

"And Jean-baby?"

"No, no. Not Jean-honey," said Dorinda. "She is going to be a big help to me."

So the men took the female children away and Varney unlocked Callie's handcuffs to loose her from the chair and he took her, too. Callie went docilely. Jean saw her profile, as she went. It was serene, and it was strangely beautiful.

Vance had vanished. Outside, Jean saw bumping across below the back windows, the blue roof of a car.

"You are sure about that cellar?" said Dorinda, to Varney. "They better not be able to get out."

"Sure, I'm sure," he said. "There's a wall been built down there. Looks like they had to shore up this crummy house. Safe as a jail." He swallowed and his little eyes flickered.

"Don't be cute," said Dorinda coldly.

"Dor, we better not stick around here much longer—"

"I'm making the phone call now," she said, "from the car. Bring *her*."

Through the floor came the sound of children's voices but the sound was slowly losing its excitement, softening to a murmur, as Jean was plucked from her chair and then Varney dragged her around corners and out a back door. He was very rough. She could feel him hating her. She couldn't help it, if he did. She kept thinking, if they'll only take *too* long, somebody will come.

The blue Continental stood on the lumpy lawn, well behind the house, invisible, now, from the street. Dorinda slipped into the driver's side. Varney jammed Jean into the car, beside her, and held Jean with hard hands.

Dorinda pushed a channel button, got an operator, placed a phone call.

"Paul Fairchild's residence." Jean could hear the answering voice. It was Elaine's.

"Governor Thomas Fairchild," snapped Dorinda.

"I'm sorry, but Governor Fairchild isn't here. May I . . ."

"Paul Fairchild, then."

"May I say who is calling?"

"Never mind. Put him on. And hurry up."

"I am very sorry . . ." Elaine was taking offense.

"Tell him I've got his daughter."

Elaine squeaked.

Jean was throbbing. Her heart was making such slow heavy sad sweeps in her breast, not so much with fear, as with sorrow, for the old man's sake.

"This is Paul Fairchild." His voice came on. It was steady. It was even bold.

"I've got your daughter," said Dorinda, "and now, you'll do what I tell you to do."

"Why should I believe you've got my daughter? Who are you?"

"You know Jean Cunliffe, I believe?" said Dorinda nastily. "Dear little Jean, who was in your house for hours, only last night? You'll know *her* voice, now, won't you?"

She thrust the phone against Jean's face. "*Tell* him."

Jean knew, right away, that this was not the time to refuse to speak. It was the time to tell a brave old man the truth.

"Mr. Fairchild," Jean said, "this is Jean Cunliffe."

"Jean, where are you?"

"No, no," said Dorinda. "Not *where*. Hit her, Vic, if she starts."

"Don't tell me," said the old man, quickly.

"Mr. Fairchild," Jean said steadily. Her voice seemed to go like a thin thread, a long elastic connection. "They do have the little girl. I'm sorry to have to say so. But it's true."

"I see," said the old man. "And they have you, too?"

"Yes, but *Harry* . . ."

Varney's fingers were on her throat. Dorinda snatched the phone away.

"Now," she said, "tell your son Thomas to fix a month's stay, at least, for Maximilian Kootz. Tell him to do it, *now*. I'll give him twenty minutes and no more. I'll call you back, and if he doesn't—"

"Within the next twenty minutes," said the old man, "I can't tell my son Thomas anything. And neither can you. He's on an airplane."

"Tell him . . . When does he get off the airplane?"

"He should arrive within the hour," said Tom's daddy calmly. "I can call his office and his home. I can leave your message."

"Do that," she snapped. "And tell him he has got to stop—"

"I'll tell him what you say," said the old man. "I can't tell him what to do."

"Oh, yes, you'll tell him what to do. Or the kid will pay for it. And Jean Cunliffe will pay for it. So you'd better."

The old man said, "I will call. I will leave the message. What my son will *do*, is my son's business."

Dorinda poured out scorn. Paul Fairchild was talking stupid nonsense, just to annoy her.

But when she had run down, the old man said, and Jean could hear his exhaustion, "My boys are men."

Dorinda said, "I'll tell you what you're going to do, old *man*. You'll stop any looking around for us. If I hear—where I am—one sound that I can't trust, the little girl will get her ears cut off. Give *me* the governor's phone numbers. We'll see who's going to tell him what to do."

Paul Fairchild gave her two numbers. Then he said, "Why don't you listen to the six o'clock news? KNX. It's about on."

"What?"

"You can't reach Tom, before that." The old man was impatient with stupidity. "You may hear some news," he snapped, "that will put your mind at rest."

Dorinda said that she would do as she pleased, and the rest of the world would do as she pleased, too. And hung up.

"What's *that* about?" She glared at Jean.

"Listen and find out," said Jean.

"Damn you! *Tell* me."

"Then would you *really*," said Jean, "stop hitting me?"

Dorinda hit her.

Jean went with the blow . . . pain was inevitable . . . and thought, maybe he's bought a little bit more time. A few more minutes. She felt proud of him.

Dorinda was out of the car, giving orders. She sent the man Cole out to the front to watch with the man she called Jake. She told Vance and Varney to bring Jean indoors.

So Jean was tussled back into the house. Dorinda did not call the governor's numbers. (He wouldn't be there, yet.) She hunted the room for a radio and found one. She turned it on. It gave forth dance music.

Jean, huddled and bent uncomfortably, handcuffed to a chair, knew what was coming on the air. The governor's statement, of course. But Dorinda did not know.

So Jean hung her head. She thought of the old man, who must be sick with sorrow, yet had been so steady. She thought of seven children and the mother, down in the cellar, at the mercy of the merciless. She thought of Harry, of help coming, and this woman waiting here, where the men she led knew that they ought not to wait. Jean didn't think Dorinda ought to wait either, from Dorinda's point of view, and she hid her face to hide her hope that Dorinda would wait too long.

Chapter 25

PAUL Fairchild (who had been put to bed after his expedition to St. Bart's) hushed the two women in his room and dialed long distance with a steady hand. He spoke briefly to someone in Tom's office. Then he dialed again, and spoke to Patricia Fairchild, giving no more than a bare outline of what was happening. "They have the child. I don't know where. The least they threaten is to kill her. Tom should know about it."

He then dialed a local number, St. Bart's. He asked for Dr. Fairchild. (Dick should know.) While he waited, this time, he looked across the room at Elaine.

The woman was huddled in a chair. She had listened, twice over, to his account—so bare, so terrible. She hadn't meant . . . Nobody understood . . .

"Did you help these people?" the old man said to her. His voice could not afford emotion. Not yet. So it was calm. But she began to go to pieces, to sob and squeak, to twist and writhe. Mei moved swiftly and took Elaine under her arms and, with the strength of ten, she lifted the hysterical woman out of the chair and forced her out of the room. Forever.

The old man watched them go. A voice soon told him that Dr. Fairchild was with a patient, at the moment. Was there a message?

"Is Harry Fairchild there? Can you have him paged?" (Harry should know.)

The voice reported that Harry Fairchild must have left. The voice was sorry. The old man dialed Harry's number. Bonzer didn't answer.

The old man's head fell forward. His sons were men, but he could not reach a single one of them. And his little girl—was only a little girl.

Mei came back, so he braced up, and called the agency.

"Got her, have they?" this voice said. "Well, we do know where the child *was*. Dr. Fairchild called in. May pick up some traces, there. We're on it, sir. Rounding up a . . ."

"Wait," said Paul Fairchild. "Wait. The woman threatened that, if she saw help coming, she'd take it out on my child. And they've got Jean Cunliffe, too. So go easy. Will you go easy?"

"Yes, sir. Very unlikely they're still at the Julian house. We'll be in touch."

"Police?" said the old man. "There's a crime, now. Give me the address where she *was*. I'll call the police. Everything has to be done . . . everything. But . . . easy."

So Paul Fairchild dialed, again, to tell the police where his child had been, that she had been kidnapped, that he could not pay the ransom, and to beg them to go easy.

Down in the depth of what was really only half of the original cellar, Callie was sitting on the hard cold dusty floor, with her hands cuffed together behind her back, and the chain between the bracelets threaded around behind one of the metal stanchions of the washtubs. These were an old-fashioned double set, with three metal supports at the front, each embedded firmly in the cement of the cellar floor. All the little hands, the small soft fingers, had tried and tried to find a way to release her, but there was no way.

It was almost dark, down here. Only siftings of light came through cracks, here and there, above them. And on the two gas furnaces—one for the upstairs, one for the downstairs, according to Southern California custom—the pilot lights burned and were illumination, of a sort. It was airless down here, empty, unused. On one wall there were the stairs, wooden, without risers. On this wall were the old washtubs, to which she was chained. Over there were the furnaces. And the fourth wall was the new wall. Across the middle of the older cellar, it rose, made of concrete blocks, sheer, windowless, except for a narrow heavily screened slot to let in what air there was. It was tight to the floor above, which it supported. It had no flaw and no exit, and all the old cellar windows were on the other side of it, now.

But Callie was speaking to her children, very softly. Sound rose through the floor from here, as she knew. Sound came down to them, also. They could hear the dance music.

So Callie, who had lived here a long time and knew what strangers could not know, said, "You've all got to go. We can't leave anybody here, to get the brunt of it. Because they'll be pretty mad, I guess."

"Mama?"

"Oh, I'll be O.K. Anyhow, *I* can't go. Even if I could get these things off, I'm too fat for your little old crawly way. But you must all go, every one, and the bigger ones must watch out for the littler ones, and the boys must watch out for the girls, and the girls must watch out for everybody, of course. And you got to be Indians, real, real Indians. Not one scratch. Not one goof, mind.

"Now you come out under the porch. Well, see, you must be very, very quiet, there. As soon as there is a chance, if you're sure nobody is going to see or hear you, then you must crawl out where it's broken, you know? And crawl along, under the shrubbery. And then you must go and wait under the bushes, around the corner, past the store, until Papa comes along.

"And you've got to stop him. Because we don't want him walking in, not knowing, do we? And *after* you do that, then we need somebody to help *me* out of here. But Papa is coming any minute, so . . ."

"We'll stop Papa," they whispered. "It's O.K." "O.K., Mama." "We know what to do." "We won't make one bit of noise."

"Mind you don't shush each other. Now, that's noise."

"We won't." "That's O.K., Mama." "Papa will come." "Won't be very long."

The little hands comforted her face, her hair.

So then she watched them, as best she could, as one by one, they went to the wall where the furnaces stood. They ducked and bent and wiggled through a space, between some pipes, that looked impossibly small. And then, with small mice sounds, not too loud, they went up the wall where there seemed no way to go. And then, flat on a tummy, one by one, each disappeared, between the joists above and the top of the old wall.

And then they were gone. Free, all her children.

Harry Fairchild had no trouble finding the house. He found the store and turned to his right. Hah—*this* house was old, had once been white, and looked to be in less than perfect repair. And its back yard must run all the way to the hill. The curb was bare before it. He parked. He looked and listened. He felt as if he had fallen into a pocket of emptiness, a hole in the busy fabric of the city. It was about 6 P.M. The store had closed. Nobody seemed to be around.

Still, he could hear music, couldn't he?

It must be coming from the house. Well then! His spirits rose. He must be here first.

So he loped eagerly up the overgrown brick path toward the porch. The porch was a low platform and, between its edge and the ground, ran the usual lattice of green painted lathe.

Seven pairs of eyes watched through the lattice how the brown shoes in the dirt under the oleander bush tilted and those toes dug in. Seven children made no sound, at all. Harry's foot was on the first step, when those toes pushed, the figure leaped from the oleander, the blow fell on Harry's head.

The second man, who had been lying deep in lantana, behind the hibiscus, joined the first man and, with grunts and mutters, they picked up Harry Fairchild and carried him into the house, by the front door.

So seven children sifted softly through the place where the lattice was broken and skinned along the ground behind the low acacia bushes, deep in the ivy. The big ones helped the little ones, and the boys helped the girls, and the girls, of course, helped everybody.

It was 6 P.M. The music had given way to a voice selling a pain-killer. Varney, who seemed to carry an inexhaustible supply of handcuffs, pulled limp arms behind the limp body and put the handcuffs on.

Dorinda looked down and, with the toe of one pretty slipper, she nudged the body as if to put a piece of annoying dust out of her way. Varney glanced at his wristwatch, and the two men who had dragged the body in here watched Dorinda. The voice on the air was talking about "quick relief."

Jean Cunliffe was speechless. Even the subvocal procession of interior words had ceased.

But then Harry opened his eyes.

The first thing he saw was Jean's face, smiling radiantly (because it seemed better to her that he was not dead). Then he knew that he was tied up, in fact, handcuffed. And so was she. He narrowed one eye. Help was coming.

The crack on his head seemed to have made his senses abnormally acute. Now he saw Dorinda and knew why her smile was usually so dainty. She had two little tusks at either side, two little teeth that were too far forward of the rank of the rest. He had never seen a wild pig in his life, but "wild pig" came to his mind. (Something mean and small, ruthless within its power, which was low, low to the ground, but very dangerous down there.)

He saw Varney, and his aura was as plain as his outline. A killer who didn't much mind what he did, from now on out. He saw Vance, so inconspicuous, so efficient. He saw the other two men, who were watching the woman and he heard Varney expressing what those two men were thinking.

"Better not wait, Dorinda. Because how did Harry-baby know just where to come?"

"Don't worry about him," she said. "He got it out of a pig." She lifted her arrogant head. Her sense of power flowed out of her. She thought she had the world in her hands. Harry seemed to know that Dorinda had lived all her life with a proud and shocking secret, and now the blind world, and all the poor, stupid, timid, law-abiding, trusting people in it, would see what *she* could do. She was blind with this notion.

"We'll take the girls," she decreed. (Somebody's feet shifted. It was protest and she didn't like it.) "Four of you?" she raged. "Hit them, if you're so feeble. We can stack them in the trunk, can't we? Move the car, Vance. Ready to get out. Wait. If his car is out there, get it out of sight. I'll listen to this."

Voices on the radio were singing a jolly rhyme, the finale of the commercial.

"Listen in the car," growled Varney.

But Dorinda said, "I told you what to do. I want to know what I'll feel like doing with darling Harry."

Harry had not moved. He hadn't tried anything. What was there to try? Now he didn't move his eyes when she looked at him. Vance was taking Harry's car keys out of Harry's pocket.

"I suppose," drawled Dorinda, "that *somebody* loves him. His daddy, maybe?"

"The one kid is enough," said Vance in his mild way, "and less trouble, Dorie."

She turned on him. "Then *you* get it out of Jean-honey, which one *is* the Fairchild brat!"

"Varney's job." Vance went away like a piece of smoke.

"Yeah, but she's some kind of kook," said Varney sullenly. "Take the four of them. No problem. But take them quick, is all *I* say."

"Shut up," said Dorinda.

Harry, hearing his brother's name spoken on the air, and knowing, now, what she was waiting for, began to wonder where there were any children here. His ears had this heightened keenness. He could hear everything, the radio, the voices in the room, a plane going over, a car outside, a bird in a tree, but he could not hear the sound of children.

Chapter 26

"GOVERNOR," the voice was saying, "there is some kind of rumor going around, to do with a child? And . . . uh . . . Max Kootz? Would you care to comment on that?"

Tom said, "I am here to comment on that. Nationwide. There is good reason to believe that a criminal group is planning to kidnap a child. They threaten harm to this child in order to force me to postpone the legally appointed execution date of a convicted and a condemned murderer.

"But I was elected to govern my state, at the polls, by the people. If I were to yield to such a threat, then no child would be safe. I am responsible to all the children, as well as to all the mothers and fathers. The execution date will not be changed by me, under any such pressure.

"If they take the child, harm the child, then they commit a crime, for which they will be accountable to the law. But another crime will have no effect, whatsoever, on the fate of Maximilian Kootz.

"I have considered clemency, as is my power and sometimes my duty, long ago, and found it not appropriate in this case. No crime will change that decision. Only the law can. Criminal force, criminal blackmail, do not govern my state. By the authority delegated to their lawful representative, its people govern my state."

Very good, Tom, thought his brother Harry. Very noble!

Pious and clear—and bound to be misunderstood. He turned his heightened senses on things here.

It was hard to remember Dorinda's beauty, the raging frustrated will had so corrupted the lines of her face.

"Jake, get outside." Even her voice was ugly. "What are you doing in here? Cole, help Vic get those four brats ready to go. They've asked for it."

Cole said, "Sure. Sure, Dorinda."

But he wasn't so sure, as Harry could tell.

"And kick these two down cellar," Dorinda commanded. So Varney, and the man called Cole, took Harry by his ankles and began to drag him. At first he wiggled and threshed, but it did no good—it was essentially self-punishment and stupid—so he soon desisted and concentrated on keeping his violently aching head from being banged again on each step of the descent into the cellar.

They dragged him over to the washtubs and then he was chained to a stanchion. There was a woman, already chained there. She said nothing.

Harry had scarcely adjusted to the gloom when the men came down again, half carrying Jean Cunliffe, who did not struggle at all. They chained her to the middle stanchion.

There they were, three monkeys in a row. A zoo in reverse. The animals were chaining the humans.

"Very odd," said Harry aloud, absurdly. Then he saw that Jean had her teeth over her lower lip, not in terror, but as if she knew a wonderful secret. She sparkled at him and he said, outraged, "What now?"

Varney, huffing from exertion, gave him a hard look and then, standing still, he looked all around.

The man Cole sidled to Varney. "Say, Vic . . ."

"Where are the kids?" said Varney.

"Wha . . ." Cole now looked around, much startled. "My God, she'll blow her top!" he said. "Jake took a walk, already. And this does it."

"They *couldn't* get out," said Varney, plaintively.

"They got out, they got *to* somebody. Ah, ah, not me. Max has had it, right?"

"It's impossible," said Varney, as if he might cry.

But Cole went up the steps, two at a time.

Varney kept looking around and around. Upstairs, through the floor, they heard Dorinda yelling, "Cole! Where are you going?"

Then she was a fury at the top of the cellar steps. "Vic. Bring up those—" She waxed profane.

Varney went to the bottom of the steps to look up, his face almost comical. "Come and see if you can see them."

"See what? See what?"

"The kids. I don't *see* them, Dorinda."

"Are you out of your . . ." She came down four steps. She stood over the deep place, black against the light, like a hovering raven.

"Better get going," said Varney heavily. "All the kids got away."

There was silence.

"Why, then, Harry will have to do," said Dorinda in a high hard voice. "Won't he? Daddy's little man."

Varney didn't find this amusing. "Damn it, Dorinda. Who's outside *now*, for all we know?"

"Just a minute." She ran up the four steps. Varney put a heavy foot on the lowest step. He looked as if he had seen ghosts, had been shaken out of his conception of what the world was all about. But he had begun to work a handgun out of some hidden place in his clothing, as if, helplessly, all he knew how to do was to kill somebody.

Dorinda came back with a candelabra. Seven candles. And they were lighted. She set this down carefully, on the second wooden step. "If you kick loose the gas connections," she said, "what will happen, Vic? It rises, does it?"

"Sure. Accumulates. It'll blow."

"Very nice," said Dorinda. "Fire, do you think?"

"House'll go. Old. Dry. Wood."

"Very nice," said Dorinda. "And no oxygen for them, right?"
"Right. Like a fire storm."

"So they can wait. While I call his daddy back, and we'll see! We'll call from the car, Vic, far, far away."

Varney sighed, turned, and went to the gas furnaces. He examined them. He lifted his foot and did some hard kicking. Almost immediately the oniony smell of gas came to Harry's supersensitive nostrils.

But what was the use of talking? Speech was a human attribute.

"And if those damned brats," said Dorinda, "are hiding in a crack somewhere, they can go, too."

Varney shrugged. He went up the steps. Dorinda let him by. She looked down at Harry in his chains. "Is the darling governor fond of you, I wonder? If not, goodbye." Then she was through the door at the top with a flash of legs and pretty ankles. The door closed. It slammed. It locked.

They could hear Dorinda's voice, high and excited. "We'll *see* what he'll do!" Feet crossed the floor above. The tap of her heels. Varney's tread. Then silence. Except for a very soft whispering, a hissing.

Harry was thinking of his daddy having to take this, when he heard Jean saying, as if she were at a tea, "Oh, I'm sorry. Mrs. Julian, this is George Fairchild. But they call him Harry."

"I'm Callie," said the woman, heartily, beaming friendliness. "Listen, it won't blow. See, the kids went to stop their papa. Then they were all going to get us help. So don't worry. They probably did, already."

And Harry said, in a voice he tried to make bright and hopeful, "Hey, that's good!" (How could he tell this woman that the children couldn't have stopped their papa? He wasn't coming. Rex Julian was in St. Bart's, with a broken head.)

Jean said, "Oh, it won't have time to blow. Dorinda called your daddy, already, Harry. He will have called somebody. Of course, they wouldn't let me tell him where." Then she seemed to know what worried him. "If she calls him *now,* he just won't *believe* this," said Jean Cunliffe. "I don't even believe it, myself. Do you?"

"No. No," said Harry. "It won't blow. Dick knows where we are. He called help long ago."

"Oh, good." Jean said. "It won't blow, then."

But in fact, it might blow.

Out on the street, in front, Varney said, "Oh, oh." Vance had the Continental waiting for them across the road. But Varney had just seen another car, hesitating at the intersection. He was deeply depressed. "We've had it."

But Dorinda clutched his arm fiercely. "Go, get in with Vance. Tell him to move when I say so. And wait a block down. *Down,* mind you. I'll fix this."

Her power was great. Varney ambled across, in a gait faster than it looked, and got into the back of the car. The other car had stopped and two men were getting out of it, looking this way. Dorinda waved to them and began to run, the tripping run of the female in high heels, attracting their attention, firmly, and crying, "Oh, please. Oh, please."

They hurried to meet her. She said, "Oh, please. Are you after the little Fairchild girl?"

"Yes, ma'am." They were giving her hard stares.

"Oh, all the children have run away! They're somewhere on the streets. We're *all* out looking for them. Please help us?"

"Who are you, ma'am?"

"Oh. Oh, *my* name is Jean Cunliffe."

"I see." Both faces accepted this. "What happened to the Kootz gang?"

"Oh, they've gone. They listened to the radio. They've gone, but now we can't find the children."

Then Dorinda waved and called across to Vance. "Go ahead. These men will help me. Thanks for stopping."

So Vance nodded and the Continental began to slip away.

"You've searched the yard, have you, Miss Cunliffe?" said one of the agents.

"Of course. Of course. I was going down, *that* way. Could you go up the hill?"

"Not in the house, eh?"

"*Nobody's* in the house," cried Dorinda. "Their mother's gone up the alley. She's just about crazy. Oh, please help us. I'm so scared. We've got to find the children."

One of the agents ran back toward the intersection. He waved and ran into the alley. The car, driven by a third agent, came along and picked up the other. Then it moved; it passed the house, it went slowly around the curve toward the steep winding into the hills.

Seven pairs of eyes watched, from under the acacias.

Dorinda tripped to the corner. She turned down; the blue car was waiting. She got in. The car moved. It picked up speed.

"It'll blow," said Varney morosely.

"What will blow?" said Vance.

"Drive," said Dorinda and picked up the telephone.

In the cellar, Harry had carefully tested all his chances of getting lose. None existed. Meanwhile, according to his lights, he kept on talking nonsense, because that was what one did. It will be interesting, he thought, to see who *is* going to get us out of this. But he didn't say so.

He had enticed Jean into an animated defense of her remark in Ireland. Very well, she was saying, she admitted that she had used the wrong verb. But the *image* had been clear, hadn't it? And it was a pity if one couldn't use a little poetic license. To complain that it was not feasible to handcuff a chicken was pretty stuffy of him. She did feel that the epitome of helplessness was a chicken, *trussed* for the roasting.

So nonsense came to a sudden and unfortunate end.

And Callie said, "My poor sister—"

Because she knew, as they all did, that it might blow.

"Listen."

The candlelight fell wickedly upon their upturned listening faces.

There were sounds now, above the floor. Tiny creakings. Small tappings.

Then the voices, the little voices, were calling softly on the other side of the door, up there.

"Mama?" "They've gone, Mama." "The door's locked, Mama." "There's a car out back." "The key's not here." "They've all *gone,* Mama." "Papa didn't come." "Mama?"

"Go away," roared Harry, realizing what had happened. The children had sneaked back into the empty rooms upstairs.

But it might blow!

"Go. Go. Get out of the house," screamed Jean.

But Callie said, "Say, would you two keep quiet?"

"Yes, yes, keep quiet." Jean's shoulder throbbed against Harry's.

So Callie spoke to her children. "Listen, kids. You can't open the door, huh?"

"It's locked, Mama." "Mama, Papa didn't come, so we . . ."

"All right, listen," Callie said. "You must all go out of the house and all the way to the end of the yard. Or else all the way up the hill. *Far* away."

"Mama, we don't want . . ."

"See, policemen are coming and they'll know what to do. But there's gas leaking out, down here and she put some burning candles on the steps. We can't put them out. So it might blow up. And I don't want to worry about you being hurt."

"Mama?"

"I-do-not-want-you-to-be-hurt," she said with wide-spaced emphasis. "I would rather anything else in the whole world! Do you hear me? All of you? Do you hear your Mama?"

"Yes, Mama." "O.K., Mama."

"Then, hurry. Hurry-scurry. Go. Quick."

"Mama, can I . . . ?"

"*All* of you."

"All right, Mama."

Then they could hear the feet tapping, hurry-scurry away. Seven pair? Oh, let it be all seven!

Silence above. The candles burned. The smell of gas was very strong. But all three prisoners breathed in deeply and puffed out sighs.

"Chow-ee," breathed Harry softly.

"Well, that's better," Jean said flatly.

Callie leaned her untidy head on the washtub and closed her eyes.

On the street, the police car went slowly by. It would turn and drive by again, assessing the situation with due caution. No car parked at this curb. No signs of life in the old house. Everything seemed very quiet. But they would go easy, as they had been enjoined to do.

In the cellar, were those candles any lower? Was it possible that those flames would gutter out? But in how many minutes? And how heavy was the invisible cloud, up there? So when it blew, would it blow suddenly?

Jean had shifted as close to Harry as she could.

"Oh, Tom's a talker," he was babbling. "Dick is the handy man, I guess you could say. I'm just a quiet fella." His shoulder was tight to Jean's. He said, because he was absolutely running down, "I wonder—should we join in song? I believe that *is* what's done."

"They had an orchestra," Jean said sleepily.

(He knew who had had an orchestra, where and when.)

"Hell of an acey-deucy game," he murmured.

(She knew who had had this game and where and when.)

Callie said, "*Why* didn't Rex come?"

And Harry could follow her train of thought, too. He felt himself as a bright nervous knot, with many long and sensitive antennae reaching out, *way* out. Understanding everything.

He said, "Listen."

Mice? Scratches. Scuffles and scrapes.

"Go back," said Callie. "No, no, loves. No, no, loves."

"It's just me, Mama."

High up there, behind the furnaces, through an opening that looked to be no more than six inches deep, but must have been, behind the masking of a beam, deeper, now there came rolling and slithering, the body of a little girl.

She was wearing shorts. Her bare legs were long and beautiful, although skinned in spots. She had flaxen hair, cut very short. She didn't look at them. She had her small feet on some toehold and she was hauling and pulling. Behind her, above, there were children's voices.

"Come on, pull harder, Nancy."

"Don't let it kink up! Hey, Joe!"

"Wait. O.K."

Bobby Fairchild was guiding the business-end of the green garden hose down behind the furnaces, threading it through the pipes.

"I need more," she shouted.

"O.K., Bobby."

Jean said in a voice that couldn't help ringing with some pleasure. "Harry, this is your little sister."

Callie said, "No. It's too dangerous. Go back."

But Harry said, "No, no. Let her. Just let her. Don't stop her."

His whole being understood. It would kill her, to stop her. You mustn't do that.

Now, Bobby was on the floor, and she had the end of the hose in her hands, and she sighted at the burning candles.

"Just a minute, Mama," she said and then called, "O.K., mob."

The children, outside at the house wall turned on the water with enormous enthusiasm. The water burst forth from the hose end and, as it did, the nozzle, not in good repair, fell off.

Bobby, braced on her good little legs, saw the water cascading in a heavy round stream to her feet, but nowhere near the high place where the candles burned.

She whipped one leg over the hose; she squeezed her knees

together; she bent and scrabbled for the nozzle; she got it in her hand.

Harry was breathless and fascinated. Jean wasn't breathing, either. They non-breathed together, in perfect rhythm. Callie said, "Oh God . . ."

The child was trying to get the nozzle back on the hose end against the heavy stream of water, but it wasn't easy. She struggled for ten seconds. Then she looked up at the flames. Her little face was calm, her gray eyes were very clear; they narrowed shrewdly. Bobby cut her losses. She dropped the nozzle on the floor.

She took a good grip on the hose with her strong little legs. She then put both hands over the streaming water and, pressing with all her might, she began to narrow the opening. She made the water into a hard fan. She shifted slightly. She tested and she gauged, and by trial and error, swiftly correcting error, slowly she brought the water fanning higher, higher. It rained upon them all.

It spattered drops. One flame went out. The child persisted. Another. Then, all fire was dead. But Bobby, calm and wise, kept the water playing to make sure.

Now, outside, arose screams and shouts from the children and the water was abruptly cut off. A man's loud voice said, "What are you kids trying to do?"

The children screamed, in anguish.

Callie called out. Her voice could carry marvelously. "It's O.K., mob. It's O.K. now."

Then she said to her fellow prisoners, gaily, "Unless we're going to get gassed to death, anyhow. Bobby, come here and lie down low, you little monkey."

Bobby said, "Well, we turned the gas *off,* Mama. 'Cause we'd watched the meterman, and he explained."

The man above was shouting, "Police Department. Who's down there?"

"Listen to the *children,*" howled Harry, out of his mind with delight.

Bobby scarcely glanced, out of her long gray intelligent eyes, at him, or at Jean. She came to squat before Callie and touch Callie's cheek with her wet little hand. "Are you O.K., Mama? Don't be mad. We didn't want Papa to be so sorry," said Harry's little sister.

The blue Continental had made it to the Hollywood Freeway. Vance driving, it was headed toward the Valley. Varney was in the back seat, a nerveless lump. Dorinda, in the front seat, was twisting and twisting, with both hands, at the purse in her lap. Then she would stretch those claws to grope the air for power, and then she was back at that twisting. She had punched all four channel buttons. All the mobile operators had told her the same thing. Paul Fairchild's line was busy. Long distance circuits were busy.

They were through the pass. Vance said, "I'm taking the next exit."

"You can take the Ventura and turn on the San Diego," Dorinda said. "Fast way to Fairchild's. I want to see their darling daddy."

Vance said, "Varney can drive."

"What do you mean?"

"You're not making too much sense, anymore," said Vance, "is why. It don't matter to Vic, so much, I guess."

"You'll drive me to Fairchild's house. Right now. Do as I tell you."

"Max has had it, Dorie."

"Then I'll get all the Fairchilds."

"Try, if you want," Vance said. "But *I* didn't set to blow up all my bargaining power. Just if the phones happened to be busy. So here's where I get off."

He pulled on his right-turn indicator.

She lifted her purse and whammed it into the side of his face. The car missed the exit lane. It hit the abutment of an overpass. It reared up, turned over, and burst into flames.

Chapter 27

NINE-THIRTY in the evening, and still Monday.

Paul Fairchild sat high against his pillows, looking passably healthy. Mei was watching him. Dick, the doctor, was watching her, thinking that he had done well to suggest that she take over here, and run his father's well-staffed house, and be nurse-companion to his father. (Elaine was elsewhere, heavily sedated, and what would become of her remained to be seen.)

Callie was watching Dr. Fairchild. Jean Cunliffe, nursing the lingering pain in her face, was watching everybody. Nobody was watching Jean.

Harry Fairchild was watching his little sister. She was a revelation to him; he couldn't get over it. Tony Mizer had been a good little guy. Deirdre had had her moments. Even Sally Jo had her potential. But this one!

The old man had been playing a little game with the seven children, who were attired in a wild miscellany of raggedy night apparel, rescued from their own house by Bonzer, when he had gone there with the extra keys to fetch Harry's car.

The old man had been trying to match a name to each child, making wild errors and ludicrous suggestions, with a streak of nonsense in him. (Like Harry's, thought Jean.) But now, as he sighed, the giggling died down, Mei stirred, Dick nodded.

But Paul Fairchild said to Callie, "What pleasure! Fine children."

"There's one fine child of yours," said Callie, "*I'm* taking a lot of pleasure in, believe me." She beamed on Dick, the doctor, who had, two hours ago, performed an operation with his usual skill. Rex Julian was doing very well at St. Bart's.

(Where Miss Emaline, at the moment, was lying in a drugged slumber. And what would become of her remained to be seen.)

Dick said, "Shucks, ma'am. A little chore of classic simplicity, to such as I. But I *am* the doctor. So I wouldn't be surprised if it was Daddy's bedtime. The . . . er . . . mob can whoop it up somewhere else? O.K.?"

"I'll show them," Mei said.

"Just one more minute," said the old man. "Callie, may I talk to Barbara, for a minute?"

"Why, sure," said Callie. But a shadow crossed her face.

Jean saw it. Jean had been feeling a shadow on her own heart, but not the same shadow as this one.

Now, one little girl went closer to the man in the big bed. She was wearing a pink flannel nightgown that was too short for her, and ragged at the neck and hem. Her flaxen hair was rumpled all over her head, all of her having been washed just a little while ago. She stood there, quietly regarding him. He did not touch her.

"You know, Barbara, that I am your real true daddy?"

(Whether he is or not, he ought to be, thought Jean. Oh, he is! He is!)

"I know it," said Barbara, gravely.

"And you know, don't you, that I never even heard that you had been born, 'til just a few weeks ago."

"I know." She nodded. She didn't hold it against him.

"Do you know that you have three big grown-up brothers? That's Dr. Dick, over there. And that one is your brother George, but we call him Harry. And your brother Tom you'll have to meet another time."

Bobby turned her head and glanced at the Fairchild boys. A grave, assessing, and then dismissing, glance.

"But I guess," said the old man, "you have a lot of brothers, already. And sisters, too."

She caught her lip in her teeth. The gray eyes were very watchful.

"And I guess you'd rather stay with *those* brothers and sisters? And—because your real mother, I'm sorry, isn't around—you'd like to stay with your mama, here?"

The child's lips began to curve but she did not quite smile. She nodded.

"And I guess your mama would rather have you stay, than not? And all the mob would, too?"

"Sure would," said Callie, softly. The other children stirred and twittered. They were all very respectful. They did not rejoice too much, or too soon.

"Well, *I* think it's a good idea, too," said Paul Fairchild. "You see, I'm pretty old, and in this old house there'd be nobody to play with. Your mama wouldn't *let* me have you all." (Oh, he was a charmer.) "I hope you have some fun here, for a couple of days, now." (Until Wednesday, wasn't said.) "While you are *all* going to stay with me. And afterwards, you can come, and bring the other kids, whenever you feel like it."

"O.K.," she said and now she smiled. Now she let him see that she was happy.

"Well, that's settled. *You* sure have got a family," said the old man lying back. "Let me see. You've got three sisters." He counted on his fingers and the little girl nodded and counted on her own.

"And *six* brothers, three big ones, three little ones. Whew!"

Bobby laughed. Her body bent. Her spine had not seemed to be stiff, but now as she bent toward him, a certain stiffness was betrayed to have been there, until now.

"And," said the old man, "you've got your mama."

"Um hum." The child stiffened, just a bit, ahead of him on his sequence.

"And you've got your papa," said Paul Fairchild, fox and charmer, "who can play the guitar, I understand?"

"Um hum." Now the child drew back very slightly, relieved, yet still waiting to understand her status, completely.

"And on top of all that, you've got a *daddy,*" said Bobby's daddy.

"I know it!" crowed Bobby. "And I've got a *father,* too. Mr. Webb, you know? I guess I've just got everything!"

She was aglow. It was true. Humanly speaking, she had everything. Bright and beautiful and beloved, and young, besides.

"So now, let Mei take you all to where you're going to sleep," said her daddy, "sooner or later, that is." He winked. "And goodnight."

He didn't touch his daughter (oh, a fox!), but Bobby gave him just a soft pat on his cheek with her cool little hand. "Goodnight, Daddy," she said with grave and charming joy, and some graceful foxiness of her own.

All the kids began to chorus. Callie said, "Scoot, mob. I'm coming, in a minute." She shooed them, and they all trooped away with Mei.

Callie said, the shadow gone from her, "I'd like to thank you, Mr. Fairchild. We do love her."

"Oh, it's best," he said warmly. "That's obvious. Now, what can I do? For her? For you? For all the rest of them? Money?"

Callie was standing. Her heels were run-over, her stockings were laddered. She pushed her hands into her untidy mop of dark hair. "Gee," she said, "I don't know, Mr. Fairchild. See, Rex makes an awful lot of money, these days. But we just never got the habit of spending it, so much. So there's this man, he manages for Rex, and there's *been* college funds set up, and all."

"Ah, ah," pounced Paul Fairchild. "But you only took in Bobby last Thursday. So I'll match *her* fund, up to full strength, tomorrow."

"O.K." said Callie with perfect generosity. "That's a deal." She beamed on him, she beamed on everyone, especially on the doctor, and she went off to her children.

The old man sank back deeply. He had done well; it had been a strain; he was nobody's fool. People of goodwill. Generously, lovingly, inclined. Yes. But how it would work out—remained to be seen.

Dick said, "Hey, since I've got the usual on, for the morning, I'm off. Why don't you two stick around 'til Mei comes back?" (But no longer, his look said.) "Goodnight, Daddy." And he was gone.

The old man, in heroic courtesy, summoned his attention toward those who were left. "Well! I haven't even heard a whole patch of it," he said to Jean and Harry. "I haven't heard about the yellow pig, yet."

"Another time," said Jean. "Then *I'll* get to come back and help tell it."

"You sure will, honey." He smiled fondly and rolled his weary head.

Harry got up. "Been a busy busy day." He was a little stiff. *Who* was supposed to adore Jean Cunliffe around here?

"A doozy," said his daddy feebly. From under a shadow.

Then Mei was back. Harry and Jean said goodnight. They went out into the upper hall. The house felt alive. It hummed in its distances. Harry could hear it, plain.

Downstairs, Dick met them. "Pat just called," he said crisply. "Daddy's phone is off. I took it."

"Who called?" said Harry stupidly.

"Pat Fairchild. Tom's *wife,* you idiot. Tom's occupied. I don't think I'll tell this news to Daddy, tonight. Max-the-Kootz has up and died."

"Huh?"

"Pat doesn't know what *of.* She thinks he up and busted out of pure pique. Known as natural causes."

"Maybe his heart broke," said Harry oddly. (The man had had a child. How did Dorinda *know* what would hurt a father?)

"Usually does," his brother said. "Only the layman thinks something 'attacks.' By the way, Pat thinks Tom is the greatest speechmaker since Abraham Lincoln. She's mad as hell at some dame who wanted to know 'Yes, but why couldn't Tom have postponed the execution?' as if he hadn't said. Poor old Tom is going to have to put up with a latterday Mary Todd, I'm afraid."

"How is Daddy?" Harry said.

Dick didn't answer, at once.

So Jean said, very low, just making thought audible. "Dorinda and those men. So horrible. And waiting for the other man to be killed. He can't enjoy that. Just can't." (This was the shadow.)

Dick said, "Should I tell him, now?" He said this with fond respect and Harry blinked.

"Oh," said Jean, swallowing, "I don't know. But at least it's over." She sighed. "Done is done. That's what your daddy is going to say." She was saying it, herself. Done is done. That is that. It's over.

"I'll talk to Mei," said Dick. "I'll see. As for how he is— Listen, once he's rested, I wouldn't be surprised if our daddy took a notion to live forever. He'll want to see how his little girl turns out."

"She's a honey," Harry said. "Oh, she's a honey."

"Makes you stop and think, eh?" said Dick. "Goodnight, Jean-honey."

Harry took Jean out to the familiar car.

"Home? Right?" he said carelessly.

"Why, sure," she said, as carelessly as he.

She hoped she hadn't been too forward, just now. Never mind. She could love anybody she felt like loving. Although, perhaps, best quietly. Much—remained to be seen.

So she mused and mulled in silence, over this long and busy day, over the four days and the thousand years of this adventure, until she noticed that the car was diving down into Harry's subterranean garage.

"Hey!"

"Come on," he growled. "Bonzer is fit to be tied, and you know it. *In*carcerated, from four to six this afternoon, in some police station, waiting to give red-tape-type testimony in the matter of his file being stolen. He feels he failed us. You've got to help comfort him."

"Oh?" she said.

"Listen, he's been marketing and laid in candied canaries' tongues, I expect."

"I'm fond of Bonzer, too," she said demurely. But now her heart was pounding. It couldn't help it.

So they went up in the familiar elevator, where Harry said to its ceiling, "Occurs to me *I* may not be the hero of this saga. For a while there, I figured I was getting on to it. Climbing down cliffs, with raging beast below."

"I didn't do any good, either," she said. "After all that trouble and strife, they just chained me to a washtub."

He looked down at her. She never said what he expected. Ninety-nine percent of the girls in the world would have bolstered up his male ego, after that lead-in. But she didn't seem to think he needed bolstering. Could take his lumps. *Was* a man. The subtlest compliment of all?

They had landed. "Me, too," he said meekly, and opened the door to the familiar landing, the small windowless cube, before his familiar door.

Harry put on his worried-cherub look. (As a matter of fact, his heart was pounding.) "Well, maybe we weren't the heroes, exactly, it not being our forte. But even so, you know what *is done.*"

"Yes," she said. "We are supposed to get married."

Then she was in his arms and nonverbal communication was going on.

But Jean began to struggle fiercely; she pulled away.

She said breathlessly, "Harry, if you want to take me to your other place, let's go. But it's only fair to tell you . . ."

(Oh, what a fool I am! The thing is to GET him. What am I *doing?* Why can't I be devious, like everybody else? Oh what a fool!)

"I am *not* going to marry you," she said, "except for keeps and children."

(Oh, now she was terrified.)

"Which I would be glad to do," she said nervously, "if you'll —say the word."

Harry Fairchild couldn't think of a word to say. Especially since Bonzer, having sensed their presence, had now opened the door and was calmly expecting his gentleman, and the lady guest, to enter with decorum, and partake of genteel refreshments.

What word could Harry say? How could he say that "for keeps and children" was exactly what he had had in his enlightened mind. Among other things! One million other things! All that wasn't going in a word.

Ah, deviosity to the rescue!

Wordlessly, Harry picked up Jean Cunliffe and carried her, in ancient symbolism, across his threshold, and put her in her own place.

Everybody took his meaning, immediately. Jean, with all her heart rejoicing, Bonzer with pleasure, although not (of course) surprise.